THE OPTIC

by

Andy G. Collidge

Published in 2013 by FeedARead.com Publishing – Arts Council funded

A CIP catalogue record for this title is available from the British Library.

THE OPTIC

Like everything else in life, things are not always what they really seem. From the simple ant to the complex human, comparisons can be made. Assumptions can be calculated and the realities are normally interpreted, but rarely does the brain collate all this knowledge completely impartially, tending to ignore certain factors to make its final outcome. This can either be more pleasing or more frightening, depending on the frame of reference and the frame of mind at the time. It seems to always be the way. Why? Who knows, but what I do know is - 'things are rarely what they seem to be.'

The eye is the only part of the brain that can be readily seen and again it has abilities that are far from obvious. It has the capability to see, show emotions and indicate intentions. More importantly it can collate information for the brain to decipher and interpret for its own ends, means and agendas. This is just its natural function, which from birth and the opening of the eyes, starts giving an almost endless supply of visual data which then passes directly to the brain.

We take it all for granted, 'we being' as in all living things that have the attribute of an optic organ of any kind. Having informed you of these simple and perhaps palpable facts, it is very interesting to note that the brain, which requires its eye or optic sensor to pass this information on, only has less than a third of its own mass actually working. A humans brain, albeit a very complicated organ, hasn't got the apparent ability to utilize its whole self as a functioning unit, and to date, we as a race, have never factually found out why…and we probably never will?
.....................................PROBABLY

CHAPTER ONE
<u>FIRST ENCOUNTER</u>

A shaft of light, or was it lights? Must be lights, as the visual experience seems to linger with its intensity, but I can't seem to see beyond them.

Christ pain, agonising pain which isn't centred anywhere. It somehow grips my whole being, accompanied by one hell of a crescendo of noise; all of this erupting together. Initially it's deafening, I can't hear anything apart from this row, but then its intensity slightly decreases in volume, becoming a very apparent droning on a single tone.

For some reason I can't see, well not as I would normally expect to. My vision is drifting at an extreme pace, from a blur tinged with shades of red and crimson, to a clearer, defined picture of faces, scenery, buildings, vehicles and fleeting images of people. Although nothing that I can fully focus on.

I can smell things that are all recognisable, but for some bizarre reason are not identifiable at this juncture. I feel like I'm taking in huge sniffs trying to gather the varying aromas, but they seem to just tickle the nasal buds, not revealing their true origins.

The throbbing of the pain is constant. I am able to identify that I am physically making my lungs draw in a breath and then letting it out again.

For an instant I felt sure that I was looking down on myself, an out of body experience I think it is called, but then in a blink of an eye, I seemed to be back inside myself, struggling to keep life within me.

The one thing that I am more aware of than anything else is that I cannot see my limbs. I am looking around me, indeed I feel that I am actually turning from side to side, but I just can't see my hands or legs. While I am labouring with this issue it also occurs to me that I can't see anything else either. I seem to have the ability of sight, but with nothing to see, just shades of pulsating blacks and greys.

Then it happens again. I rise up from within myself and I can see my body floating limply in the darkness. Staring down at it, the image that I see of myself seems lifeless but whole, undamaged and totally still, almost if asleep, but in an incredibly deep slumber. I gain distance from what I am watching and I can feel myself trying to ' will' my conscience back into the motionless body below me.

But deep inside of me I know that this is not going to happen, we are to be parted. My god is this it? Is this death, what the hell happened, how did I get myself into this situation?

Slowly the pains that engulfed me start to diminish. The blaring, droning starts to desist, the reluctant aromas disperse and my sight instigates an entirely different aspect of my surroundings.

My previous visualization of myself drifts away slowly, almost menacingly, and I feel fear well up inside of me. As thoughts of death and other finalisations seep into my already questionable feelings, I am aware of; although I would be lying if I said I could see them, of more flashing lights and images. The inner me, identifies that these are not corporeal apparitions, these are most definitely in my mind, and I find myself just watching, viewing the display, waiting for some kind of outcome.

Although I am conscious of a sense of dread and foreboding, I feel as though I am being orchestrated along my passage to wherever I am now bound. This is accompanied by a strange feeling of serenity in the way that I know I must accept this experience and await its final placement.

After a while of, well all I can describe it as is drifting, watching all the while, seeing nothing but blackness shimmering within different intensities, I experience a garbled onslaught of voices and noise. The sounds are not intrusive this time, but manic. There is clattering, beeping and mild metallic clicking and the voices, quite loud with a reasonable amount of urgency. I cannot distinguish meaning to any of the dialogue. I also feel as though I am being subjected to various pressures which are being applied to points of my body, but I feel no pain or importance to the awareness.

5

When this finally passes, I feel tiredness overcome me, a sensation that I don't seem able to fight and the drifting of my presence disperses into nothingness that engulfs all and every part of my awareness.

I awake with a jolt, and I mean 'I am awake,' firing on all four cylinders and raring to go. Now I'm alone, I don't know why or how I know this, but the feeling inside me is certain of this fact. 'I am alone' and there is a distinct dread that accompanies this sensation.

I very carefully and methodically take a look at my surroundings, standing on a fixed point while slowly turning in a 360 degree circle assessing my proximate situation. I see heavy foliage, almost like the stuff you see in jungles (not that I've ever been to one but can assume from what I've seen on TV.) This place is like an extremely dense forest, with only shards of light filtering down through the intensely tree covered skyline. The light itself is weird, not daylight, not dusk light but a shimmering almost artificial radiance that makes it difficult to focus on anything too distant. Squint as I may the horizon is only a blur.

The one thing that I can see is a path in front of me, but again its destination or even its course is ambiguous to determine because of this shadowy illumination. I also hear a distant drumming, no wrong word, a thudding, thumping, extremely deep within its acoustics. What the hell is that noise?

As I strain to see further, so the more indistinct the horizon becomes. I feel that it is time to move on, not that I really know where I came here from but this path seems to be the way forward but wait, there are questions to be asked here. I again feel fear welling up inside my guts. How the hell did I get here and where the bloody hell is here?

I don't seem to be able to remember anything prior to being stood in this place. How can this happen? I am a very methodical person, everything in black and white for me, people who talk 'grey areas' are people who seem to like living their lives in indecision. I've always felt that a person who wants to achieve needs to step out and be seen, always moving forward. So why am I in such a situation that everything that is happening now, and has been happening for the last few moments, all seems so completely alien to me. I am completely hesitant, unable to remember any recent past before this point. Sure I have memories, distant, remote but nothing recent. I must move on, staying here is not going to achieve anything and is certainly not going to answer any of my questions. The answers must therefore lie in front of me.

"Come on Andy, just get positive," I hear myself quietly say.

I slowly, very slowly move forward up the path, come track, I can't help but feel that this has been especially set up for me alone to travel. The air is thick to the point that I find it hard to take a deep breath and fully inflate my lungs. The shrubbery around me doesn't move. I stop, move towards the green undergrowth and kick at it. It breaks and cowers at the invasion but makes no sound as it splits and falls. Very odd, but this is side tracking me, I need to keep going.

Every step forward is placed in a positive way, tentative but always with purpose. My trepidation must be held in check. I know the course I must take, so positive thoughts and aggressive actions are the order of the day, with a splattering of caution also being applied.

Ahead is the drumming noise. That sound is what I must find. So far it feels the only thing fully tangible to me. I need to go onward, find out what this constant thumping is. At least it's something to aim for, concentrate on. I need something in this whole unfamiliar scenario. Everything so far, short lived as it is, has no resemblance to anything I know or understand. This mystery must unfold in what lays ahead.

After walking for what seems an eternity with the continual droning, drumming getting closer all the while, I encounter a sharp bend in the pathway, almost a 90 degree turn. Immediately I move for cover in the undergrowth, adopting a crouching position and cautiously negotiate the unseen. Bit by bit I move until I can see what lies ahead.

The path here seems to enclose me with its dense foliage and the undergrowth almost completely covering the track. Even the trees here have a hand in making this part of the journey problematic. The taller trees are overhanging my position and the immediate way forward I liken to wild, dense and completely unkempt woodland. The smaller trees push out sideways as if fighting for their right to light in this overcrowded part of the forest.

Stopping for a moment I stare at the way forward, recognizing that my progress is going to be difficult. As I ponder the situation, I consider the option of leaving the track and cutting my own way through the scrub. In less than a minute my evaluation of this problem has been concluded. If I were to score a new route my direction would be compromised, especially as I haven't got a frigging clue as to exactly where I am in comparison to the drumming, so this possibility isn't going to be an option. Stay on the main, and I use that term loosely, corridor.

On I go step by step with great effort, as I have no implements but my body's own in order to cut my way through, so its hands and straight forward brute force and ignorance that drives me on, crushing back the green barrier.

The distant drumming that I initially heard and have followed, has now become a positive thumping sound, more like a heartbeat and by my estimation cannot be more than forty or fifty meters in front of me. From my position I can see that the trees are cropped back ahead as though someone has cultivated this part of the forest, and the illumination ahead seems a lot brighter. I also feel that a little more caution is now required, so I resume a crouching position.

The closer I get to the source of the noise, the easier the going becomes. The thumping sound now starts to echo, resounding around me as though I were enclosed inside a drum. I collapse onto my belly, crawling along as low as possible. Making no sound at all would be good because whatever is up there, I have this terrible dread that it's all going to be bad.

As I slowly edge forward towards the perimeter of the undergrowth, and also may I add, towards the end of any cover that I have, I pause before parting the final shrubs that hopefully are still camouflaging me.

"This is it" I whisper to myself, "whatever is out there I'm about to meet and it's just about to meet me too."

So far it doesn't seem to have noticed me, otherwise surely it would have made its presence known by now, so whatever I do next may well surprise it. Do I want that? That could cause a confrontation and as I don't know what I'm dealing with, it could all go tits up and possibly extremely bad. Then on the other hand the element of surprise is always seen to be an advantage. I could just stand up and be recognized, but then again not knowing what it is that's out there, it might not want to recognize me, just see me as a threat and that would be that. Bloody Hell what to do. I'm not into all this covert and annalistic crap. Vigilance; just keep your head, keep calm, take this opportunity and get on with what you've come to find out.

I move, almost snake like to the point of no return, making very little noise, yet every inch forward sounds to me as though I'm an elephant in a nitro-glycerine factory. I make no false or jerky movements whatsoever. I know the next few blades of grass I part are going to be my final camouflage, but I feel I'm ready to make this first contact. Just as I initiate the final negotiation to the clearing a huge booming voice speaks out.

"I have been waiting for your presence being, come forward".

Shit so much for my clandestine efforts. I remain still. Stupid really because it's obvious it knows I'm here, but my reaction is to stay still and hope that perhaps it will go away. A little naïve maybe?

"Waiting is one thing and tolerance is another. Testing me is not wise. Come and face me now. I have been waiting."

Considering my extremely limited options at this juncture, I slowly get to my knees. Now I can see it, or rather him. The voice sounds masculine, or is that just a sexist assumption. Some women have deep voices too.

What is before me is, what I can only describe as an eyeball sat on top of an exposed brain. The image is quite repulsive to view. The eye itself has the ability to rotate like a head, but the base or brain part so far has remained perfectly stationary. The eye like a human eye blinks and I can see the pupil focusing, and at this moment in time, on me.

The brain part of this thing pulsates, it looks like liquid moving to and fro around the brains torso. The optical part appears to be joined to the base, but it also has the ability to move completely independently from its bottom half. Its gaze is now most definitely upon me.

Okay, I need to really go for this, with direct and firm questions.

"Who and what the hell are you?" I manage to utter in what I can only describe as unbounded fear. It really could have been better.

The reply initially is of as little help as everything else in this nightmare.

"I am the OPTIC".

Great! An apparition that grunts in monosyllables and explains absolutely nothing. It is obvious to me that I need to be more precise with my enquiries.

"What do you want?" I ask trying to keep an even tone to my voice. "Why am I here, what is this place and how the hell did I get here?"

"Ah, all important questions," The Optic menacingly answers, "and apart from one, you should be able to master and answer yourself in time. The one single request I will enlighten you with at this time, is to why you are here. It is quite simple. You and I have been together since the moment you were born. I knew of you and learned about your world at the same time as you did. As you grew, so did I, but in completely different ways, ways you did not know and could not possibly understand. Your knowledge of me however is negligible and unrecognised and I, at my own doing, kept myself as a distant ghost in your imagination, never letting you understand why we were as one. I will tell you, that although we were together from your birth, I was already a grown entity with a job to do. You were and are my job, my task, my reason for existing. UNTIL NOW!"

I take in all that the Optic has said and in the brief pause between its sentences I try to comprehend what the hell it is trying to say to me, the meaning I mean, it seems to only talk in riddles.

I attempt another inquisitive question. "Until now you said. Why until now, what has changed, why are we meeting now? I need to know what you want from me. Indeed I need to know what is going to happen next".

"NOW!" the Optic booms, "NOW YOU WILL TAKE YOUR JOURNEY ONWARDS UNTIL I AM HAPPY WITH THE OUTCOME!"

"Happy with the outcome," I blurt out "what's that supposed to mean? Jesus, are you going to give me any direction at all? I have no idea what you're talking about or what the bloody hell you want!"

"SILENCE!" the Optic yells so loudly that it actually hurts my ear drums. "LET THE JOURNEY BEGIN."

The solitary eye of the Optic is now glaring fiercely at me. I see red and blue veins bulging within the off-white part of the eyeball, the pupil grows larger as I stare at it, becoming darker and blacker with every second that passes. At first I try to stare back, but like the stupid kids game we used to play at school of trying to stare one another out, I start to blink. It truly begins to hurt inside my head. I drop my head to my chest in an attempt to alleviate the pain. There is a soft hissing sound. I lift my eyes to see what is making this noise, especially as it's increasing in volume. The Optic is still in the same position as before but now it appears blurred as though I'm looking at it through water, fuzzy and wavy. I can also see little shards of light emanating from the brain part of the Optic, dancing about in all different directions.

The hissing noise is originating from the Optic. As it reaches deafening pitch, I drop to my knees with my hands over my ears, screwing up my eyes and distorting my face. Then dropping to the ground and rolling myself into the smallest ball that I can, believing this is the way to stop this audio violation, but it just gets louder and louder until I really can't stand it anymore.

No wait, I now feel faint, very light headed but I know I need to stay with it. I can't black out, I must not black out.................and then comes the darkness, silence and finally nothingness.

CHAPTER TWO
<u>MOMENTS OF DEGREES</u>

As I begin to come too, I realise that I have remained tucked into a ball as though still trying to evade the booming voice of the Optic. My head is pounding, a real thumping headache far worse than a great night on the tiles. Typical, I get a hangover without any of the initial foreplay. My luck entirely!

Still on the ground I unwind myself and start to stretch out. I don't feel stiff at all, implying that I haven't been here for too long. Ah there's a question, HERE, where the hell am I now?

Having stretched fully out making sure that everything is working as it should be, I timidly rise into a crouching stance. Surveying my immediate area, I see that I seem to be on the side of a steep river bank. There is foliage here, various reeds and weed type plants, all much bigger than I've ever seen before. I look left then right, up and down and then straight across.

In front of me is the water itself, the closest part of the river to me appears to be quite still, further out towards the middle it is running fast, a very definite current there and then over by the far bank it appears to be fairly calm again.

I survey the opposite bank and then something catches my eye. It looks like feet and the lower part of a pair of legs. I strain to make out the indistinct image as this bank is a good fifty feet away from me. No, it isn't clear. I'm going to have to get closer, over there to discover exactly what this is.

Okay let's take into account the options I have at this time. Firstly I have no real idea of the depth of this stream, river or liquid barrier or of how strong the current is going to be, especially when I reach the central part of the waterway. Attempting to swim it without knowing more about the dangers would be a reckless action to say the least. Gazing to my left and right doesn't furnish me with any better ideas either. The portion of the bank I am crouched on is fairly flat, but behind me it's steep and a fair way up, while before me leading down to the water, it's almost a sheer drop. I need to find more height to gain a superior vantage point, so that's what I'm going to do.

With this choice made I start to cautiously climb. Using the various types of vegetation as hand and foot holds I laboriously scale the steep bank. Eventually I reach another flattish spot, about half way up from where I started; a good resting spot I think to myself. I ensure my safety by pushing as far back into the bank as I can and then start trying to locate the foot and leg that I saw earlier on the opposite bank. I can't see it now at all. I glance down towards the point that I started from and then I realise that on my ascent I have actually climbed diagonally. Noting this fact I again start to scrutinise the opposite bank, taking into consideration the deviation that I have made.

Finally I spot my goal. There it is, but from this view point my objective has become a little clearer with a fuller picture. Now I can see feet, legs and part of a torso. It is definitely another person.

"HELLO OVER THERE, ARE YOU ALRIGHT?" I yell.

Not a thing, no retort and no movement whatsoever. The body doesn't stir. Great, why did I think for one moment this was going to be easy?

I continue. "IF YOU CAN HEAR ME BUT CAN'T RESPOND, MOVE YOUR LEGS OR FEET SO I WILL KNOW THAT YOU ARE AWARE OF ME".

I wait and watch for a few seconds but there is no reaction to my directive. I conclude that whoever they are, they are either unconscious or.......dead. Now I definitely need to get over there.

The flat plateau area of the bank that I am on remains level to my left, proceeding to contour the bank for some distance. I advance along it in an attempt to gain a further advantage and possibly find a way over to this other person. My path widens and then narrows at will but it remains traversable. I travel along it for possibly two or three minutes. This takes me around a slight bend in the river. The person on the opposite bank is now out of my view causing me to experience anxiety within me and that feeling of dread deep down inside my guts; but I don't know why. It must be that for some reason I feel that if there are two of us in this nightmare then our chances must be greater. The chances of what, I really don't know.

I look back down the bank towards the water. The gradient here is not so steep and I feel sure that I could clamber right down it to the water's edge. I gaze out to the flowing water. Here it really doesn't look any more dangerous than it did further down the bank but I need to make a move to see if I can actually get over to the other side to this other person. I begin my decent. As I warily find foot holds that I think could take my weight so I get nearer to the water's edge, when suddenly I lose my hold on a piece of vegetation that rips out from the earth and I slide the rest of the way down. As I tumble out of control I manage to turn myself from facing the bank, to having my back towards it. It is a natural reaction, as if sliding down on your arse is a far safer and less damaging alternative. I come to a grinding halt at the bottom of the bank with my feet dangling in the water. My back is covered in mud, for that matter my front is pretty filthy as well and the worst thing of all, my arse hurts. I brush myself down and try to clean my hands off. A funny thing to do really as very shortly I intend to get into the water and swim across the river, which hopefully will do a far better job of cleaning them than I'm doing right now. Anyway, I'm down now. Let's get on with the swimming thing. Again trepidation rears up in the pit of my guts. I once more watch the water for any signs of a potentially easier route across. Nothing is over apparent although it does cross my mind that the current appears to be flowing towards where the other person was lying, so if I do and it is extremely likely that I will, get dragged with the flow, at least then I'm heading in the right direction.

A very positive attitude, I think to myself. Odd how such a tiny bit of feasible luck can be such a joy in the face of everything else that seems to be against you. I feel a small smile flicker across my face. Thank god for humour.

Extraordinarily alert, I begin to wade into the shallows. The ground underfoot seems firm enough so far. As I slowly walk to the point where the water is above my knees the river bed becomes a lot more uneven, softer to the point I feel that I'm going to stumble or fall.

Oh to hell with this. I bend my knees and push myself off into a shallow dive towards the middle of the river where I assume the current is going to be the strongest. Swimming as strongly as I can, I reach the central waters and yes, I feel I am being sucked along with the current. As I think I am getting past the worst part of this bathing experience, it begins to feel like something is holding me back. I increase the strength of my swimming stroke trying to overcome this hurdle, but no headway is being gained. It's my left foot, something's got hold of my left foot. I kick at it, I wriggle to try and break free. It doesn't work. Panicking I completely submerge myself, endeavouring to see what is holding me back and potentially dragging me under. As I try to see through the water, something I have never been able to do well; open my eyes under water, I am able to make out long flowing green strands. Three or four of these are the cause of my dilemma, firmly wrapped around my legs. Bloody hell I'm tangled in the reeds. My initial reaction is to kick out to try and struggle free and then I remember my father's words when I was a little boy while he was teaching me to swim in our local river. It was a sheltered spot but he always impressed upon me that if I should get stuck and caught up by the reeds, I should relax, not struggle and they would slowly release their hold. With his wise words echoing around my mind, this I do. It's so difficult, especially feeling as though I'm completely running out of my held breath, but unexpectedly I find myself floating upwards to the surface. I'm free. It worked, I have broken free! As I break the water's surface I snatch at the air, it feels like my lungs have burst as I gasp for breath.

Now I start to panic swim, that is to say I don't have any direction in mind, I just need to get to dry land. Within twenty or so strokes I finally reach the river bank and pull myself up onto it. As I lay here attempting to get my breath back, I look about me trying to ascertain which bank I'm now actually on. I'm going to be bloody pissed off if I'm on the same side as I started on, but as luck would have it I'm pretty sure I have actually crossed the watery divide.

Inside a couple of minutes, I again feel ready to move. A great excitement swells up in me, am I really going to find an ally to take along on this journey with me. That would be great. Then the dreaded thought also crosses my mind, what if the person I saw isn't a person

15

at all, perhaps it was just a ploy to try to get me to cross the river in the hopes that I would fail and meet a watery grave.

SHIT, perhaps it's really the Optic. There are way too many variants here. My choices are limited. I either try to find whoever or whatever I saw across the river or I leave it well alone and just keep moving to see if anything becomes familiar or makes any sense to me. Two options and the only one that carries any logic is to continue towards meeting the new arrival in this nightmare.

Traversing the river bank yet again, I glance to the other side from time to time to see if I can recognize anything over there, anything at all that will put my mind at rest or confirm to me that I am indeed on the correct side of this river to be searching for the body. Having travelled for about 10 minute and recognized nothing, I can only conclude one of two things. One I am on the wrong frigging side, or two when I swam to the shore it was further up the river and I had therefore passed the point where the body was. Immediately having had these thoughts, I turn and make my way back to the spot where I initially left the water.

As I approach that point again I begin glancing across. Within a couple of minutes I am looking across the river to the exact place where I started my horrific swim. Now I know I'm on the right side and the body wasn't far from here. It was higher on the bank but it was around here somewhere.

I scurry up the bank using the reeds, weeds and foliage to gain height. As I approach a small clearing, I can see where the undergrowth has been laid flat. I glance back across the river. Now I am in full view of where I awoke. This is definitely the spot where I saw the body, but where the hell is it?

A real frustration begins to take over and I call out. "CAN YOU HEAR ME. DON'T BE AFRAID, I'M LOST TOO." I strain my ears hoping for a reply. Nothing. "FOR FUCKS SAKE TELL ME WHERE YOU ARE, I'M NOT GOING TO HURT YOU!" I blurt out.

That is really going to help, a bit aggressive. I need to calm down. I slump into a sitting position to reassess my situation and as regards to what to do next, when unexpectedly I hear something.

"Who are you, and what do you want?"

I turn quickly, looking up the bank and there they are. This is a female, I would have said in her early twenties, fair, blondish hair about five feet eight inches tall and looking extremely apprehensive. As I look at her for some reason she seems familiar, as if I know her. The questions she asked seemed pretty familiar too.

"My names Andy and I hope that all I want is the same as you."

"And what's that?" she retorts.

"To understand what the hell is going on because I really don't have a clue. I just woke up here, I don't know where here is, I haven't seen anybody else except you, oh and a real weird looking thing like a giant eyeball on a brain that calls itself...", but before I could finish, she ends the sentence for me.

"THE OPTIC."

"You've seen him?" I blurt out. Obvious really! Why did I even say that? It really isn't going to inspire her confidence in me at all if I keep stating the obvious.

There is a moments silence before she answers. "Yes I've seen him. He's terrifying, his voice is deafening and what he said doesn't make any sense at all to me," she softly explains.

With a much gentler tone of voice I reply. "Well I am in full agreement with you there, he's a real piece of work. What's your name?"

She tilts her head to the side and looks down at me. "Bump," comes the reply as if I should know.

"Bump!…..that's a very unusual name, is that short for something?" I question.

She looks at me a little puzzled and says, "No it's not short for anything, it's my name. I've always known myself as Bump. What's wrong with my name?"

"Oh nothing, nothing at all, it's a great name and I must admit, completely original. You've got a great name, really. Okay then Bump, there are two of us now and I reckon that between us we can sort this riddle out. Are you up for it?"

A small smile appears on her face and again it's almost as though I know this person. I have seen that smile before.

"Okay," she replies. "I'm up for it."

I begin the upward climb to reach where she is standing. It's not a long climb but difficult to obtain secure foot and hand holds. Shortly I reach the top. I extend my hand towards her to shake her hand. She pauses for a moment looking at the extended hand, she takes it tentatively and says, "Nice to meet you Andy." As she utters these words she is looking straight into my eyes. There is absolutely no blinking, no flickering, it's a full on stare.

"It's great to meet you too Bump. Come on let's move on and see where we go."

As she pulls her hand back I see her expression change. A concerned look encompasses her face.

"Which way, which way are you going to choose? Do you know this area, have you any idea where we would be safe?"

I can see that there is little trust at this point and who can blame her. In point of fact why am I so willing to put any faith in this person, I've only just met her and so far nothing seems to be what it is. I attempt to calm the situation down.

18

"Woo woo, let's not get into a conflict situation here. I am aware that we have only just met, I know that neither of us has a clue where we are and I definitely know that I am not your problem. I do know however from what the Optic has said, that I am supposed to be taking a journey. To where, again I don't bloody know but staying put here isn't a journey and I feel that moving on is going to provide me or us with some answers. Now, you said that you have met the Optic. What did he say to you?"

Bump's head drops and with a short pause she starts to relate her meeting with the OPTIC.

"I've met it only twice over the long period I've been here…."

"Over the long period," I interrupt urgently. "Over the long period. How fucking long have you been here?"

Bump slightly backs off as I interrupt her in this semi aggressive manner and she replies, "I don't know, I can't remember being anywhere else, I seem only able to remember here."

As she states this I start trying to recall times before waking up here. I have definite memories, although try as I may I cannot remember how I got here or anything that must have preceded my route to this place. I'd like to say that it's all a fuzzy memory, but it's not. I have very distinct memories of my family, where I live including previous places that I've lived, my jobs, childhood pranks, loves and hates, but here, I've never been here before.

"Sorry for swearing and sorry to interrupt you, but I was taken aback by what you just said. Please carry on and I'll keep quiet until you've finished".

She smiles a small smile and continues. "The first time was a long time ago. I was very young but I have no idea of my age, in point of fact I don't know how old I am now but anyway, I was sleeping down by the river when I was woken by a strange hissing sound. As I awoke, I rubbed my eyes to clear my vision and I saw this huge eye like thing hovering over me. I was petrified and tried to back away from it when it spoke."

19

It said. "How, what……. You should not be here…………GO NOW, LEAVE MY DOMAIN!".

"Its voice was booming, very deep and low but now I understand that it was shocked to see me. At the time I didn't realise this, I was just scared of it. Having said its piece the hissing started again and it began to move away, fading as it went."

"You said you were asleep at the river?" I question. "This river?"

"No," she replies. "I don't know really, it could be although just a different part of it. The truth is that every night when I stop to sleep, it's a different place every time, it's always been that way. I have even tried not moving for the whole day but somehow I always manage to end up in a different spot. I really don't know how this happens, but I can assure you it does, and it will."

"You said you don't know how old you are. Look at me and tell me how old you think I am?"

I ask her to do this, not because of the old age game of 'guess the age' but because the thought has crossed my mind; does she have any concept of age?

She stares at me for a short period of time and then very apprehensively says, "I truly have no idea. I am aware that very many days have passed you, just like me, and I know that periods of days make weeks, and then weeks make months and months make years, but having never ever tried to keep a record of these things, time is only measured for me by the ending of a day."

"You have been here a hell of a long time Bump by the sounds of things. Please carry on with your second meeting with the Optic."

"It was only a few days ago, no not that long, possibly a day ago. I was walking towards a large ridge entirely covered in grass. As I approached it so the grass started to turn a yellowy brown colour and then the entire ridge began to shake and change shape. Rocks pushed up though the ground and flames flickered all around. Not blazing flames but more like lightening, although red and blue. I very carefully

20

started moving away from this. As I slowly backed away I could see the OPTIC unwind itself from under the ground and protrude out towards the surface. This time it had a different shape. It was like a snake and the only reason I thought that it was the Optic was because the entire head was just one eye, exactly the same as the one I had seen all that time before. I backed into the long grass and hid. I must have laid there for a long time before I managed the courage to take a peep out. I crawled forward until I could see. The whole landscape had completely changed and there was no sign of the Optic. I didn't go on that way. I made my way back the way I had come, but even that had altered. I can't say I recognized any of it, but that was quite normal." She looks at me and gives me a half smile and a little shrug of her shoulders. "Until now," she continued. "I haven't seen anyone, in point of fact the only real person I've ever seen or met is you."

I've got to admit, I really don't know what to make of her story. If this has been the whole of her life and she hasn't ever met anyone else but me, how has she survived? There has got to be others here somewhere. Millions of questions need answering here but no answers are openly apparent.

I question Bump further. "What do you mean that I am the first real person you have ever met, are you saying you have seen other people but haven't been able to talk to them?"

She glances up at me with a confused look, "No the others are like shadows, you're not like them, they don't seem to be able to see me at all. They certainly do not stop to talk to me. I've tried to converse with them, called out to them, but they don't hear me, I don't think they even know I'm here or care for that matter. As I said they are shadows. You are completely different. I don't know why you are here, but from what you've said, the Optic wants you here. I'm pretty sure that he doesn't want me here and you and I meeting will really annoy him, of that I'm sure."

I take the time to consider what Bump has just said and I feel at this time more conversation would be futile. I need to break the mood, time to get going, move on.

"Hmmm," I begin. "Well let's move on, wherever it takes us, in which ever direction your little heart desires and see if we can find this Optic character to discover if we can really piss him off."

Bump's face seems to lighten up, again a small smile. "Okay," she says. "But you decide which way. I feel that I'm not going to be much help directing you anywhere and I don't want to get it wrong and put us into danger. I don't want it to be my fault. That is why I questioned your decision earlier. I am frightened of either of us getting it wrong."

There is a short pause, then I take a deep breath and say, "Wrong, right. I don't know if there is any wrong or right here. As I've already said, I'm not sure of anything here and I'm certainly not sure of the way forward. Nevertheless we are going to travel somewhere. So let's rock and roll."

Bump looks at me a little puzzled by this statement but says nothing. So having relayed my words of wisdom and strength, I take a good look around at our surroundings. The river is immediately behind us, which is exactly where I remember leaving it, while in front is a small area of sparse, grassy land that soon tapers off into a desert type terrain. Now this I haven't seen before.

"Was that lot there earlier Bump?"

She turns slightly and gazes out over the terrain towards which I'm pointing. "I don't know, I never really looked out there. I can't say I noticed one way or the other. Why, is it important?"

"Dunno, probably not."

 I gently take hold of her hand, which is noticeably quite cold and head for the sand.

CHAPTER THREE
<u>CONSEQUENCE OF THE ACTIONS</u>

The sky is what can only be described as 'perfectly clear'. There is not a cloud in sight and the sun is at its highest point, big and bold with a hazy look about it. I am unable to even interpret a wisp of wind and as we walk onwards it occurs to me that although the sun is beating down on us from on high, it's actually not hot in the slightest.

I glance over at Bump, there are no signs of her sweating and there are also no signs that the supposedly baking hot sun is causing her any discomfort whatsoever. Well it wouldn't. The bloody big ball of burning gases high in the sky isn't hot, not even remotely warmish really. How very odd. I actually feel incredibly comfortable, personal temperature wise. I just automatically assume that it will get hotter when we reach the desert sands. Don't get me wrong, I'm hoping not, but all the things I know, have read or seen on TV about deserts, state that they get very hot!

We walk on. After about ten minutes or so we abruptly reach the sand. I stop, crouch down and take a handful of the grains. Yep sand. The shrub land just seems to stop and the sand starts in almost a precisely drawn out line. I gaze left and then right. Yep one great big straight line, shrub then sand, all very orderly. My handful of sand feels cold and exceptionally smooth. As I allow the grains to slip through my fingers I gauge the texture and take note of its colour. I've seen yellow sand, orange and red coloured sand in various countries that I have visited. I've even heard of and seen photographs of black sand, but this sand is nearly every shade of the spectrum. There are traces of greens, blues, purples and even pure white particles here. Pretty as it may appear, I have never seen or heard of anything like this. As I look out at the sandy landscape in front of me, I can see the misty, hazy quality where the heat and the moisture meet, giving the impression of a vast area of sand, sand dunes and blazing sun that is going to kill us unless we know exactly what we are doing. We need to bring water with us. I turn and look at Bump. She is standing quite still gazing out at the multi coloured waste land.

"We need to take some water with us Bump, didn't think of it before, but if we intend to walk across this expanse, we will most definitely need to take water with us."

"Why?" she asks.

"What do you mean why? Without water and food we are going to die out there, unless it's a much shorter distance across the desert than I think it's going to be."

A really funny question to ask, I can't help thinking to myself. Then it occurs to me that since I arrived here, which must be quite some time now, I haven't felt thirsty or hungry for that matter.

She is now looking directly at me, her gaze most disconcerting although her features show nothing but gentleness. "Food and water? We won't need those. While we are here we will never need those."

This statement concerns me a lot. I question her further. I need to identify exactly what she is implying. "What do you mean we don't need food here?" I hopefully say this in a nonchalant and calm manner.

"Oh, I can't remember the last time I ate or drank. I honestly can't recall ever wanting to eat or even ever seeing any food, not as such anyway."

My face must look perplexed by this admission as it takes a couple of seconds for these words to sink in. Before I further this conversation, again I look up into the sky. No birds. I quickly turn and survey the brush land we have just travelled. I cannot see any sign of life. I think back to the journey here and I can't recall any indications of wildlife.

"Have you ever seen any animals or birds anywhere since you've been here, or indeed any other forms of life?" I question her.

She smiles and says, "Of course I've seen birds and animals." There is a short pause. "And fish, but they never seem real and I'm often not sure if I'm dreaming when I see them."

"Well surely if you saw them in a dream then you were asleep. You would know this when you woke up. You are obviously aware that the things you have seen in your dreams are not real. The memory of that vision stays with you, but only in your thoughts. If you've seen animals and stuff for real then they become factual. That's how we learn."

Bump just stares at me, her face one of complete misunderstanding. "Andy things here are not as clear cut as you obviously think they are. Sleeping and being awake are almost exactly the same, you just move to different places in your sleep. When you wake up you are in reality, then at that point the dream ends, but it doesn't really end, you are at the same point, but at a different place. The dream world and the waking world are the same. You'll find out soon."

"What the hell do you mean!" I stutter in total miscomprehension.

"At some stage," she continues, "you will feel lethargic. I don't think we actually get tired here, so to speak, it's just that something in us tells us we must rest. That's when you will go through the process of going to sleep. Then when you wake up, which is just another pre ordained function and whatever and wherever you dreamed about, is where you are going to be. It's as if nothing stops in this world, there is no pause, just this ever moving story that we are part of."

Wow, now that's what I call a deep statement. How are you supposed to take that in and comprehend it? Just as I was beginning to think that Bump may be a little simple and not overly bright, she comes out with a report on this nightmare we are in as if she had actually invented this world herself. There's another thought, or should I say concern. DO I TRUST HER?

I smile at her and gently take her by the hand. We start walking into the desert sands. "So if we keep walking, we won't feel thirsty or hungry. Is that right?"

"That's right," she retorts in a chirpy manner. "We will walk right across these sands and the only dangers that we are likely to come across will be the Optic. Everything else, as I said, it's like it could be there but isn't. Do you understand what I'm saying?"

Having listened to her interpretation of things, I really don't have to consider my response for very long. "I've got to say, I haven't a frigging clue. Everything you've said is completely alien to me. Don't get me wrong, I understand all the words, it's the concept that I struggle with. Everything that I have known in life thus far is being challenged by what you have just said happens here, but as you've said, I'm probably going to sample it all for myself before too long."

Bump bursts into laughter. "I think it's going to be very weird for you but I also believe that you will handle it okay."

"Why?"

"Because you are here and also because you have direction in what you are trying to do. I have been here as long as I can remember, but I don't know why. I don't know anything different and don't know how to change things. I believe that you do. You are here for a reason, you said that, and that's why we are going to find out what this place is, then possibly we can leave together and I will be able to identify all the things that you talk about."

Again I feel that her conversation is rather deep, but nevertheless she does seem to have placed her trust in me. I'm still not sure whether that's a good or bad thing.

As we trudge through the sand and head deeper into the desert, every now and again I glance back to see if the way we are going is putting any distance between us and the river. Indeed it is. After an hour or so I am unable to distinguish where we started from. As I stare forward all I can see is sand and dunes. The going is difficult as the sand is soft and our feet sink into it making every step a trial. The sun beats down, but the heat coming from it isn't how I imagined walking through a desert would be. I don't as such feel tired and again, I don't seem to be experiencing the drained feeling that one usually associates from the suns heat. Also, Bump was correct, although every now and again I feel that I am thirsty, the contemplation soon wears off and I find that I can carry on going without experiencing any ill effects. The whole thing is strange. It's as if I am indeed here, but not completely. Now whose thinking is deep?

After walking for what seems to be an eternity, the desert sand appears to become still softer under foot than before. I notice that Bump is taking her paces much more slowly and deliberately. She is also looking rather intently as to where she will place her next footstep. As I watch her for ten or twelve steps I ask, "You okay?"

She comes to a standstill and says, "Yes thank you. Are you?"

"I think so, but I have been watching you over the last mile or so and you seem to be extremely cautious with regards as to where you are walking. Initially you didn't seem to care but now, well as I said you seem much more vigilant."

"Ah I see, you are not talking about my condition as such."

Now this statement takes me aback for a second. Her response is a little too robotic in content for my liking. I continue, "Now that's a strange answer."

"Not really," she says. "If you had stated the precise intention of your question then I could have given you the appropriate reply. Instead I had to decide exactly what you were enquiring about. I decided it was my health and physical condition, and that's just fine at the moment. As for the ground, the surface is becoming exceptionally soft and powdery. It's becoming more difficult to walk. I've seen this before."

"You have, when?" I enquire still amazed at the way she is speaking. It's very factual and cold, not at least how I expected her to respond. As I said, almost akin to a programmed response.

She continues, "I've seen this many times before and it usually means the Optic is close and also that he knows you are close too. He likes to play games."

"Games, what kind of games?"

"Horrible games, they scare me but I think they are meant to scare me."

27

The expression on Bump's face says it all really. I can see the fear in her face and she is very obviously agitated. I walk over to her and cuddle her up. She feels as though I'm holding a statue. There is no response whatsoever on her part but she doesn't pull away either. I attempt to side track her fears. "Well shall we turn back to where the ground was firmer Bump?"

"No point Andy, he knows we are here. Whichever direction we go the ground will be the same now. We have no choice. We will have to participate in his game."

"You talk as if this Optic thing has control of everything around us. Is that what you are telling me, that it has the power to change and alter things at will?"

"Precisely that, haven't you got it yet, we are in 'the Optics world'."

This announcement is spoken with complete conviction and she gently pushes me away to say it, looking intently into my eyes. "We are part of his world, he's already said he doesn't want me in it, but you were invited. He likes playing games with me, trying to terrify me, but at the moment we don't know what he's going to do with you. At this time we are together and I cannot identify what he's going to do with us both here together."

"Okay, okay, let's not lose our heads and let's keep calm. So from what you have just said, it doesn't matter which way we go, the outcome is going to be the same. The Optic is going to do something to us, right?"

"Maybe, he doesn't always, but it's likely that he is going to do something, something to frighten us."

As I gaze in the direction that we have been travelling towards, I think I can see trees ahead. I squint my eyes hoping to clarify what I am looking at. Yep, it's trees. We need to get closer to see more clearly. "Can you see that, far over there Bump?" I say whilst pointing in the general direction of this mirage.

"I can now," she replies. "But I'm sure it wasn't there a few moments ago."

"Well we both see it now, trees mean water and it looks like a great place to take a breather while we are surrounded by nothing but sand. What do you think?"

"Breather?" she enquires.

"Yeah, breather, take a rest."

"Oh....I see now. Okay let's go and take a breather then, if you want to."

I can't help but smile at how Bump puts things sometimes with a genuine naivety. This comes across to me as an amusing type of humour. We plod on but this time with definite direction. We are heading for the oasis.

CHAPTER FOUR
DIRECTION TO NOWHERE

The oasis is a mile or so away, that's the nearest that I am able to gauge its distance at, but as we head towards it we seem to never actually get any closer. After what seems like a good twenty minutes of walking, I can't help but feel we have covered absolutely no ground at all towards reaching our goal.

"How long do you think we've been walking?" I suddenly blurt out.

"I don't know. You talk of time, but time is nothing here," is the reply I get.

"What the hell do you mean time is nothing here. Time is probably one of the greatest inventions of man. It is what governs the day and night. It is what people use to establish perimeters within their day and most importantly time is the paradox of the past and the future. Have you any concept of time at all?" I must admit to feeling that this little outburst of mine is quite impressive. I await her retort with great anticipation.

Bump suddenly stops walking, looks slowly at me with her head slightly tilted to the left. "Time? How long? These are questions that only people who are ruled by trying to achieve an objective within a specific instance ask. Here there is no instant that needs time, can you not see that? Why do you think that everything we do here is totally alien to what you seem to know or believe? You seem hell bent on finding a logical reason for what occurs here. It's almost as if you assume that it's all linked to something in your past. You seem to remember before we were here. I don't so therefore your precious TIME means nothing to me, or to anything that is here! Okay"

Wow, yet another incredibly deep statement and delivered with such vigour.

"Yeah it's okay, you really do need to calm yourself. I only asked a simple question, but if you have a genuine issue with time, Jesus I won't mention it again. Shit, I'm sorry."

She stops walking and turns to face me with the trace of a grin on her face, then her head droops downwards. She half looks up and says, "No, I'm sorry. Sometimes you ask questions that not only do I not know the answers to, but often I don't even understand. Time, you have talked of time before. Until I met you I never thought of time. Don't get me wrong, I know what time is or at least something inside my brain says I should know, but I cannot put the concept into perspective. I know you are going to think that I'm mad, but I do not know how to evaluate this time concept."

Again I am taken aback by her statement. Not only by the fact she states that she doesn't identify with time, but by the way she describes so eloquently how she does not comprehend the subject matter. How can she not understand time but still have such a command of the English language as to express her lack of knowledge so fluently on such a simple subject as time, or am I being naive? "Would you like me to explain time to you, and please don't get mad?"

She bursts into a rapture of laughter."By all means," she giggles. "As you feel it carries so much importantance please explain time to me so that I can understand why you consider it to be so vital and relevant to what is happening here, and to us."

I must admit when she puts it that way, the whole subject matter seems to crumble within my mind. With Bump's giggles it causes me to feel that I definitely want to explain the concept of time, and the more I give it my undivided attention, so the more I realise that to elucidate time to her is going to be almost impossible. The whole perception of time took me years to understand from childhood, how the hell am I going to enlighten a person in a few short bursts, of my interpretation of time. What a stupid idea. "Bollocks to it, I understand time and you don't. That is just fine, at least one of us does, so therefore we are in fairly good shape. Let's press on and get to this watering hole."

Bump again bestows me with a smile and quietly says, "I'm really glad we've found each other. Alone I was lost without any direction, just moving around this place and never knowing what was going to happen next. With you, I know that we will find the answers. I feel warm with you."

I smile at her, take her hand and say, "It's great to have company on an adventure and even better to have a friend. Come on you, let's get going, time is a wasting, not that we give a toss about time eh?"

Once more she erupts into laughter. "You're funny, but I'm with you, let's get to the water." We continue.

After what I can only describe as yet another eternity of seeming to encircle the oasis many times over, it suddenly appears that we are upon the final approach. I can clearly see and am able to gauge the size of not just the water, but also the various types of vegetation, trees, reeds, rushes and sparse grasses. As I get even closer I observe that the trees are Elm. ELM? I do not know too much about an oasis I've got to admit, but all the ones I've seen on television or in books, hey don't they have palm type trees around them, not Elms? As I stare harder, I'm sure that I am able to see that there is even an Oak in there as well. How bloody odd. "Have you ever been here before?" I question.

"Nope, I'm pretty sure I haven't," she replies.

"Have you ever seen an oasis on your journeys?" I ask.

She stops and I see her perusing the question. "No I haven't, in point of fact I never knew that this place had the name of an oasis until you called it that, but as soon as you gave it that name, I was able to recall that oasis was the correct title for a water hole in a desert. It's as though you have prompted me into recalling something locked far away in the back of my mind. You've done that on more than one occasion since I've met you. Weird isn't it?"

I feel my face physically frown. "That it is, that it is, but I don't reckon weird is the word to describe it. I'm not sure what one word if any can actually describe it."

We move on. The nearer we get so the slower my approach becomes, but this time it is of my own doing. Let's not throw caution to the wind. I try to see everything. My eyes feel like they are out on stalks. I have this real gut feeling that this is some form of trap. I don't know why, perhaps it's because of the time it took to finally reach this place. If I was to put it into a time frame from the first instance that I saw the oasis, I would have estimated it to be a couple of hours of walking at a medium pace. It has actually taken a good five, possibly six hours to get here. WHY? All I am able to conclude is that either I had judged the journey length completely wrongly or we were intentionally held back on purpose for some reason whatsoever. I'm going to go with the total paranoia theory; there's trouble here.

When I am within a hundred yards from the water's edge, I stop. The small lake is almost perfectly circular in shape, with the trees precisely spaced out around the banks of the water's edge. I see rushes and reeds standing up in the water, again most strategically placed. The neatest little pond I think I've ever seen and that's strange within itself, but hell, how many times have I said that recently?

The water is an exceptionally deep green and seems to ripple from its very centre, as though stones has been continuously dropped there causing a never ending cycle of almost perfectly small tidal waves. It's most hypnotic. Perhaps that is it's intention. I drag my stare away from the water. As I am looking out over the topography of this area, I glance over to Bump. She too is staring at the waters, her eyes fixed on the spectacle, with her torso inclining slightly towards the direction in which she is looking. She appears totally mesmerized.

"Bump!" I shout. "Are you still with me?"

Suddenly she shudders, blinks wildly and shakes her head. "Yeah, yeah, I'm here, I'm okay," she quietly replies.

"There is something odd about that frigging pond, so don't look at it," I order.

"I couldn't take my eyes off it," she stutters. " I think you're right, I was feeling quite weird and drawn towards it. I couldn't stop myself."

"Yeah I know, just don't stare at it. Only glance at it if you have to."

She looks at me and grins. "Aye, aye captain."

"Come on you, you sarcastic mare," I counter.

I decide that our approach should be one of completely covering the entire area, to obtain as informed an overview of this location as possible. I want to be able to see if there is anything at all hiding around those unobvious corners. As for the water, well I already know that it has hidden agendas within its perfect beauty.

We stick very closely together as we encircle the area. Moving closer to the waters border I observe that the sand changes its consistency. It becomes noticeably finer, colder in temperature. Although we are moving slowly, it feels harder to make any headway, as the grains appear to suck our feet further down into them. As we get within ten feet of the water's edge we enter the sparse tree line. I was right earlier, there are Elm trees here and the one I'm actually touching is an Oak. By the size of this tree it must have been growing for a minimum of fifty years. The circumference of its trunk is at least twice my reach, so I would gauge it's diameter to be over eight feet. Height wise, this tree must be forty feet high and is heavily laden with foliage, implying it to be an extremely healthy tree. So what the hell is it doing here? I know I'm right in saying that Oak trees do not grow in deserts and as we appear to be in the middle of one, at an oasis, which must be the only oasis in existence that sports a bloody Oak tree.

I turn to Bump and ask "Do you know what kind of tree this is?"

She looks at the trunk of the Oak and up at its height and stature, then she turns back to me. "In a word no, but you're going to tell me aren't you? I do know it's a wooden one."

If I didn't know better I would have said that her last words were sarcasm. "Nope, I'm not going to tell you now, you can stay happy in your ignorance." Is my defence. On saying this I slowly focus my attention on her face. I can see annoyance. She takes a pace towards me and there you go, I felt it, she gave me a little kick. I start to giggle then within a second I compose myself as I again become acutely aware of our surroundings. "Just kidding, just kidding. You're right, it is a wooden one and it's called an Oak tree but they don't grow in deserts."

She frowns a little and then questions me. "Where do they grow then?"

Well I have really got to say, out of all the questions, retorts or enquiries she could have made on the subject of trees, I didn't expect that one. "Good question, well I know for sure they grow in England, Britain as a whole. I'm sure I'm right in saying that they grow in temperate climates and this isn't a temperate climate," is my explanation.

There follows a brief silence and then it comes. "Why isn't it?"

"Why isn't it what?"

"What you said, that temp, tempo…… that climate thing?"

Ah for Christ sake, this is another conversation that I wish I hadn't started and it is definitely at completely the wrong time. "You are just going to have to trust me on this, it shouldn't be here. I'll explain the rest of it when we are on safer ground. Okay?"

She gives me a nonchalant nod, so I presume that is fine for now.

I take a long hard look at the path to the waters' edge. Nothing appears to be amiss. So it's time to take the plunge, well in a manner of speaking. "Stay here, keep me in view, I'm going to take a closer look at this lake and whatever you do, DON'T look at the water. Okay?"

I turn to Bump giving her a little smile. She nods again and returns my smile.

I traverse the trees and head down the slight, sandy incline to the water's edge. The sand becomes heavier the nearer I get to the water. This is to be expected I suppose, the sand must be wet? At the verge I kneel trying to gauge what I feel are the dangers of this water, while still trying to maintain a three hundred and sixty degree vigil on my immediate surroundings. Everything around me is still. I can see Bump crouched right behind the Oak tree with her head sticking out of the side intently watching me. All seems safe enough. Time to take a look at the water.

As I look down so the ripples stop. I abruptly edge away from it but I don't take my eyes off this new found calm. Remaining very still, to the point that I realise I am holding my breath. I'm trying so hard not to make a sound; in fact being invisible would be great right now. Nothing happens. I glance around at Bump, she's still at the tree watching me. I can see the fear and apprehension written all over her face. I gesture to her that all is well. She nods. No sound has been made. This whole scenario is incredibly tense and eerie.

Almost in slow motion I approach the water again. By now the water is completely still with its surface reflecting back at me like a mirror. I can see myself clearly. For the first time since I've been here I can see myself. But it's not me. To justify that last statement, it's not the me that got up this morning, or whenever the last time that actually was and I saw myself in a mirror. I am or was a man in my mid fifties, fifty five to be exact, with greying hair, mainly sideburns and temples, with a bit of a belly on its way. This reflection shows a man in his mid twenties. It's me okay, but thirty years ago. How the fuck can this be so. I stand up. I can see my attire. I have on a short sleeved buttoned up shirt and a pair of jeans. My hand moves to my neck. I have always worn a crucifix, a gold chain and crucifix, but it's not there. Have I lost it? I look down to my left hand to where my wedding ring should be. Not there either. Now that ring hasn't been taken off for years, it won't come off, I've grown into it, the knuckle of my third finger left hand has grown and the ring will not pass over it. No way have I lost that, no way has that just fallen off. So who am I looking at? What's going on? I slump down onto my rear. I have nothing on my feet. Why haven't I noticed that before? Suddenly I feel a touch on my shoulder. I immediately swing round and grasp what's touching me. I yank it forward in front of me. As I let go I see Bump go base over apex and into the oasis. Brilliant, I think to myself. Straight away I grab out to reach her, catching her wrist. She partially enters the water but I manage to catch her before she falls completely in and pull her to the shore. "Christ sorry Bump, you made me jump," I apologetically blurt out. As I pull her to safety we both slump down and sit with our feet dangling in the water. I can't help thinking that all the caution we have shown in exploring this oasis has just gone completely out of the window.

"I didn't know what was going on. You fell backwards and you looked so strange. I thought the water had got you. I was scared. I had to come and help you," she said.

As I glance towards her I see tears in her eyes. I lean over and gently brush them away. "It's okay and I appreciate the gesture, but I saw something that I just don't understand."

I get to my feet, still paddling at the waters edge and say to her, "I need you to answer a question for me as honestly as you can please, and I mean honestly. Can you do that?"

Before I have finished the question she is dragged backwards from me at great speed, by what is not visible. Just as I make a move trying to grab her, my feet are pulled from underneath me. My whole body hits the ground with an almighty thud and I am dragged back into the water. As I submerge beneath the water, the last thing I see is Bump disappearing over a sand dune. As I'm dragged downwards I try to kick at whatever has hold of me, but I soon realise that both of my legs are held by the entity, whatever it is. Again I find myself following my father's advice, not that I seem to have any choice here, and I desist in my struggle against the power in control of this event.

Suddenly I become aware that I am no longer being pulled down, I am now floating upwards, towards the surface. I glance down, deep into the water and I see the image of a mermaid with long flowing hair and a beautiful face, beckoning to me to swim down towards her. I feel my breath ebbing. I need to reach the surface, so still looking down at her, I start to swim upwards. Before my very eyes the attractive picture of this stunning mermaid, turns into a one eyed, veracious, distorted featured, nightmarish image. This picture increases my urgency to reach the surface, to say nothing of the fact that it appears to be coming up after me.

I break the surface of the water in a blind panic. The rush of fresh air is apparent and most welcome, but reaching the bank is of greater urgency to me, not knowing how close the Optic is behind me. I immediately enter into the front crawl, the swimming stroke I know to be my best and also fastest. I head for the shore. I actually manage to reach the shore without interruption, and hauling myself out of the water I turn to see if my pursuer has emerged. Within seconds the Optic shoots out from the centre of the oasis, flying into the air a good ten feet above the water's surface. He hovers there, suspended by nothing, glaring at me with his one eye and spitting at me from out of his broken toothed mouth. He then coils himself up, launching himself towards me. As soon as I perceive his intention I dive back into the oasis just as he shoots over the top of me. I instantaneously turn in the water and return to the bank, watching the Optic disappear into the distance. I wait, pensive for a couple of minutes, waiting to see if he's going to come back. When I feel confident that this little skirmish is over, I call out to Bump. "BUMP, WHERE ARE YOU?"

I hear a muffled sound from behind me and I turn seeing the small dune that she disappeared over earlier. I run in that direction, over the top and see her, well the back of her head poking up from the sand. I rush to where she is, placing my hands either side of her face saying, "Jesus Bump, are you okay?"

She nods and mumbles, blowing and spitting sand out of her mouth. "Please get me out of this, please," she pleads.

I start frantically digging, throwing sand in every direction. Slowly but surely I manage to free her arms until I am able to lever her out of the sandy hole.

"What the hell happened?" I question. "I saw you being dragged off but I couldn't help you because at the same time I was pulled into the oasis."

"I know," Bump replies. "I saw you go in. I don't know what had hold of me, everything happened so quickly. One minute I was being dragged over the sand, the next I was up to my neck in it, unable to move. I couldn't call out, it was hard enough just to breathe." She brushes herself off and we walk back towards the water's edge to enable her to clean herself up. I however stand guard, always watching for the Optic.

"Remember the question I asked you before we were attacked?"

She hesitates for a moment looking straight into my eyes. "Yes, of course I can."

"I want you to look at me and describe as best you can, what you can see, exactly what you see."

Again her gaze is extremely direct. She gets to her feet taking a couple of paces away from me. She stops, turns and the only way I can describe it is, she proceeds to scan me like a machine, from top to bottom. This scanning process takes no more than a minute but it is a completely systematic action. When she seems to have finished her inspection, her gaze again meets mine but this time with her head very, very slightly tilted backwards, as though to give her a height advantage and an air of superiority. "Right," she says. "Here I go. Ready?"

"Yep and be as honest as you can."

She swallows and gulps as if she has a dry mouth and then begins. "You are at least a head taller than me and wider across the shoulders. You have dark brown wavy hair, no facial hair and blue eyes. You have a deep voice, white teeth and you know a lot," she pauses. "And you're my friend."

While looking at her I notice, as she says the last part about being my friend, how her head lowers. It also occurs to me that her description was very basic, just like a small child would have described it. No detail at all, but hell it doesn't matter, she has basically described what she can see and in essence, it is not the same me that I look into the mirror every morning and see. Therefore I can only conclude that it's my thoughts, brain and consciousness in a body that was mine a good thirty odd years ago. This just gets weirder and weirder.

Bump is now looking at me with her head tilted to the side again. "Was that okay? I was as honest as I could be."

"That was brilliant but can you take a guess as to how old I am?"

"About the same age as me I would think. Why?"

"That's a good question, but I know how old I am. I am fifty five years old. When I saw myself earlier in the reflection of the water, what I saw was a twenty year old. You say that I am about the same age as you, well you are no more than twenty five years old. Don't you see, before I woke up here I was at least thirty years older than I am now."

Her face is a picture of complete confusion. Her eyebrows are frowned and this in turn causes her forehead to crinkle. Her eyes are almost squinting, her nostrils slightly flared and her mouth is clasped shut making her look as if she has only one lip, that one being the bottom one which is protruding.

It's at this point that I really take notice of her, her features, her stature and her dress. On her feet she wears nothing, her blouse or top is of a buttoned up type, yellow, short cap sleeved with button down, pleated breast pockets on either side. This is tucked in loosely to a pair of khaki coloured shorts. She is of slim stature, roughly 5 foot 2 inches tall with light brown to blonde shoulder length hair which is parted in the middle. Her eyes are brown. She has pale, translucent skin. Her voice is for the most part, fairly soft and she is quite well spoken. There is very little or even no accent to indicate where she originates from. She speaks English, obviously, so I can only conclude that she is from England, but as for brogue, nothing is evident.

"Listen Bump, It's time we got out of here. This place isn't real and I reckon we were directed here for the sole purpose of me getting a real fucking shock by seeing myself in those waters. Job done. If indeed that was the intention, who or what is orchestrating this little funfair has achieved its little game."

Her persona now changes as she stares straight at me. "Where to now?"

I scan the horizon of the direction that we haven't already travelled. In the distance I can see what appears to be something resembling a raised plateau. From this distance I cannot gauge the size, height or make-up of this range but for me it definitely seems to be the direction in which we should go. I turn to her pointing in the direction of the plateau. "That's where we are going. Can you see that lot over there?"

 She is gazing in the direction of which I am pointing. "I can see them, but why there? What makes you think that's the next place to go? What makes you think there are any answers up there?"

I slowly turn back to look at the plateau. "Because everything we've done thus far, every direction we've travelled, I had previously

40

assumed were our choices, but I am beginning to wonder if that is actually the case. I feel that we are being led, directed. There is no going back, we need to press on."

She smiles at me, laughing out loud. "You're funny you are, but I'm with you, so let's go."

Well there goes another deep and meaningful statement from my only support, companion and friend. I've got to admit that our little conversations, as obscure and totally off the wall as they seem to be, are my only sanctuary inside this world that is dominated by ambiguous direction. This is the Optics world and I'm only just beginning to understand how his mind works. He said, "Let the journey begin." Well ass-hole I'm walking your road but the further along it I go, the more I seem to understand you. Believe me, if I obtain complete understanding, you will rue the day you started this fucking little game.

CHAPTER FIVE
HEADY HEIGHTS

The mountains ahead appear to be, if I was to put it into distance, a couple of miles or so away. I can see where the sand comes to an end and where more undergrowth begins. As we distance ourselves from the oasis, I glance back and feel dread as to what has just occurred there. I don't know why, but the apparition in the water has unsettled me. I wonder if that was the intention?

I look at Bump and say, "Are you alright?"

She looks back at me and says, "I am now. I was very concerned for a while back there. You looked frightened and strange which scared me. Having explained to me what made you like that, I now understand, well sort of anyway. Now you're back to the fearless leader again and that's why I'm fine."

God she's comical at times. I can feel the smile cross my face as I slightly shake my head.

As we walk on I look up at the mountains. They look enormous, high and pretty stark. Pondering on their stature and appearance, it occurs to me that the desert looked pretty stark too. Now there's a thought. Does this mean that we are going from one boiling pot of fat into another? Well maybe it does, but I'm on that journey the Optic told me to take, so I can only hope that following instructions will give me my answers.

We walk for a further mile or so and the mountains become bigger and bolder. The desert ebbs away and the shrub land starts under foot. It's a bit like the shrub land we encountered on our first meeting with the desert. At least that's consistent, but now the shrub land looks as though it progresses forward into tall grassland, not a jungle but like pampas plains. As we get closer, it becomes apparent that the grasses are at least ten to twelve feet high and completely motionless. They just stand tall and straight, no sway whatsoever.

"Well that lot is going to take some getting through," I say to Bump as we are on our final approach.

She looks at me, smiles and says, "I don't think it will be as bad as you think, but we'll see when we get there and attempt to get through it."

Now that's a true enough statement if I've ever heard one. I can't argue with that kind of logic.

"True enough fair maiden, true enough." I retort.

Finally we arrive at the grassland. The grass is indeed 10 to 12 feet high, immensely dense and thick. I stop for a minute, look at Bump and say, "Any suggestions?"

She looks at me, looks left and right saying, "We can try to go round it but I don't think we are going to be allowed to."

I look at her a little mystified. "You don't think we are going to be allowed to?"

Having not taken her eyes from me she replies. "No. If he wants the grasslands to go on for twenty miles, then they will go on for twenty miles. If he wants them to go for ten feet, then they'll only go for ten feet. We are here and this is what we must go through."

She suddenly stops and freezes, looks at me and runs straight at the grassland, pushing her way into it. I follow behind her to see where she has gone, but she's just inside the first layers lying on the floor.

Looking down at her I say, "What's the matter, what the hell's the matter?"

She looks straight at me with her staring huge wild eyes. "Leave me alone, don't talk to me, leave me, I'll be right here when you get back."

Immediately I back away, turn sharply and start looking around. I intentionally make some space between us because of her obvious fear. Fear of what though?

Then I hear it. "You are finally here." A booming deep voice. A commanding voice. "I've been waiting." It's the Optic.

I turn slowly and there it is. It's not the same as before, it's not a big eye this time. The eye is still most evident but now it's a little slimmer and it's hovering. This time it doesn't seem to have a base although the eye is surrounded by matter. The matter is almost transparent, glowing but with no definite shape. The lights inside it react like lightening, dancing and flickering, but the eye is most intense, gyrating, expanding and dilating like a zoom lens being focused in and out. This time, I'm really going to try to make this thing talk to me.

Nonchalantly I say, "So you show your ugly eye again do you, you really do have some front you ugly bastard."

This statement causes a moment of complete silence. The Optic's eye squints slightly, so slowly, making the seconds seem like a century. It is focusing itself directly at me, its pupil becoming ever larger. I can only await the Optic's retort. "What do you think of my world, being?" It says in a sneering manner.

"Oh, I'm a 'being' am I?" I taunt. "Nice, you really have a way with words don't you asshole. From that grunt I can only assume that you don't have too many beings visit you here that often. I wonder why? Could it possibly be your winning personality. I don't know. What do you think?"

"YOU WILL TALK TO ME WITH RESPECT!" his voice booms. The volume and sheer force of his voice is deafening, and yet again it takes me to my knees, my hands over my ears and I almost beg, "For Christ's sake, for Christ's sake. You came here to talk to me, not burst my fucking ear drums, so talk to me. What is all this stuff about, trying to get me to bend down because your voice is so frigging loud. What's the matter with you? I'm here for a reason, you've made that perfectly clear, the only thing thus far that is clear. You obviously want me here, so tell me what it is you want me to do. I'm taking your journey, for want of a better word, I'm going through your little games, I'm jumping through all your fucking hoops. So what is it you want?"

There is a moments silence, which is quite pleasing and then the OPTIC starts to narrate. "You and I are almost the same in the sense that we are in the same place at the same time. We have always been in the same place at the same time. You are a Being and I am a Being, all enveloped in your Being. Do you understand?"

Do I understand? No. I know that the words were all English but I haven't got a clue what it's on about. I am beginning to believe the subject matter is all a little bit too deep for me. So I tell him. "No mate. I'm sorry; I'm not with you at all. If you're going to talk in riddles then we're not going to get very far are we. I really do need you to be a little bit more upfront with whatever your problem is with me. I have no problem with you as such, how could I, I hadn't met you until recently. As far as I'm aware, I've never pissed on your parade, so why are we even conversing like this? I have no idea. It's you that seems to be pulling all the strings around here. I just really need to know what the fuck is actually going on."

"You will continue your journey. You will eventually understand, but you've got to find that out for yourself because I cannot tell you. I cannot even hint to you, you have to find out for yourself, and when you do find out, that is when I will appear to you for the very last time. Do you understand?"

I look slowly at the Optic and say, "Well sort of, I think."

I don't know, this is all extremely bizarre. I turn to look back to where Bump sneaked into the long grass. When I look back again there is no Optic. It's gone. For a minute I just crouch down on the ground and look around. Where the hell did it go! I didn't see it coming and didn't see it go. That means it simply just appeared! So how does it do that? I really don't know. There are way too many questions and no bloody answers. I get to my feet and walk over to where Bump was and to my surprise, she is still lying there.

"He didn't see me, did he?" she says.

"No it doesn't look like it. At least he didn't say anything to you."

"So therefore he thinks you're on your own."

"Look," I say. "You're on your own, I'm on my own. Firstly he tried to pull me into an oasis and he buried you up to your frigging neck, which implies that he knows there's two of us. Just because he was talking to me and ignoring you, doesn't mean he doesn't know you're there. I think he knows you're there, it's just that you are of no importance to him for some obscure reason that I don't understand. It's me that he seems to have issue with. It's me that he seems to have some objective with, but I don't know what or why that is. For some reason you seem to currently be surplus to his requirements. As you said, I don't think he wants you here and he's going to ignore the fact that you are here, but all the time you are with me, it strikes me that you are in a lot of danger."

She looks at me with very saddened eyes. "What are you saying? Are you saying we are going to split up?"

I will have to give this some thought, quite serious thought, but not right now. What I need to do now is to reassure her and get moving again. "No. No of course not. We don't split up, we stay together. We started this together, we'll finish it together. Chin up you."

She looks at me, sporting a big grin on her face now. Very pretty girl when she smiles.

"Come on, let's get through this grass and keep going. If the Optic wants this game played, let's play it and win."

So with a new found vigour we head for the grass. We enter at the exact spot where Bump threw herself in earlier and start to break through. It is heavy going, pushing the grass both aside and down. It quickly becomes apparent to me that the further we penetrate into the grass; in reality we should be forming a track with the flattened grass, but obscurely when we turn around, the track behind us has completely disappeared. The grass is upright again. A couple of times I stop, retrace my step, knock it down again, look at it and nothing happens. It doesn't move. Then I move away, turn my back and within seconds as I turn back to check, so it's stood back up again. Huh, weird, very weird, but par for the course here anyway. What the hell, I need to press on, so that's precisely what we do.

Having eventually worked our way through the long grass we finally reach the edge of the mountain. Here there's a short expanse that's lacking in grass, there's bits and bobs of tufts of grass around and large stones, but it's extremely sparse. We negotiate the boulders, traversing through the stones to the foot of the mountain. Here we stop and look up. It appears to be quite a steep path up but still climbable. It's obvious there's some form of track here which makes me think that other things must have used this trail to have actually carved this out. Bump and I look at each other, nothing is said, but the joint understanding is there, and understood. We start on our hard trek up.

All the while with every step, we are climbing higher and higher. I can see over the vast lands that we have just crossed, the oasis and the trees, but the desert just goes off into the distance a million miles away and I am unable to see beyond it. I can't see the river, but feel sure that on reaching the top I probably should be able to. We keep climbing upwards. The path is arduous, difficult and several times I have to help Bump with various parts of it. There's very little conversation between us on this stretch of the journey because we are both short of breath. About a third of the way up we come across a small plateau. We stop and rest.

I actually say, "Let's take a rest here. We've come up a long way."

She looks at me smiles and says, "Yes if you need to."

What does she mean, if I need to? That's a funny thing to say! I look at her and reiterate my thoughts, "What do you mean, if I need to? Don't you need a rest?"

"No, no I don't," she states assertively. "There was a time I thought that I wanted to rest, but now I don't and nor do you if you think about it. You just believe you need a rest. It's like when I told you about sleep." She pauses for a second and then asks. "How long have we been here?"

This question gives me food for thought if that's the right expression. I need to provide an accurate and decisive answer.

"Well there doesn't seem to be any night or day, your observation on that subject matter may be correct. Having said this, I really do not know for sure."

She continues, "No night will come. We have been here longer than what you call a day. Do you need sleep, are you hungry?" Again Bump has posed a good question.

"Well now you mention it, I think I am hungry. Yep I reckon I could eat."

She smiles. "But you are not, are you? You are not hungry at all?"

"How do you know that? How can you justify that statement?" I ask slightly agitated.

A little smile flickers across her face but her answer is definite. "I know because I am not hungry."

I must admit, with this conversation I begin to feel my hackles rise. I feel an argumentative attitude coming over me. "Well just because you are not, doesn't mean that I'm not hungry," I snap back at her.

"But I know you are not, you just think you are." Her reply is as fast as my agitated argument is becoming. I need to bring this conversation into perspective.

"Okay, this is getting very confusing. I think I am hungry and I could eat some food, let's just put it that way."

"Yeah I dare say you could but there isn't any food, so therefore you couldn't eat anyway! You just walked through a desert and you didn't need any food or water. At no point did you ever indicate that either of these things did you need."

"No, you are right. I have got to acknowledge that neither food nor water were an issue. I can't recall even thinking about them, but having said that, when I got to the oasis I wanted to taste that water."

"Hmmm", she mutters. "That's because you think you needed to."

At this point I can honestly say, I am totally pissed off with this dialogue. To be perfectly frank, I can't see any conclusion to the debate. Fine, I'm going to end it on my terms. "Ah okay, I think I see. So what you are saying is I don't, hell, we don't have to sit here and rest at all, it's just me having a stupid moment. However to adhere to my obvious failings, you will humour me so that we can sit a while, taking the rest that I don't need and you don't need either. Am I right?"

Bump gives me what I can only describe as a sideways look, but she says nothing. Feeling that I have obviously reached an advantage point in this war of wills, I make a commanding statement. "Okay, then let's carry on! Let's get up this bloody mountain!"

She is staring at me, her look one of verbal attack. Then she brings her defence to the fore, jumps to her feet, smiles a huge grin and says, "I'm ready, I'll lead the way then," and off she goes clambering upwards. Did I win that debate? I am not so sure. She certainly has a way of making an argument, if that's what it was, into an objective situation.

Off we go again. I follow her onward and upwards, travelling for another good hour or so. By now we are three quarters of the way up, when all of a sudden the track peters out to almost nothing. From here on in it's going to be a steep climb. We start to climb, I've taken the lead now and bit by bit we ascend the final stretch. It's not a sheer face by a long shot but it is incredibly steep and extremely difficult to ascend, but nevertheless we continue to climb.

When we finally reach the summit of the mountain, I pull myself up onto a rocky ledge, rock that is completely covered in grass. It appears almost as though the stone has had a short, cropped, velveteen haircut. I know that sounds bizarre, but this stone absolutely compliments the soft, green lush grass as they blend inseparably into each other. I lean down helping to pull Bump up the last few feet. We both look over the lip of the mountain gazing down at our particularly long and difficult climb, and also at the view it now affords us. The only recognisable features properly visible are the oasis and the route to the base of this mountain.

I take her hand and say, "We made it."

With a huge smile on her face she retorts with, "I knew we would. Are you still hungry?"

I just burst into a rapture of laughter, "Oh, you can be a real bitch when you want to, can't you?" She simply chuckles at my comment.

Slowly we turn away from the panoramic view towards our goal, the one we climbed this lump of rock to see. In front of us now there is woodland, not jungle but woodland. It appears like an orchard, with all the trees planted in order as though someone has intended them to be in perfectly straight lines, with exactly the same distance between each one. Interesting!

I glance back again to see if I can see the river, but no it's too far away. I can still see the oasis, more or less, but the funny thing about it is that the trees that were there before, are not apparent anymore. There's no sign of the trees. They're gone.

I look further down to where we previously saw the Optic through the long grass but there's no sign of anything there, and even the long grass seems to be different. It's hard to put my finger on what it is, it's not that important, or at least I think it's not. I turn my attention back to the orchard looking at the trees in their orderly fashion and also at the fact that they're not overly high.

I look at Bump and say, 'What do you think of those trees, give me your thoughts."

She looks at them and then turns to me and says, "What do you mean, what do I think?"

I slowly turn towards her and repeat the question that I really did think was pretty straight forward. "What do you think of those trees? What species are they, the one's right in front of us? What kind of trees do you think they are?"

She gives her full attention to the woodland and then delivers one of her incredibly factual answers."Well they are wooden trees of course, what else would they be."

In essence you can't fault her single layered logic, but I can't help thinking that these 'one liners' of hers are totally fucking unhelpful. "Yeah I know they are wooden, it's obvious they are bloody wooden, but the way they are all in precise positions, in rows, do they not remind you of anything?"

She is still staring at the trees. "I don't know what you mean Andy, I don't know what you want me to say."

Okay, I think it's best I prompt her thoughts, "Do they not remind you of an orchard?"

She looks blankly at me for a second then says, "Orchard, orchard,..... orchard as in apples and pears?"

"Yep exactly, as in an apple orchard. Does that not remind you of an apple orchard?"

She turns to me, semi smiles and says, "I've never seen an orchard, I've never even seen an apple so I don't know."

For a minute I just look at her and say, "You've never seen an apple, what never?"

"No," she replies.

"Have you seen a pear?"

"Nope."

"Have you seen a plum, an orange..............a cherry?"

"No, I have never seen any of those things."

These statements absolutely astound me. How can she have never seen any of these things. She is a mature twenty something woman. I don't understand how there are these huge holes in her knowledge of essentially basic subjects. For some reason I feel the need to find out more, so I pursue the topic.

"Right ok, so you've never seen any fruit from a tree, not a walnut not an acorn nor a coconut?"

"I don't know what any of these things are. What is an acorn?"

"It's a tiny little nut that comes from an Oak tree."

At this point the light dawns on me that I'm actually labouring something she's never seen, so I need to be much more constructive. "Well you have seen trees, right? I know you have because of the ones at the oasis."

Her eyes start to light up as if now we are actually conversing on a subject matter which she is fully au fait with. "Oh yes I've seen hundreds of trees."

"Great. Did you notice that there were lots of different sorts, different kinds?"

Again that little frown. "Well most of them are, depending on where I am."

"What do you mean depending on where you are?"

"Well the one thing that I know is, if I see one type of tree, it's the same as all the rest of the trees in that particular place. You say they look like apple trees here, so I said yeah. You know a lot more than me, so I assumed you would be right in what the trees are called."

"Well they are all apple trees. That's exactly what they are."

Now Bump seems to gain a confidence blast. She puts her hands on her hips, smiles and lets rip. "So, here we are looking at, as you put it 'an orchard' and all the trees you can see are all apple trees. Well when we went to the grass it was all grass, and when we went to the sand it was all sand. Don't you see?"

"I'm at a bit of a loss here, can you please explain what you are trying to tell me."

She looks at me with a frustrated but superior look and a wry smile crosses her face. "Oh Andy, haven't you got it yet, it's because they are what you want to see?"

"What I want to see?"

"Yes exactly that. You want to see apple trees, so you are seeing them. At the point you first set eyes on those trees, in your brain you decided they were apple trees, so they all are." She moves right up close to me and places her left hand on my shoulder. "You will get it eventually, you are seeing apple trees because you wanted to, you saw an oasis of water because you wanted to see something in the sands, so therefore you saw one."

I have to give this verbal onslaught some serious thought, as this is quite deep stuff. Where does she think it all up from? "Ok I think it's time to press on. I really don't know what to make of what you've just said. I need to consider it much more thoroughly."

She just smiles at me, but as her smile reaches beaming point, so it starts to disappear and replace itself with a concerned, fearful look. Her whole bodily structure becomes tense and her eyes start flickering from left to right.

"Bump, what's up?"

Her whole being is completely still, like a child's, as if by being in this state it makes her invisible.

"Talk to me, I need your input here." I state with some urgency

"Andy I've got that feeling again."

"That feeling? Are you talking about that Optic type of feeling?"

"Yes, yes. Something is going to happen."

Now I sense myself begin to tense up as well and I start looking in all directions, even up and down. I have no idea how the Optic is going to appear. I do know that I have never seen his arrival or departure as yet, and that in itself is a major worry. "When is it going to happen, got any idea, talk to me?"

"I don't know, I just get this feeling and then he comes."

"Do you think it's imminent?"

"I think it's going to happen any minute."

"That's what I just bloody well asked! Let's get away from the edge of the mountain."

We both move away from the mountains edge and pensively head towards the woodland. Just as I am about to suggest that we make a run for the trees and the cover they may afford us, the closest trees to us begin to uproot themselves from the ground. I come to a grinding halt and grab Bump to stop her advance towards this totally unacceptable vision. Fucking trees that move! I've got to be in some sort of special effects movie. As the lumbering, wooded apparitions head straight towards us, so the smaller branches fall off leaving only the larger boughs. When they seem to have shed all the branches that are surplus to their requirements, their intention becomes acutely clearer as they head directly towards us, swinging their remaining huge limbs in what can only be described as a terribly menacing manner. Escape route. We need an escape route.

I look to the left, nothing and then I look to the right, also nothing. Then all I can think is, we've got to go backwards to where we have just come from. Not a great option, but as far as I can see, the only one we have. We slowly start to back away until we are right at the edge of the mountain top.

"I'm not going that way, there's no way I am going that way." Bump blurts out.

My quick reply to this is, "I don't think we have got too much choice here sweetheart, so we'd best start moving our asses down the mountain and let's do it now!"

With my eloquent suggestion she starts to go over the edge, endeavouring to make a hasty descent. I follow her. In my obvious haste I lose my footing, followed by my hand hold and to my horror I begin to slip. The gravity of this situation can only speak for itself. Within a second, I'm out of control falling down the mountain. I pass Bump and see the horror on her face as I continue on my downward path. As I tumble I attempt to cling onto things. I grab at brushwood and try to hold on but nothing holds me, most of what I fumble and grab at just comes away. I eventually tumble all the way down hitting, bumping and crashing into things, until eventually I come to an abrupt halt at the exact same spot where we initially rested on our way up. I lay quite still thinking, "My god what have I done to myself, everything hurts."

I rotate my eyes enabling me to look up. I can see the trees hanging over the edge, the branches swishing back and forth. Bump is around ten to twelve feet out of their reach, and it looks as though where she's perched is relatively safe for the moment. I know I've got to get to her, but firstly I need to find out what damage has been done to me. I think to myself, I've got to be careful here. If I have broken something, anything, I am going to be in deep shit. I need to actually test everything out. Slowly but surely I move my fingers and toes and then my ankles. Then I try my knees, hips, elbows, my neck and then finally my back. Much to my surprise, my initial evaluation of my medical status is good. Everything seems to be working, so I will go to stage two. I pull myself to my feet. Having done this I give myself a good stretch in all directions. Everything seems to be as it should, nothings broken. I can only count myself lucky, tremendously lucky.

I gaze back up to the top. I must have fallen a good two to three hundred feet, well more or less, and taken the most bippity-boppity route on the way down that there could possibly be, and nothing has really harmed me. I look at my hands, at the very least they should be scratched, but no they are fine, what's going on here?

I attempt to climb back up, now with renewed vigour. There's something extraordinarily odd here, and the one thing I do know is that yet again I'm not hurt. I wasn't hurt when I was dragged under water in the beginning at the river and I wasn't hurt when I fought whatever it was in the oasis, and again I am not hurt having fallen two or three hundred feet down a mountain! By the look of things it seems that physically I can't be hurt. I have to get back up there, so I start climbing quickly, again there's no lack of energy. As I approach the ledge that Bump is crouched on, I slow down so as not to cause her to jump. When she spots me, I see the horror in her face. She looks straight at me and in breathless panic says, "Andy, Andy make them go away. You can make them go away."

I look at her perplexed and gasp, "What the hell do you mean, I can make them go away?"

She glares at me with an intensity, "You CAN make them go away."

I stare back up the mountain. All I can see are at least forty huge branches thrashing in our direction. Pieces of the edge that they are standing on come tumbling down at us, as well as bits of grass, broken wood and foliage. While I am observing this situation, I say to Bump, "Well why don't you make them go away, why don't you make them piss off right now?"

"I can't Andy. This is not my world."

I can't help thinking blood hell, I haven't got time for this. I don't need another deep and meaningful conversation at this moment in time. I need to actually get us somewhere safe. While I'm having these fleeting thoughts it suddenly occurs to me that the thrashing of the trees has ceased. I look back up, and yep sure enough, the walking wooden tops are not in situ having a go at us. This of course poses yet another problem. While they were up there, the obvious choice of escape was down. The choice now is either up or down. Left and right are out of the question due to the severity of the mountain side. It's up or down. It's time to make an executive decision.

"Bump I'm going up to take a look, okay? Just stay here, I won't be long."

She nods confirming that she understands the plan. So up I go, slowly, surely and with extreme caution. When I reach the point of no return, which is slightly below the ledge at the top, I can't help wondering what the hell I'm doing here. The trees would be able to reach me without any effort at all. With this thought, I realise that caution is not really needed. If they are there, I'm a goner for sure, so I might as well go over in a flurry of fool hardiness and take them by surprise.

I place my hands over the top, very slowly in an effort to remain invisible and place my torso and legs into a coiled, crouching position. When I'm happy that I feel ready to attack, I uncoil and spring myself up and over the top. I feel my whole body has turned into a mass of hard and readied muscle, but as I enter into a battle stance I observe that the trees are all back in their original positions. The trees that were swishing about all over the side have gone, they have actually rooted themselves again! I calm myself down, return to the edge and look down at Bump. "Come on up, it all looks safe enough up here now, c'mon up."

She warily retraces her footsteps up. When she is within my reach, I grasp her hand, pulling her up to safety. She gathers her bearings, crouches and looks around. "Are they going to move again?" she asks.

"I really don't know." I answer

"You have made them stop then."

"I don't think I made them stop, I don't know why they stopped. Bloody glad they did though."

She clambers to her feet and walks right up close to me. "It's important Andy, you've got to be sure. You've got to be sure that you have made them stop," she states urgently.

"Bump what is this thing that makes you think I can make them stop?"

Her head lowers, then immediately springs back up. "I don't know why exactly, but I am sure you can make them stop. You can control things as well, all sorts of things if you try."

I turn away from her, focusing my attention on the trees. "Look at those trees, there's no breeze, no wind, yet the leaves shimmer. I can't feel any wind, I can't feel anything like that and yet the leaves are shimmering. Can you see that?"

She simply nods her head.

I start walking towards the trees and as I reach the first one I stop. Having stopped, I feel a knock in my back. I know it's Bump, she has followed me so closely, watching everything else around her except where she's going. "I've stopped Bump." I inform her.

"Oops, sorry," comes the reply.

I look back at the tree. I push it, with slight apprehension obviously, but I give it a good push nonetheless. Nothing, so to make sure, I think to hell with it and give it a kick. Well all that succeeds in doing is to hurt my foot. It's solid wood, so I can only conclude that it actually is only a tree. Bump is giggling at my action. Funny as this may seem, I still ask myself what the hell did we see? What the hell made us jump off a frigging cliff? There aren't too many things that could get me to do that, yet they managed to do so.

CHAPTER SIX
__INTERPRETATIONS__

We slowly and cautiously commence our journey through the orchard, acutely aware that something else may just appear to come to life, that shouldn't actually do so. We walk for some third of a mile and finally the orchard begins to peter out. We encounter no incidents or any cause for concern, although we do not speak or utter a single word. A gentle stroll in essence, but carried out in cautious silence.

As we leave the trees we enter into an exceptionally flat area with grass so perfectly short that it would have made a great football or rugby pitch. If somebody could have used a lawnmower on it in little straight lines, it would have really looked the part. However at this moment in time it looks like one enormous lawn. Looking across this expanse of grass I am able to see for a good five or six hundred yards. Where the lawn ends, a jungle abruptly starts. From this distance it looks to be reasonably thick with heavy, dense foliage. It reminds me a little of the first time I found myself in this world in a similar jungle. Perhaps I've completed a full circle and returned to where I started from. I look at Bump who is also surveying the area.

"Have you ever been here before. Do you recognize anything?"

"No, I've never been here before, but that's the whole point, every time I visit a new place, I can never seem to find it again. It changes. You met me at the river and I had never been there before. We travelled across that desert and I'd never been there before either. I had never seen that oasis until we were just there, and as for the mountain and orchard, that's all new to me too."

"Okay I think I get the message, it's all new to you, and all new to me as well."

I look to my left, it seems to go for miles, just flat grass and then I look to the right; guess what, goes for miles, just flat grass.

I look at Bump and say, 'What do you reckon? Do you want to go straight across or to the left or the right?"

She looks at me and smiles. "We are going whichever way you want to go, it's all up to you?"

"Okay then, oh faithful companion, let's go straight across. It's a wide expanse and we should therefore be able to see danger from a fair way off. The big problem that I can foresee here is that we can also easily be seen. We will be out in the open, no cover. What do you think?"

I can see she is pondering my statement. "No cover, I don't think that matters. If the Optic is watching, he already knows we are here."

"If he's watching? Do you not think he can see us anyway?" I question.

"No I don't, as sometimes I think he is not here."

"Where do you think he is then, when he's not watching? Where do you think he goes?"

She calmly turns towards me, smiles and says, "I don't know exactly where he goes, but there's obviously more than one place that he has to be, otherwise he would have found us many times, and he hasn't. So I don't think he can see us all the while. I believe he can only see us when he enters into this room."

I put my hand on her arm and proclaim with interest. "In this room? You think this is a room?"

"Well that's how I have always thought of it, as different rooms, that is."

"So where we have been so far is all one big room?"

She laughs out loud. "No, no, no, we've actually been in three rooms and this is the fourth."

My mind is buzzing with this concept. "So every time we go through something, like the river, that's a room?"

"Yes, yes, yes, that's it!"

There's a short pause and I continue, "The desert is a room?"

"Yes".

"The mountains were a room, and this is just the latest room?"

"You've got it," Bump says with definite glee in her voice.

"So," I conclude, " if I go back through this orchard to the mountain, and then climb back down the mountain and walk through the long grass, go back to the oasis, pass the oasis, back through the desert and finally get to the river, I can go back through all of those rooms."

Now she frowns and her face becomes saddened. "The doors are shut on those rooms. Once you pass through them, you can't go back."

I stare at her, searching her face as if we are just playing some sort of a guessing game against each other. "Come on Bump, are you are off your rocker, I have a good mind to walk through that orchard and go back to the edge of the mountain so that I can show you."

Her posture and pose become slightly agitated. "Okay Andy, if you don't believe me, let's go and do just that."

"Really?" I reply, a little surprised.

"Yeah let's do it then you will see, then perhaps you will understand what I'm trying to tell you." She has definitely got a strop on.

"Right, let's go." I order in a defensive but assertive manner.

We both turn and look at the orchard. It's still there, so we start to retrace our journey back through where we have just come from.

We walk. We walk and we walk, for what seems like an hour and it remains purely an orchard. I know it didn't take us this long to walk from the top of the mountain through the orchard originally to where we reached the big playing field, but the orchard this time just goes on endlessly. Although it looks like my theory is going to be overturned, the good news is that the vegetation this time isn't coming to life!

61

Eventually, with imminent defeat over this argument, I come to a halt and look straight at Bump. "We've been walking for at least two hours now, would you have said?"

"If that's how you gauge it," she replies in an almost superior tone of voice.

"And we should have been at the mountains edge ages ago, shouldn't we?"

"I told you that door was shut, we are in a different room now."

At this point I need to concede. "Hmmm ok. I am wrong and you are right. I apologize."

She flings her arms around me and hugs me.

"So you think we ought to go back?" I submit.

"I know we have to go back," she knowingly states, " Otherwise we will be walking in this orchard forever."

I have to smile at this as Bump knew all along that she was right. I am stupid really to have even questioned her knowledge. After all, I'm the new kid in town here.

She continues. "You have to keep going, as you are the one who has to take this journey and the doors will shut behind you. You cannot go back to any of the other rooms. They are locked now. There remain only new rooms to visit and explore."

I must confess I am still a little mystified by this interpretation, but I turn positively, heading back the way we came. Within less than twenty minutes we are back to the grass and the big playing field. "Well we are back, and it didn't take us very long at all."

She smiles. "I told you so."

"Yes you did, but I wasn't sure you were right, so I had to see for myself. Now I have, now I know, so we will call them rooms as that's what you call them, okay."

She nods.

Looking back at the orchard I say, "Well as you say we have completed that room, so we need to move on don't we?"

"I think so. You point the way forward, you are the one who knows where we are going."

I glance across to her and laughingly say, "Bloody hell, I haven't got a frigging clue where we are going, but let's 'rock 'n roll' anyway."

Again she begins laughing. "Rock 'n roll, what does that mean?"

"Ah Bump, that's a phrase I use when I want to get something done."

"I think I understand then," she retorts raising her eyebrows.

As I look out over the grassland, I kneel down to feel the texture of its individual blades. They have a damp feel, almost as though a morning dew has not long ago settled upon them. I have no idea what time of day it is now, so this is just an assumption, something I feel I should evaluate because yet again, I have that same feeling that this isn't real. "Do you reckon we can jog over this to the other side?"

"Jog?" she queries.

"Yeah, jog,...........trot, run."

"Oh yes, I can do that okay," she states assertively.

Glancing away from her and back to the grassy expanse, I caution, "Because I reckon we need to. Like I said earlier, there is absolutely no cover out there."

She gives me a wry smile. "Yes of course, I know what you mean."

With these words of wisdom we start jogging across this vast and open grassland, not fast but at a steady pace. As we proceed, both of us are extremely vigilant within our surroundings, watching in all directions. When we reach the half way point, we begin to feel a slight breeze. This is something I haven't felt since I've been here, there has been no sign of wind of any intensity before, but there is now. We carry on jogging but we pick up the pace a little. I glance over to Bump. I can perceive from her face that something is wrong, I know she can feel it; understatement, she knows it. I get a gut feeling about certain things, she seems to have an intuitive ability when it comes to happenings in this world. I break into a run but as I surge forwards I realize that she is falling behind. I slow up. As she reaches me I take her hand. "Come on, we need to get going, we need to get some cover."

"I know, I know," she screams. There is intense panic in her voice.

We have now passed the halfway point of this expanse and the closer we get to the jungle, so the more the breeze turns itself into a definite wind, then the wind into a gale. It's becoming hard to push against it.

I can see the jungle quite clearly now. The wind is blowing through the forest directly at us. All the vegetation contained within the heavy foliage is leaning our way and in some cases it is being uprooted or torn from the trees. The whole lot is bearing down upon us. As the inevitable happens, the jungle debris, Bump and I all meet, it feels as though we are being hit and battered by a myriad of sharp objects, little razors. It really hurts. I look down and can see where the flying substances have scored and marked me. Unbelievable, I can fall down a cliff face and not get a scratch but now I'm being lacerated to pieces by leaves and flora. Glancing over at Bump I observe she is suffering too. I grab hold of her, throwing her to the floor and then attempt to shield her from the onslaught. "Keep your head down and stay behind me!" I yell. The gale has become so strong now that it has the ability within it to carry my words off into the distance before they can be heard. As we lay huddled on the grass I am able to see the matter that is being thrown at us. Not only are there leaves, grass and small branches, but small stones, some as big as a cricket ball. The only upside is that all this debris is now flying over the top of us at about what would be waist height. It has become so dense that it has managed to block out a fair proportion of the light. I am still just about able to see our goal, the forest with its cover and hopefully, safety. "Follow me, stay low!" I bellow.

She nods assent to confirm that she has heard and understood. I start to crawl as low as I can, right on my belly. She tags on behind.
Ultimately after one hell of a crawl we achieve our intention and reach the jungle. As we approach the heavily laden forest, so the wind stops, I mean stops dead, it doesn't subside, it just ceases, exactly the same as it started. No warning or notice, from a howling gale to a total calm. I can only assume it has been turned off at source, that's what it feels like anyway.

We stumble to our feet and begin to examine the damage caused to us by the flying fragments. On inspecting myself, I can't see a mark on me. I can feel that certain parts of me are sore, but there are absolutely no visible signs of cuts or bruises. How weird as I was able to see them on the way over and now they appear to be completely gone. My healing powers are obviously at their greatest ever. Perhaps in this world I am indestructible. Bump is fine as well, although I do see her wince when she rubs her knees. "Are you still all there, is everything functioning?" I joke.

"I think so, a bit sore in places but no cuts or bruises."

"Have you ever seen anything like that before?"

"No, I can say without any doubt whatsoever, I have never seen anything like that before. The speed it came at us or the speed it disappeared."

Having listened to her emphatic answer, I don't think there is anything else to say on that subject. I once more look out at the vast lawn. Our surroundings are now completely still, the wind has gone and as before, there is no evidence of even a breeze. I turn back to the jungle that lies before us. It's like a solid wall of foliage, to the point that I can't ascertain a way into it. I push at the outer layer which reacts like an elastic barrier. The branches give to a certain point and then no more. As I release the pressure it instantly springs back to its original state, showing no evidence of my assault.

"Well I don't reckon this is the way in, there must be an easier path. We will just have to skirt around the edge of this lot until we find a suitable way through it." She nods in agreement. I glance left and then right. "This is your chance to shine. Left or right, you choose."

"Right," she says without hesitation. "Definitely right."

I look directly at her, tilting my head to one side and I ask, "Why right, you seem so sure? What makes going right your decision?"

She begins to titter. "Because right means correct, so going right must be the correct choice."

What an astounding piece of logic. No factual substance at all apart from the play on words, but a definite basic logic. "Then fair maiden, right it is."

She sports a huge smile covering her entire face as she takes my hand and off we go. We stay very close to the jungles perimeter for fear of another storm erupting. The going is incredibly easy as underfoot the grass is short. As we walk along, trying to find a way into this forest, I can't help but notice that where the jungle starts and the grass finishes is once more an exactly defined line. Again it's very apparent that everything is over orderly. I survey the grassy area. It looks like common or garden grass, so who keeps it cut? Surely unless it was being cared for, it would be the same as the grasses we encountered at the base of the mountain, long, wild and overgrown. The jungle is also well kept. At no point thus far has the foliage dared to encroach over its line towards the grass.

After quite some time we finally discover a small but accessible hole in the jungles shell. The orifice is just about big enough for me to crawl into. Bump being smaller than me should manage it fairly easily. I drop to my knees trying to gain a view through to the other side. No good, I can't see. I get onto my stomach. This is better. I can perceive that the length of the tunnel from start to finish is no more than about ten feet. At the other end there is light, it's quite bright really which leads me into thinking that this must come out into some type of clearing. "This is it, this is the way into the forest," I state getting to my feet.

She is looking straight at me. I can see concern in her eyes as she glances down at the opening.

"You okay?" I question.

"I think so. It's just that while we were walking around the forest, everything was so peaceful. Now we have to enter another room."

"And that bothers you?"

"Of course as it means that we have to encounter more of the Optic's games."

My heart sinks at this thought. "Look we have to move forward. As you have already said and indeed shown me, if we stay in the same room nothing can be achieved. Our journeys end is through this tunnel and probably even further on, but to get there we have to keep going."

She hangs her head and says, "I know."

"I'll go first. You stay here till I'm all the way through. I'll call you when I'm ready. Okay."

She nods and semi smiles.

I drop down onto my belly, enter the opening and slither along the passageway to the other end without any incident. As I reach the point of exit, so I stop. I do not want to throw caution to the wind here. I slowly edge my way forward, attempting to gain a better view of the clearing. It is very bright out there, but I can't actually see anything clearly.

Finally I leave the tunnel but I remain perfectly still so that my eyes can adjust to their new surroundings. I will also admit that I'm hoping by lying still, I'll also be invisible to anything that may be in here. Within only a few seconds my vision has accustomed itself to the new light. I discover that I am stood in an immense clearing, so large that I can only just distinguish the far side of it. The area which is encircled by the jungle has stumps strewn about all over the place. It's as though someone or something, has recently lopped all the trees in this area.

There is the odd 'boulder' as well, colossal stones, standing a good twenty feet high. The ground I'm directly standing on and also that within my immediate surroundings is earth, extremely dry and dusty dirt. It is obvious to me that no rain has fallen on this vicinity for some considerable time. I cannot see anything that could immediately concern me, so I call back. "Okay sweetheart, come on through." She makes no reply but I can see and hear that she is on her way through.

As I crouch to see if I can help her through the tunnel, I catch a glimpse of something moving. Immediately I spin around attempting to focus on whatever it is. It appears to be one of the huge boulders about forty feet away from me, it look likes it is actually changing shape. I urgently feel I should call out a warning to Bump, but at the same time I also feel that this will focus attention on exactly where we are. I slowly drop into a crouching position without taking my eyes from the shape shifting stone. Suddenly it begins moving towards me, not as you would expect though. You would expect it to roll in some sort of manner, but this one has levitated and is hovering forward in slow motion. Then it happens. I feel the dread in me swell as the centre of the stone opens and an eye becomes awfully evident. It's the Optic, I know it. Just then it spots me and within a fraction of a second is directly upon me. It's hanging in the air about five feet above, glowering down at me. The final velocity at which the Optic approached me made me step back and fall in a totally disordered position.

"Ah, there you are Being." The Optic booms.

In front of my eyes the Optics whole being changes from one shape to another. There are no defined lines to its essence, apart from the eye. Everything else fluctuates with the spectrum of lights dancing around it inside a misty outer form. Accompanying it is a damp smell of old cut grass in the air. I have smelt this before, but I can't at this moment in time anyway, remember when.

I try gesturing to Bump not to emerge from the tunnel but it's too late, her head literally pops out of the hole like a tortoise emerging from its shell.

At this, the Optic sees her, abruptly lurching back, its enormous eyeball squinting. Within a second his demeanour has changed into a hateful, menacing stare. "YOU. YOU AGAIN. HOW MANY TIMES HAVE I GOT TO PUT UP WITH YOU IN MY WORLD! THIS TIME I WILL BE RID OF YOU!" The Optic shrieks. Before it has even finished the sentence Bump is yanked from the tunnel and tossed like a weightless rag doll into the middle of the clearing. What grasped her I couldn't say, it appeared as a jelly matter, extended from the Optic's substance. Her flight path was far above the ground and immensely powerful.

"You fucking bastard," I shout and lunge at the Optic, swinging punches as fast as I can put them together.

"Be still Being!" The Optic commands, pushing me to the floor as though I were an annoying insect to be brushed away. "I'll deal with you when I have purged myself of this virus that persists on dwelling here," its voice sneers. Within a split second the Optic is floating over to where Bump has landed. I rise to my feet as fast as I can, running to where she lies. The Optic gathers height and I watch helplessly as Bumps body is lifted from the ground. I try to go faster, but as I approach, a tentacle of radiance strikes out at me, throwing me sideways. On hitting the ground I right myself immediately and once more attempt to attack my target. Again I'm thrown backwards with that same force. The Optic is now so high that I am barely able to make him out. As for Bump, she is not that far below him, being swivelled and tossed around back and forth. Then I hear her scream as the Optic releases its grip upon her, and lets her fall.

I feel intense anger engorge me. I attempt to dash to the location where I calculate she will fall, but again I am thrown backwards. This time the strength in which the tentacles exert their power over me is a good deal stronger. The points of contact are excruciatingly painful and sharp. My resistance to their clout is insignificant in comparison and I am hurled a good thirty feet or so away from my objective. My landing is awkward and at the very least I must have broken something this time; furthermore I experience that I'm being restrained there in position. I lie still unable to do anything, it's even hard to breathe with the pressure that is being applied to me, but for the life of me, I can't see what has taken a hold of my body and is forcing me to the ground.

All I can do is watch like a spectator on the sidelines. I can see Bump falling, her arms and legs kicking and clawing at thin air and the Optic racing down just behind her. My mind tells me to do something. I have got to save her. Got to free myself, fight that fucking thing.

"NO................THIS CAN'T HAPPEN; MUST NOT HAPPEN!" a high pitched voice suddenly shrieks out.

As I helplessly watch, I see Bump violently change direction, as though grasped by something invisible and wrenched sideways. The Optic stops in mid flight and before my eyes changes shape. It's whole nature of structure shifts to a humanoid outline, but gigantic at least ten feet tall and extremely muscular. The head though it has a nose, a mouth, ears and hair has retained that ultimate feature, the one eye. It looks like a Cyclops, not that I've ever seen one in the flesh until now, I'm purely relying on pictures and drawings to form this assumption.

Bump is most gently laid down in safety. As she nears the ground, her speed rapidly decelerates, almost reaching a stop. She is then placed tenderly on the earth, but I can't see by what. Did the Optic do this? As I stare at this miracle, I see glistening, twinkling illuminations around her body, similar to the Optics tentacles, but these have no outline.

I return my gaze back to the Optic; Oh Shit, he looks furious, totally pissed off. He is still airborne, hovering, but almost immediately he launches himself towards the ground. When he lands, it is with a deafening thud and everything around me shakes. Dust rises instantly forming a cloud around him, but I witness his whole body coil like a spring taking up the impact. Having contacted with the ground he unravels himself into some massive stature, roaring with his deafeningly, deep voice in the direction of Bump. He then proceeds to stomp towards where she is lying, lashing out at the undergrowth and boulders, smashing pieces off everything that he strikes. It is quite terrifying to watch; the raw power the Optic possesses. As he demolishes all in his path towards her, I can see that she isn't moving.

Again, I try to lift my spirits and my strength to overcome whatever is holding me. Suddenly I spurt forwards onto my feet. I was released. I am now upright and able to see her lying motionless on the grass with the Optic almost upon her. As he approaches her resting place, he lifts his gigantic arms above his head, joining his hands together to form a club. "YOU ARE DONE, I WILL BE RID OF YOU, I WILL PURGE MY DOMAIN!" he bellows.

"NO YOU WILL NOT TOUCH HER. TO HARM HER BEING WILL RESULT IN FAILIURE WITH WHATEVER YOU ARE WRONGLY ATTEMPTING TO ACHIEVE!"

It's that high pitched voice again. There is another player in the Optics game, and it's obvious to me that he didn't know about it. Whoever or whatever it is, this participant is firmly on Bump's side and it's pissing off the Optic big time. Also whoever or whatever it is, seems to have powers that match those of the Optic.

The Optic stops dead. His gaze fixes upon one of the larger boulders. His eye squints, his nose wrinkles and flares and his teeth grit. I can hear the terrible grinding from where I am. He takes a couple of paces towards the stone which he is so intently staring at, then stops inspecting the object at length. His head stretches forward from his shoulders, peering at the rock, then without taking his sight away from the boulder, he side steps towards where Bump lays.

"Tut tut, I am warning you, I request you take heed." The voice is still high but now it is gentler, still very menacing.

The Optic glares back at the boulder, his head moving from side to side, his eye widening and then narrowing, his forehead riddled with lines and his mouth snarling as his tongue flickers in and out. At least the teeth grinding has stopped. Again he takes a pace towards where Bump is, but this time the boulder that he showed so much interest in, starts to visibly shimmer. The Optics full attention is now alerted to the rock and his gaze does not falter. He doesn't blink, he doesn't move and from where I am, he doesn't even seem to be breathing.

All of a sudden there is a colossal crashing noise, similar to hundreds of crystal glasses being shattered simultaneously; vociferous isn't the word, deafening possibly. My hands cover my ears and because of the nature of the sound, I instinctively attempt to take cover. As soon as I realize there is no immediate danger to me, I stand up to view the source of the commotion.

71

The Rock that the Optic was so obsessed with is now changing shape and as it does so it becomes startling apparent that it's transforming into an exact replica of the Optic itself. As I observe this, the only conclusion that I can factually make is that this must be another Optic. Two Optics, outstanding, I would just love to know where this is going to leave me.

Then the thought occurs to me that perhaps every time I have met 'the Optic', that in fact they were not the same Optic at all but possibly different ones. Nah, I don't think so, the conversation between us had a definite continuous association. I can only conclude this is a different Optic and the first Optic, my Optic is really pissed off with the new one showing up. The game's afoot. Brilliant! Conceivably I may have an ally, Bump certainly has and it has saved her from my Optic, but thus far, it's done nothing for me. Why am I calling it my Optic, the frigging thing has caused me a whole world of discomfort and pain; I can honestly say I hate it; him; whatever. Optic one, that's what I'll call him. Optic one and now Optic two. It's funny what flicks through your mind when everything is going tits up.

Optic one is now poised in an extremely aggressive manner and as I glance over to Optic two, so is he/she/it.

"You are as I am, what are you doing in this domain? This is mine not yours, you should not be in here." Optic one questions.

Optic two replies submissively. "Yes, we are the same and yes I should not be in here, but my subject is in here with you, and as you well know, we are to be as one, always together until the natural parting."

"That parasite is yours!" Optic one snarls. "How can this be? We enter only one host and stay with it throughout its life span. How can two hosts be in the same being? HOW CAN TWO DIFFERENT OPTICS BE TOGETHER IN THE SAME PLACE? This was never meant to be. We are the same, but we should never exist in the same being. Take your being and depart.....NOW!"

Optic two starts becoming agitated. "Listen and listen well. The female being has no form to expand within, it died at birth. Her essence was passed to her twin and with it, so was I. How this can occur I have no idea. All I know as a fact is that we both spawned within this host. I am more than aware that this is your domain, which is why I have remained indistinguishable inside your world. Now I have no choice but to be entertained by you and show myself. I will not, cannot permit you to destroy the female being that I was propelled to restrain and protect."

Optic one seems to relax a little at this dialogue, although the second Optic looks as if it's ready for anything.

As for me, I'm at a total loss. I haven't got a frigging clue what they are on about, however I do see the potential of the situation though. While these two are having this deep and meaningful conversation, I begin edging my way towards where Bump is situated. The two Optic's continue conversing, allowing me the time to reach her. As I gently caress her head in my hands, her eyes abruptly open, staring at me intently.

"Well hello you," I gently whisper.

"Andy, I knew you would come to save me," Bump quietly retorts.

A lovely sentiment but I can't help feeling this isn't the time to tell her who did actually save her or what the hell is going on. "We need to move and we need to move now, but extremely quietly. Can you do that?" She nods and we slowly move away from the two debating Optics. Our progress is painfully slow as we don't wish to attract the unwanted attention of either of the Optics. They both remain deep in discussion which suits us fine, as the longer we have for our retreat, so the greater the distance between us.

Finally without detection we make it to the edge of the clearing on the opposite side from which we entered. As we advance to the border of the clearing, we encounter the jungles edge once more. I am fully aware that we urgently require an exit out of this arena, so we gradually start inspecting the border of the forest looking for that all important and essential way out.

After what feels like an eternity of trying to stay hidden while attempting to escape, we spot our potential exit. Again it is low to the floor and again it appears to be in the form of a tunnel. This time I'm not going to bother checking the frigging thing out first, I'm just going to go for it. I signal to Bump and point to the proposed route that we will be taking. She nods and in I go.

This passage is larger than the first, lined with many numerous, sharp barbs. As I look forward, although it is fairly light, I am unable to see its conclusion. Ahead is completely pitch black. At first I am able to crawl on my hands and knees, but within a few yards my route becomes restricted and I have no choice but to resort to slithering on my belly to make any headway, and also importantly to avoid being scratched or lacerated by the thorns. I can hear that she is immediately behind me by her shuffling and grunting with the effort she is applying to move within this confined space. The thought does occur that if this channel eventually leads to a dead end, the way back will be arduous to say the least. Negative thoughts Andy, all will be good, just press on boy. Time passes as we struggle along the uneven, thorny passage and as we sluggishly travel it remains intensely black up ahead, yet strangely within our immediate location there is more than sufficient light to be able to see.

When the tunnel widens out a little and we are able to crawl again, it is quite a relief and I decide to take a short break. Bump's going to have a pop at me though. "Let's take a rest here." I state.

"Still think you need to rest do you Andy?" she jokes.

I knew she would just have to have a slight dig. It's definitely a woman thing. "I use the word rest without thought dear lady. I think we need to take store of how things are going. Like where are we, why it is light exactly where we are and not anywhere else and lastly, why is it taking so long to get to the end of this bloody tunnel?"

I can see her looking around us taking in her surroundings. She even peers back from whence we came, and then gazes past me in the direction we have been travelling. She stares straight at me and shrugs her shoulders.

"I hadn't noticed about the light until you just pointed it out, I must admit it is a bit strange though. As for the length of this tunnel; we entered it having never seen it before or having gone through it before, so therefore why would we have any idea how long it is, or how long it's going to take us to get to the other end."

Well what can you say to that one. I just sit there and look at her. Her name should have been 'Little Miss Logic' not Bump. A statement that is as factual as the world itself and no bloody help whatsoever. Brilliant. I am at a complete loss as to how to reply to such an account. She is still looking at me, but now she has a childish grin on her face.

"Right okay, let's continue shall we?"

"The rest is over already?" she inquires in a jibbing manner.

"Are you trying to annoy me because if you are, I'm going to leave you to the Optic next time?"

"Now would I do that?" she laughs sarcastically, "Besides, you're my friend and protector." Suddenly she glances towards me; her face incredibly perplexed, almost concerned. "You are the only person I have ever met and the only friend I've ever known. I know without a shadow of a doubt that you would never let any harm come to me."

This proclamation brings me up sharp. "I didn't save you back there. I was trying to but the Optic was holding me back. He actually had me pinned to the ground for a while. Did you see who did save you?"

Her eyes look questioningly at me. "No, when I woke up and opened my eyes, you were the only one I saw."

It is at this point I feel the need to choose my words carefully. I take hold of her arms, looking directly into her eyes. "The Optic was going to kill you. It was really a hundred percent pissed off when it clamped eyes on you coming out of that other tunnel. It pulled you high into the sky and dropped you. Do you remember that?"

"I remember all of that, but when I was falling I think I just blacked out. When I awoke and saw you, I assumed you had caught me."

"Caught you? What from that height! Christ if I had done that we would probably both be dead. I would be a squashed red stain in the middle of that clearing and you would be a broken mass of bones on top of me."

She roars with laughter, obviously my description was a little flippant.

"No it wasn't me that caught you."

"Then who was it? Did the Optic change his mind?"

"No, I can honestly say the Optic certainly didn't change his mind and that's a fact, but the other Optic stepped in and placed you safely and gently down on the ground."

"THE OTHER OPTIC, there's another one?"

"Yep, we now have two Optics in play, but the new one seems to be completely on your side. It saved your life and then stood against the original Optic. They were toe to toe at one point, that's when I sneaked over to you and dragged you to safety."

"So you did save me, I knew it was you. You saved me from two Optics!"

I can feel a heavy, fuzzy headache coming on here. I can't help thinking that I must have a speech impediment or something. Why can't I get her to understand? "No Bump, Optic number two saved you from being smashed to pieces from the fall; that's the Optic you obviously didn't see. After you were safely on the ground, number one Optic, the one that is really pissed off with you and has a real hidden agenda with me, still wanted your blood and he was coming for it. Number two Optic faced him down. The two of them seem to have a lot of friction over you. I just seized the moment, got to you, brought you around and then we made our getaway, which is why we are here. Okay, do you understand? I would love to say that I'm the hero of the moment, but I'm afraid that I'm not, I'm just the guy that saw the opportunity to get us out of there while the two Optic's were having their little squabble."

She considers what I have just said, stares for a few moments pondering my oration and then replies, "Andy, I have always told you that you can do anything and everything you like in here. I don't know why I know this but I ABSOLUTELY DO KNOW this. Two Optics. Very well then, there are now two of them, but if a second one has emerged, then it can only be by your doing, your wishes. It has only materialised because you have requested its presence or by your thought you wanted it here. You say it saved me. No, you saved me."

"What the hell are you talking about? If this place adheres to my wishes, then why the fuck am I here, why the fuck are you here? I would have wished us both out of here long ago. If I can do as I please in here, why can't I get the two of us out, why can't I make us safe? This so called journey I'm taking is definitely not my idea, it's not fun, but I still seem to have no choice but to do it. If I have such a hold over the orchestration of the workings of this environment, why aren't I controlling the Optics; why are they not doing my bidding?"

Her facial expression turns extremely serious and she places both her hands on either side of my cheeks. "That's easy to answer Andy, but you just haven't realised how yet. It will come. I know you will control things here and then the Optic or Optics will bow to you. This world will know its owner."

Do you know that all throughout my life I had previously believed that I had a pretty good grasp on things? I even indulged myself in the fact that I had the ability to converse and answer most questions that were posed to me in an intelligent and concise manner, until now. Her interpretation of my abilities throughout this situation, indeed throughout this world, are to me outlandish and to say the least, totally incomprehensible at this moment in time. I need to put this conversation to rest. We need to keep moving, we are not that far removed from where the Optics were having their little tiff. "If I ever get the supremacy you believe I have, then I will put us in a world that is safe, kind, warm, inviting and free of bloody Optics. Okay?"

A huge beaming grin crosses her face. "I'm with you and I know, I am sure that it will come. I just don't know when."

"Come on then sweetheart we need to move on, or as you so eloquently put it, we need to get out of this room and into the next one."

CHAPTER SEVEN
THE REASONING

We clamber along through the prickly tunnel and finally see light at the end; this is the first time any kind of illumination has been seen in front of me, but it is still so far ahead. I can only conclude that this room is about to shut its door behind us and a brand new one is there to challenge us. Great thought eh. I pause for a moment letting Bump know what I have seen. I witness a definite glow in her eyes, a happiness if I'm not mistaken. We trundle on and finally reach the end.

As I pull myself out of the last remnants of the tunnel so I emerge into, well how to describe it, a loft, a junk room, an attic. A jungle to an attic, you really couldn't dream this shit up, but then again, the longer I am in this world, the more I am convinced that the whole thing is no more than a bizarre dream. I must admit though, waking up would be good, because if this is a dream, then it's way too realistic for me, and besides, I had always been led to believe that dreams were supposed to be constructed from things that you'd previously seen or that you feared. Thus far none of this shit has ever been in my life and I have certainly never had fears about this sort of crazy world. Nothing about this place has ever even remotely crossed my mind before.

I uncoil myself and stretch, immediately looking for some form of cover. Just to the right of the exit is a pile of boxes, the kind you use when moving house, some made of cardboard and some made of exceptionally light, splintery wood. There are at least twenty or more stacked up forming a low wall of sorts. This is the point that I will make my way towards, and pretty quickly too. As Bump emerges from the hole, I motion her to join me immediately; which she does. I whisper, "Have you ever been in here before?"

"Nope and why are you whispering?" she blurts loudly back at me.

Ah well, if there was something in here that we were trying to avoid, it would, without any doubt at all, know we are here now.

"For Christ's sake, do you want to keep it down a bit? It would be lovely if we could be a little more covert in our efforts and that way perhaps these uncanny things that keep happening to us won't get the chance, because they won't know we are fucking here."

Her head drops as though severely reprimanded, and although I do feel bad about this, I can't help feeling that I haven't done anything wrong. "Look, sometimes we really do need to keep things to a minimum, no noise, so we can try to get the edge over these things that are happing here. We now have two Optics to contend with, and who knows, although we left them arguing, by now the two of them could all be buddy buddy, good mates and united in being after our blood. We just don't know. What we do know is that you and I are against all odds here. We do need to be careful and most of all looking out for each other. Okay?"

Bump raises her head with saddened eyes and nods submissively.

"Come here you," I gently order and I give her a tender cuddle as she buries her head into my chest. While I am doing this, I am also surveying our new surroundings.

We are in a roof space. The walls are no more than three feet high with the pitch of the roof tapering upwards to a point and then returning downwards to the other wall. I can see thick oak beams running the length of the void, and smaller rafters that every eighteen inches or so reach upward to the apex of the roof. Width wise the room is about twenty feet across, lengthwise I am not sure. The light isn't that good further down the room, so it's hard to tell. All I know is that this is a very large loft space, so the chances are that the building below is going to be quite sizeable as well. "Come on Bump, let's investigate our new room eh, at least this one IS a room."

She moves away from me with a slight smile on her face. "Okay let's take a look around," she says softly, crouching down right beside me with her eyes dancing from left to right. Well I must be winning; she is now doing the whispering thing brilliantly.

I slowly poke my head around the side of the crates and boxes. All looks still and totally unsafe if you know what I mean? I've just watched huge rocks turn into Optics, so it is acutely obvious to me that anything could happen here.

I glance back at the tunnel we arrived through and it's not there. Why doesn't that surprise me; Bump is absolutely right, completely bang on, out of one room and into another. There's no going back, the door just slams shut and that's that. You are in a whole new world. I turn back to her and say, "We will move one at a time, wherever I go, you follow when I give you the nod. Understand?"

"The nod?" she queries with a puzzled look.

"Yes the nod. When I'm looking straight at you and I move my head up and down, the nod, I will be nodding. Okay?"

"The nod," she echoes. "Got it."

Bloody hell, this is really hard work at times.

Although the light is somewhat dim in here, I am able to see an array of different objects which I can move to afford me some cover. The closest is what looks like an enormous stack of books neatly stacked to resemble a pyramid. This is going to be my first objective and even as this thought is passing through my mind, I dart over to the mound of books.

Arriving at my destination, all ten feet away from my earlier cover, it occurs that yet again, everything is flawlessly assembled. I glance down at the floor. There is no dust, no residue of the static years, no nothing. It's an exceptionally clean and tidy floor. The volumes that I shelter behind all have their spines facing towards me. I draw back a little allowing me to read the titles. Every book is identical as I survey the mound of literature that I'm cowering behind; all beautifully bound hard backed books, about the size of War and Peace, not that I have ever read it, but I have seen the book on various occasions. Strangely though, these books all have the same title, "I Want to Leave".

I thrust my head around the side of this paper barricade to inspect the route ahead. The next item of evident cover is a piano another twelve feet further on, right in the centre of the room. I look back to Bump and nod. She is studying my every move with unwavering intent; I know she sees me nod, but she isn't moving. She is looking fixedly in my direction as if awaiting a command.

81

Then it occurs to me, one downward movement of my head isn't going to crack it, Bump is waiting for me to start nodding, like one of those dogs you see in the back window of a doom brains car. Fine. I make definite up and down head movements that are completely over exaggerated. Then without any further hesitation, she lurches into action directly towards me. On arriving at my position, the only surprise to me is that she didn't manage to knock me over with the momentum she had applied to her journey; all ten feet of it!

Right the next stop will be the piano. Again I tentatively scan the area that I am about to traverse and when satisfied that the coast is clear, as quietly and as quickly as possible move from my cover and head for the piano. On reaching it, I look from both ends evaluating my next forward movement. As this instrument isn't exactly big enough to supply a decent amount of cover for the two of us, I don't signal to Bump to follow me just yet.

This vantage point affords me an excellent view of what lies ahead, being probably about halfway along this loft space. Not too far ahead, about fifteen feet or so, I observe what looks like a hatch, but there is no cover in the way of furniture etc. surrounding it. If I were to inspect it, I would be extremely visible and therefore incredibly vulnerable. Past the loft hatch I can distinguish various stacks of items, from furniture, more books, more boxes to dummies and clothing busts. I need to have Bump with me so that we are both closer to this hatch. I turn to her and nod. I see she is watching me like a hawk yet she remains still. Not again; I overstress the nodding for a second time, and once more she swiftly moves to where I am stooped.

"Bump we really do need to get this signal thing worked out. I am only going to nod the one time. I will make eye contact with you and then nod okay. THEN you come to me."

"Got it," she enthusiastically states. "That's how we'll do it; good plan."

All I can do is shake my head in total incredulity at this avowal. What on earth makes her brain tick. Some of her statements are incredible. "Can you see that hatch?" I question.

She peers around the piano and having spotted the hatch, returns to her original position and gives me a sideways look. "You mean that door in the floor?"

I hold my breath for a second then emit a slight sigh, "Yes I mean the door in the floor. It's called a hatch, in this case a loft hatch, mainly because the room we are in, is called a loft and the door to this loft is called a loft hatch. Are we clear on this now?"

She is staring at me intently. "Yep I have definitely got it, the door over there in the floor, you call it a hatch, I call it a door in the floor, but whatever it is called, I see it."

I chuckle to myself. What a brilliant reply, but this is really not the time to be too flippant. "You keep watch here, I'm going to see if that 'hatch' opens, okay?"

"Okay," comes the reply.

Cautiously I leave my cover and tip toe over to the loft hatch. As I reach it, I stoop down to examine its make-up and structure. The door is made of wood and so is the frame. The hatch itself is about four feet square, pretty big for a loft hatch. It is hinged at one end, with a pull rope at the other end enabling someone to yank it open.

I quickly look up, scanning the area in front of me; all seems still. I glance back to where Bump is and can see her looking back and forth, also ensuring that all is well.

I grasp the rope, giving it one almighty tug. As I do so the door starts to lift. Christ it's heavy, but bit by bit, inch by inch it very gradually begins to open. Suddenly the strain of pulling on the rope lessens, as I realize that Bump has broken her cover to help me. After a couple of minutes with both of us hauling on the tether, we have the trap door completely open, laying back on itself on the floor. Both of us gaze down through the open shaft. Well if the phrase 'knock me down with a feather' was to be said, you could have done it easily.

As we stare at the opening below, we look away and then at each other in perfect unison. What I am seeing isn't what I would have expected; I would have expected a hallway, possibly another room but not a panoramic view of the clearing we left not that long ago via the tunnel that led us to this loft. And to cap it all, both the Optics are still there. "Are you seeing what I'm seeing Bump?"

"Yes I think I must be. How can this be, we didn't climb up at any stage did we, certainly not to get this high?"

I am a little perplexed at what she has said; she doesn't seem confused at what we are actually seeing, more with how we managed to be so high up. I can only assume that the fact she sees the Optics in the clearing we have just left, isn't such a strange thing to her, but on the other hand, the height we are at, well now that is. Oh well I have to admit that is bloody strange as well.

We must be fifty feet up and looking down on a perfect circle that is the clearing. There is that odd smell of cut grass again and I can hear what the Optic's are saying quite clearly, even from this height. "Can you hear them Bump?"

"Yes I can. How can we hear them from here, I don't understand?"

"Me neither, but let's listen and watch for a while, perhaps we'll get some insight into what the hell is going on."

As we observe from our advantaged seats, I suddenly spot us below crawling away from the Optics. I nudge Bump and point this out. She gazes down with her mouth open in total amazement. We are watching what happened about an hour ago, as though we were part of an audience watching a television program or a film. I focus back to the Optic's, listening to their conversation.

"We were all allocated a single domain, how did you get here and why are you interfering with what's going on in mine?" bawls Optic one.

"Firstly, I have been here since the Being you are supposed to govern was born. I have just never informed you before or allowed you to find me. I knew I shouldn't be here, and yet here I am. I am the Optic for the female, and my presence here is obviously related to the fact that she is here also," Optic two retorts.

84

Optic one's stature and stance takes on a more aggressive nature. "You have hidden yourself and that other thing inside my domain since the beginning. This is TOTALLY UNACCEPTABLE. YOU MUST GO, LEAVE, BE GONE!" he booms.

Now Optic two is also muscling up. "Where, WHERE? Where do you think I should go? How do you propose I make my exit? HOW?"

Optic one steps a pace closer to his opposition, his single eye stretched open wide and his voice is intensely menacing. "I can destroy your host, she has no substance here, she isn't real and because of these facts I can annihilate her."

"Yes that is possible and yes you could try, but I will not allow it. I am her guardian, as you are supposed to be the guardian of the male. She has no substance but she does have essence and my whole worth is to suppress her brain by two thirds, as yours is for your host. We are not, hypothetically able to harm our wards."

Optic one appears to calm himself slightly while he absorbs this statement. He physically deflates. "You are right. I cannot harm mine and you cannot harm yours, but we could harm each others. The fact you are here is not correct and could be detrimental to my host. Two of us contained in the same brain, it has never been heard of."

Optic two also relaxes slightly. "The whole point of me not informing you as to my presence was so as not to alter or change the environment you had already set. The female has made no difference to anything, as she has no idea who she is or what she is. She is like a double-sided mirror that looks inwards; she has only ever seen her own reflection in the subconscious world you have created. You have seen her on several occasions and more or less ignored her. There has been the odd instance where you have growled your displeasure at her, but until now, you have never shown that you wished her any harm. Why now?"

Optic one turns aside from the other Optic, taking a couple of paces away he stops and turns to face him directly. "The girl was insignificant, wandering around in this tiny corner of his brain, he had no knowledge of her and never would have but because I brought his essence into my domain, she then became apparent to him."

"You brought him in here?" Optic two interrupts. "Why would you do a thing like that? The host was never meant to meet an Optic. We are what they laughingly call, their souls. They were never meant to know we exist, let alone mingle with us. Why have you revealed yourself to him, WHY?"

"You dare to question me!" challenges Optic one. "You have no right to question me, you are not even entitled to be here. Tell me, have you tried to leave?"

The second Optic lowers his head as if ashamed and quietly answers the jeering question. "No, no I haven't."

"Why, why haven't you just left this domain? You know it's not yours to oversee, so why haven't you left this being and taken the journey to our own world."

While I'm watching and listening to all of this, my mind is completely befuddled with questions that I can't ask and that I can't answer, and to be honest, I'm buggered if I'm going to shout down and ask. They have now started talking about a different world; are we talking aliens here? They are also saying that we are all in some corner of my brain, which I can' help but feel means that this isn't me. I mean, does this explain why I don't even look like me? Confused as I am, I keep listening.

Optic two is pacing back and forth with his head forward. Right in front of the first Optic he stops dead, looks straight at him and answers the question. "When my host ceased to live, I was ready to make that crossing from here to our world but when her essence, her life force, carried on functioning and passed into her twin brother whilst still inside the womb, I felt an obligation to follow. You and I, all of us Optics were taught many things, about how to control these beings, to restrict them from using the complete power of their brains, but when this occurred I was not sure exactly how to react to it. Her impulses showed she was still thinking, so I could only assume that I still had a job to do. I followed her here. At no point since I have been here, have I had any reason to think that my job was over. Her life force learns and although she has no tangible brain to limit, the impulses she gives off are that of a living organism. What would you have done?"

Optic one slumps backward to the ground and sits. "I would have left, I would have taken the bull by the horns and journeyed home. I do not understand your actions, it is as if you almost care for these beings. We are forced to restrain them without their knowledge but also to allow them to live their life span. Why bother, who decided on such a ridiculous arrangement. They are puny and our race could destroy all of them with the stroke of a hand. I do not want to be here. The only way to leave your host is, either when it dies or if it commands you to leave. That is the ruling. Correct?"

Optic two's eye starts to squint and he towers over Optic one. "So that's what this is all about. You want to leave and rather than wait for your host to expire, you have chosen to pre-empt your ward into telling you to leave."

Optic one glides to his feet. This whole action takes place in a split second, with the two of them almost nose to nose, both look ready to fight. Optic one thrusts his muscular arms in the direction of the other and shoves him backwards about ten feet. The second Optic remains upright but stumbles backwards with the force of this thrust. As he stops, regaining his composure, his face distorts with anger and he lets out a distinctive growl. "If you dare to interfere with my plan, I will dispose of you as well as that puny female that you accompanied in here. The only good thing about what I do is that no one can see any of my actions; not in here," threatens Optic one.

"You are correct about the ruling, there are only two ways we can leave a host but until now an Optic has never been able to draw his host into his domain. What I will tell you, and I think you really need to know, is that this scenario you have created is riddled with flaws. If things had been normal, it would have been just you and your host, but they are not normal, are they? You have the female in here; you also have me in here as well. I am an OPTIC and although I have chosen to be undetectable until now, it must be obvious to you that I have been blessed with the same powers you have. You threaten to dispose of me? Be very cautious."

With this retort to Optic ones warning, Optic twos presence begins to glisten and sparkle, his massive structure distorting and within an instant disappears into nothing.

Optic one stretches out, bearing his chest like a rampant gorilla, leaning his head back and yelling full pelt at the skies. Halfway through his triumphant ritual, he cuts short his conquering bellow, as he spots us watching from on high. I had a really bad feeling this might happen. His jubilant cry turns into a ferocious howl and he spirals like a spring, swiftly leaping into the air directly at where we are hiding. I don't wait to see if he can make it this far up, I instantly grab Bump and push her away from the trap door, fly to my feet and with new found strength, lift the door from its counter lever position and slam it firmly shut. Immediately this is done, I run to the piano and start to grapple with it in an effort to force it over the trap door. Bump too regains her feet and in an instant is helping me to manoeuvre the musical lump onto the hatch.

"Push for fucks sake, push!" I yell.

"I fucking am!" she replies angrily.

If this wasn't such a critical time I think I would have erupted into laughter over her attempt at colourful metaphors; this is the very first time she has attempted to use such language and without sounding too prim, it's totally out of character. Nevertheless, it does get her point across.

The piano grinds across the surface of the loft space, but on its approach it catches one of its casters on the uneven floor, totters and tilts until it finally turns on its side and topples over onto the trap door. Couldn't have placed it better if I had tried; outstanding, I love it when a drop of a hat plan comes together.

Within a split second of the piano slumping down onto the trap door, there comes an almighty crash below it. I can only assume the Optic actually managed to leap all the way up here.

The piano jolts off the trap door, leaping about three feet into the air and then regains its location in almost exactly the same place it was disturbed from.

"Ah, you want to play?" the Optic screams.

Play, no, no way. I start franticly looking around for some kind of escape out of this situation.

Bump grabs my arm. "Come on, let's get out of here."

I must look like a mad man as I focus on her, but she seems to have some direction in this predicament, so I'm with her. I slip my hand into hers as she heads straight across the loft space in the opposite direction to which we came. As we flounder about, bumping into various stacks of disused, unwanted and forgotten remnants of what's stored up here, I nervously search forward to see where we might be heading.

After the first few minutes of indiscriminate movement, it becomes very apparent to me that this loft space, this room is just re-inventing itself time after time as we move along it. I keep seeing the same objects and articles we have already passed. I yank Bump backwards, she tumbles to the ground. She struggles to her feet, her eyes are wide open. "What are you doing? We need to keep moving, we need to get out of here, we need to be safe. Andy we need to be safe!" Her voice moves from shock to concern and finally to despair as she bursts into tears. "We need to be safe, please make me safe, I know you can, please do this for me!"

"Calm down, I'm scared too, but we need to get some idea where we are going. We could be running, shit, steaming into worse danger than we are already in now. Let's slow it up a bit, get some bearings."

Her head is dancing from side to side, up and down, left and right, in all directions as she is clearly attempting to locate the exact location of the Optic. "He's going to kill me, he's going to kill me Andy!" she screams.

"No, there's no way I'll let him do that and come to that, the other Optic won't either."

89

I survey the loft area in front of us and I notice a light, a bright radiance emanating from the rafters and tiles above, about forty feet or so further down the room. "Just there, do you see that, the light in the roof?"

She focuses along the room and then upward to the roof lining. "Yes, I see it."

"That's our way out, just there. All we've got to do is to get up there and out of this loft space."

"Okay?"

Precisely as I conclude this sentence, the loft hatch erupts into a million pieces as the Optic pokes his hideous head through the remaining orifice. He initially glances down the section we are hiding in, but for some reason doesn't see us. He then turns in the other direction and focuses his attention on something down that end. He hauls his massive body through the decimated trap door, heading in that direction, again smashing and gouging at everything in his path. Why he didn't see us I have no idea, but he's gone off in the wrong direction and that's good enough for me. "Let's go while he's distracted with whatever he saw at the other end. I certainly don't want to be here when he finds out that we're not up there."

She is visibly shaking but quietly utters, "Go and I'll follow, let's get out of here."

Immediately I begin moving along the loft space as silently as I can. Shortly I am below the shaft of light. I glance back and nod to Bump. Hallelujah at last the one nod does the trick and without any hesitation she comes scurrying down the expanse towards me. When she joins me, I clasp my hands together to form a stirrup, gesturing my intent to hoist her aloft and into the rafters. She grasps the notion and without any indecision, puts one foot into my interlocked hands as I boost her up until she is able to get hold of the rafters. She then heaves herself up and onto them, leaving her just a short reach away from the beam of light. When she's up and stable, I too launch myself at the rafters.

With my first couple of attempts I manage to reach them, but can't quite grab and take a grip on them. My landings are not good, both times I make a hell of a noise as I hit the boards causing the floor to vibrate. I cringe at the commotion I have made and peer down the room to see if the Optic has heard me. He falters for a second, slightly turns his head, but then proceeds with his wilful obliteration of everything in his original path. Something up there has really caught his attention and my little clatters are apparently of little interest to him. Don't get me wrong, I'm not complaining in the least, but I am very mystified as to what the Optic is so enamoured with at the other end that he doesn't care about what's happening down here.

On my third attempt, I finally manage to obtain a decent hold onto one of the rafters. Having got a wholesome grasp of the beam, I wriggle and twist myself up until I'm in the same location as Bump. When I reach her she has a broad smile on her face. I grin back. "Are we having fun yet?" I joke, raising my eyebrows. She doesn't answer, but I am able to see the relief in her face. I have always maintained that a little levity when things are not going too greatly, can actually help.

Having attempted to relax Bump's state of mind with my warped humour, I slowly endeavour to find a point in which I can stand on the rafter; I am currently rather precariously perched on it. She watches me but doesn't move or say a word, she just gazes with that purposeful look of hers.

When I finally manage to achieve the right balance, I slowly stand upright, adjusting my stability as I extend my frame towards my objective. When almost there, I reach the chink in the tiles which is allowing the illumination through. This fracture is no more than six inches by two, but it is enough of a hole for me to start ripping at, to enlarge its aperture.

As I proceed, the debris from my efforts begins to drop to the floor initially making a sprinkling sound, but as my labours intensify, larger fragments plummet and these cause a more definite crunch as they hit the ground. I know the Optic is going to hear these things clattering around, so I can only assume that it's just a matter of time before he will investigate, regardless of what he thinks is up at the other end; I'm

91

making way too much noise to be ignored by him for long. I need to complete this job fast.

As I advance the size of the hole, finally it reaches the point that I believe is large enough for us to escape through. Again I gesture to Bump to come up here with me. No words are spoken as she nimbly moves position until she is right beside me. "Through you go." I order.

"What me first? You normally go first to check that the coast is clear?"

Unbelievable, this observation and declaration is not what I expected. What I expected was for her to go for the hole, lock stock and two smoking barrels, just to get out of here. Just goes to show how completely wrong you can be; after all, assumptions are just like assholes, we have all got one; and my supposition fell far from the mark. "Just get through that fucking hole, if I need a deep and meaningful conversation about who goes first, I'll tell you. Now move!"

She literally jumps to it, negotiating the opening without too much effort at all, she passes through it and onto the outer roof. As she disappears through this hole and I get ready to make my attempt at this exit, so I hear a huge commotion heading towards me. God I knew it, I made way too much noise and now the Optic is right up my ass. I glance up at the hole, crouch down and look at what's approaching me. Yep, it's the Optic and he's coming fast; way too fast for my liking. I only manage to catch a glimpse of him as he's rampaging towards me, but from that glance it appears that he has once more changed his shape. This time he looks feline but he has still retained only the one eye, not that the façade bothers me too much, just the speed at which he is advancing.

I make my leap at the hole and reach it but I am unable to maintain a positive grip on anything at all. With my hands groping about I eventually find a stretch of exposed purling, that prior to my recent destruction, previously held some tiles in place. I clutch at the severed remnants, slowly slipping when I feel an optimistic clasp on my wrists. Bump has hold of me, she is tugging, trying to drag me through the hole.

The Optic is almost at my feet when he suddenly staggers backwards, his face turning from anger into complete and utter rage, almost torment. Without hesitation he lashes out at whatever stopped his momentum, in an unprecedented manner he is ripping and lacerating at mid air from what I can see, but for him, something behind him is the definite target of his rage.

As this battle takes place; if you can call it that as I can only see one participant, with the help of Bump I manage to swing myself up and onto the roof. Having moved myself clear of the hole and to comparative safety, I really can't help myself, I grasp hold of her and hug her with all my might. "Christ Almighty, thank you." I must admit at this point I feel quite emotional. I really did think that the Optic was going to have me for dinner this time.

Outside on the roof I take a look around. It's comprised of old fashioned slate tiles, which of course have a tendency towards being extremely slippery. The gradient of the roof is some forty five degrees, reasonably easy to walk up, down or along. The sheer expanse of this roof is massive. From where we are I am unable to see either end of it. I glance down and then up. Up is towards the ridge and it's closer. I feel we may just get a better picture of what's around us from up there. I take hold of Bump's hand and slowly we proceed towards the apex. The tiles are indeed quite slippery and do hamper our progress but finally we reach the top.

The Optic hasn't emerged from the hole as yet, but I can still hear a violent fight going on inside.

When on the crest of the roof, I scan both left and right. "Which way do you reckon?" But before she can answer I pre-empt her with, "I know, I know, right, because it's got to be right. Right?"

She giggles but we don't waste any time. We take the right option and scramble along the ridge tiles. As the opening we used starts to fade from our view, so does the row the Optic was making. Hopefully this means that we have travelled a reasonable distance.

We stop, I choose my footing carefully and standing as erect as possible, I try to see the end of the roof. Yes, there it is, about another couple of minutes away. "Not too far now, let's keep moving." I state. We continue precariously along our elevated path. As I now and again glance left and right, I can see where the roofs gradient finishes but what lies beyond it is a green haze. I can't make anything out as such.

Finally we reach the end, and as we approach it, we both drop down to our bellies in order to traverse the last few feet. We inch our way forward, me leading with Bump fairly close behind. I can feel a wind start to pick up. All the way along this roof there hasn't been a hint of a breeze, but now there is a definite wind whipping up. I cautiously sneek my hands over the edge of the tiles, followed by my head. Initially I am forced to blink my eyes with the impact of the wind, but eventually I am able to fully open them, staring at our latest panoramic view.

Out directly in front of me are clouds, huge fluffy white and grey clouds. These are enveloping mountains covered in snow. As my eyes drop down I realise that we must be over a mile up, with the wall of the building which we are presently perched on, seeming to go on forever downward, disappearing eventually from view.

I feel my entire body deflate; this nightmare is hell bent on making it impossible to escape the Optic. I really don't know what to do next. I slowly pull Bump up to where I am so she can also see the predicament that we now find ourselves in. "What now, how do we get from here to safety?" she gently and hesitantly inquires.

"Christ, I don't know. Something inside me says jump. The fate down there can't be as bad as the one the Optic has in store for us up here."

"Well you had better make your mind up quickly because I can see it approaching along the roof after us."

"What?" I stutter. I glance back over my shoulder and indeed there he is moving erratically towards us. Every now and again he slips sideways as though he has been pushed, he then lashes out at thin air and clambers back onto the apex. There is something distinctly odd about what's going on around him. There must be an explanation as to why he's not just here like he was before, appearing and then disappearing at will. For some reason he is not able to conjure his troublesome black magic at will, he has to pursue us in the old fashioned way and I don't think he likes doing that at all. In point of fact I think it is really pissing him off. Good, anything that causes that thing a problem has my vote every time.

Okay back to the task in hand, or in this case the limited choice in hand. To confront the Optic would be foolish, especially having Bump with me. It's obvious that he's really got it in for her and I am under no illusion that I'm no match for him, even if he is distracted, which he undeniably is at present. Choice two is to jump. Great options I conclude, a bit like Hobson's choice, both of them as bad as each other. I turn to Bump with a meaningful look. She stares straight into my eyes and starts shaking her head, at first slowly and then more urgently. "No not that, we will be killed if we fall from this height. Are you out of your mind? No, I'm not going to do it."

I must admit, I would just love to have a discussion with her as to how she has been able to interpret my intention purely by looking into my eyes. Quite impressive, but I feel that we seriously need to apply some urgency to our escape, regardless of how radical it may be.

I grab her firmly by the hand and stand up. Over her shoulder I can see the inconsistent actions of the Optic, but unfortunately he draws closer with every one of my heart beats. Bump attempts to break my grip on her, but my hold is fast; there is no way I'm leaving her here for the Optic to decide her fate. Live or die, we go together on this occasion, as selfish as it may seem. I take a pace backwards, surging forwards towards the edge of the roof, dragging her with me. As I reach the two step ultimatum, I launch myself away from the building, never letting go of my clutch on her, she's coming with me whatever the cost and however much she struggles.

As we free fall through the sky, I attempt to attain a sky diving position that I had seen a few times on television. I take hold of her other hand and we are head to head and hand in hand. Bump has her eyes clenched firmly shut. I can see this clearly, being so close to her as we are buffered by the downward rush of the air and the velocity of our speed as we fall through the atmosphere.

As we plummet, our descent seems to take forever to conclude. I am expecting the ultimate crash, the one that finishes this nightmare but it doesn't seem to come. We have been falling for quite some time now. I survey my immediate surroundings. Around us are clouds, big fluffy meringue type white and grey clouds. We have entered and exited several layers of them. I try to see what's below us, where we are heading, where we are going to land, in essence the final place we will come to a grinding halt from this descent. As the clouds periodically clear I can glimpse water, sea to be precise, an ocean, a huge watery expanse that looks as though it is going to be our landing place. The thought suddenly occurs that we might just survive this. This could be a landing that we will be able to walk away from, or at best swim away from. Shit can Bump swim? I really fucking hope so because if she can't I've got a hell of a lot of life saving to do in order to keep her afloat.

Then suddenly I recall the mountains I saw from the roof top. Where are they? The wall of the building we jumped from, shouldn't that be right beside us? We couldn't have wandered that far away from it; in point of fact, at one stage I was worried we might be blown towards it. For a few moments in my mind it was a major concern. Not here now though, just disappeared yet again.

As we drift downwards I feel calm. We have been falling for so long now. The force of the air is pushing, tugging and buffering at us. The deafening sound from the velocity of our travel becomes the norm. Even the unstable sensation of nothing around me, it all becomes quite serene. I glance over to Bump, she has opened one eye and is frantically trying to appraise her circumstances. Suddenly her focus happens upon me and she opens both her eyes. From the look on her face I can guess that her next sentence isn't going to be one of praise or congratulations. "What the hell do you think you're doing? Are you trying to kill us both you crazy bastard?"She pauses for breath, just for a second as she gets her bearings. "And why are we still floating in mid air?" she yells to me. I can only just hear her because of the racket of the heavens we are drifting through.

To answer her, I take as large a breath as possible enabling me to obtain the volume I require for her to hear me. "I don't know why we are still up here. What I do know is that eventually we will land in the sea. Can you swim?"

"SWIM? No I can't bloody swim, but then again I can't fly either you fucking idiot."

A good answer although a little more direct than I had anticipated. She has acquired a fair knowledge of the use of colourful metaphors. To date I don't remember hearing her swear but now we have a miniature onslaught of bad language. I can only assume that this must be my influence. She has learnt this from me and that's not a good thing. "Okay, in which case when we hit the water keep a firm hold of me. I will keep us afloat; understand?"

She really does not look happy. She looks directly down and as she perceives her status, starts to struggle against me, trying to loosen my grip. Panic kicks in. Although I am weathered from this plunge, I endeavour to keep hold of her. I know that if we were to part company and hit the water she would probably drown. I must keep her as close as possible. "For fucks sake will you just stay with me. Together we stand a chance, on our own we are done for." It's no wonder she has picked up some bad language really, is it?

She glares at me intently, then pulls herself up into my arms until we are embracing. "I know I should trust you but I'm terrified. A brother and sister should trust in each other, shouldn't they?"

This statement, the brother and sister bit, shocks me. I don't know why it should really because she heard the same conversation between the Optics as I did. She has now made it very clear that she understands we are related, indeed we are kin and this will make us so much stronger. Together we will be harder to fight, much harder to beat than we ever would if parted.

I glance down again to the watery abyss below. It's apparently clear to me that we are now only seconds away from collision. "Keep hold of me, don't you dare let go."

Her eyes are full of tears, yet her expression is one of total obedience.

"I will never let go of you, I've finally found out why I'm here and for the first time in my existence, I am happy."

I offer her the best smile I can under the circumstance and then take one final glance down. Oh shit this has just got to hurt!

CHAPTER EIGHT
__TWO SIDES TO A COIN__

I try getting beneath us in an effort to take the initial brunt of our collision with the water, but because of the speed which we are now moving at, it is almost impossible to manoeuvre my position to protect Bump from the impact. Just as contact is imminent, I manage to arrange myself so that my feet are pointing downwards towards the water; at least the entry will be as streamlined as I can possibly make it. Bump is above me, head close to mine and the rest of her stretched out above me. At least we're in line so I should break the water's surface first making her entry a little easier. "Take a big breath," I yell with all my might and then follow my own advice to the letter.

I hit the water with tremendous velocity, plunging deeper and deeper down into its depths. I still have hold of Bump, I can feel her grip but I can't see her because I have my eyes firmly closed. I can't help but feel totally amazed at how little it hurt, hitting the water so hard and fast, I seemed to have penetrated its surface with no ill effects at all. Nevertheless, we still appear to be travelling deeper into its depths and as much as I attempt to stop our descent by kicking my legs, the downward spiral continues. The pressure on my ear drums and my chest is becoming unbearable. I peer through my closed eyes to see if I can see Bump. In the darkness I can just make out a shape that I'm still clinging onto and can only assume she is still with me. Finally I hit the bottom, the sea bed I presume, then with all the might that's left in me, I push up to begin our accent. I can't hold my breath much longer.

I sense that I've passed Bump, now I'm dragging her up with me. She feels limp. I keep my eyes open as much as I am able to, straining to see what's above. I can faintly make out a blurry light. It must be the surface. Christ I hope it's the surface because I recognize I haven't much time before I run completely out of air and probably drown. My initial momentum up from the sea bed towards the surface has completely worn off now and I am basically floating towards the surface. Bump feels heavy but I maintain my grasp. I still can't see her as such and feel that she may have passed out; at least I hope that is all it is.

At last my head breaks the surface of the water. I get that exhilarating feeling as new fresh air cascades into my lungs. Instantaneously I pull Bump to free her head from the water. As she emerges she is laying face down in the water. I grapple at the limp body endeavouring to turn her over. Getting a decent grip on her torso, I give her whole body a swift yank sideways. As I manage to move her half the way over, her head turns directly towards me. There is no face, no nose, no mouth or ordinary features. The whole head is just one eye.

I throw myself back into the water away from this ghastly, staring, gawping apparition. I kick my feet at it. It's the fucking Optic, I know it. "Where's Bump you useless tosser?" I bellow at the ghoul like figure.

"Ha ha, how caring you are," the Optic booms in its sneering manner. "And how aggressive and disrespectful you are as well. A lesson in basic manners would seem to be in order you pathetic Being."

As it utters these words I feel a massive pain around my chest, followed by a tightening sensation. I am lurched backwards and physically thrown. I hit the water four or five times before I eventually stop; God knows how far I have travelled. I imagine what has just happened to me is something like when I used to skim pebbles across the waters of a lake. I regain some kind of composure, looking about me to see where the Optic is now. No sign of him and there isn't any sign of Bump either, which concerns me much more. "Bump, Bump, can you hear me?" I bellow as loud as I possibly can, whilst treading water.

"Oh Bumpy, where are you?" Mimics the Optic mockingly.

I slowly turn myself in the water and yet again I come face to face with the Optic. It appears that he is no longer hampered in his movements and able to use some sort of supernatural powers to get around. Still I must seize this opportunity of being this close to his person. I tread water, and inch towards him. "What have you done with Bump, what have you done to her?"

His head sized eye peers directly at me. "What have I done with her? Huh, you assume that I have done something to her. A typical reaction from a lesser Being."

"Well excuse me but I thought it was you who was trying to kill her earlier, or was I mistaken, was that purely foreplay and you love her really?"

The Optics squinted eye transforms into a fully opened stare; I think I've pissed him off good and proper with this blatant show of disrespect. He edges towards me now. "I have done nothing to her. If she were here, I would rip her essence to death and be rid of her for good. She is a virus that should not be here. As for your protectiveness towards her, I do not pretend to understand it. She lives in this domain by my grace. NOT YOURS, MINE! You and I are almost the same, I've told you this before; she is nothing like either of us, be sure of that."

"If you haven't taken her, then where is she?" I question.

"I DO NOT KNOW AND I DO NOT CARE!" The Optic bellows at me.

During this conversation I have managed to get quite close to the Optic. As he bobs up and down in the water, for a split second he disappears from view with the waters swell. As he returns back into my sight, I swing the hardest punch I possibly can straight at his big revolting blood shot eye. As my fist makes a connection it enters the pupil and continues on its course. There is no resistance as you would expect, it's like punching a pile of goo and he doesn't even flinch. This is obviously not going to be recorded as my finest moment in battle and I have a sinking feeling that his retort is going to be a lot worse than being flung across a bit of water.

"As my host, you are a great disappointment." The Optic's words are spoken with scowling menace. I grit my teeth and close my eyes. I don't even bother to try and distance myself from him.

"Just get on with it you useless pile of shit," I taunt; I might as well talk as if I have no fear.

I wait as long as I can for his expected wrath, but am unable to contain myself any longer so I open my eyes and yell, "I might be a fucking disappointment to you, but you are not even worth a thought in my mind you dickless bully!"

I then realise that I'm shouting insults at no one, he's gone, I am all on my own in the middle of an ocean. For some obscure reason, I felt better when he was here because at least I wasn't lost at sea. Bloody great! Oh well, pick a direction and start swimming is the next course of action I suppose. I view all around me, the full three hundred and sixty degrees, not a thing in sight. I start to swim. I figure it doesn't make any difference which way. The one thing I do know is that I'm not taking a journey; the Optic is orchestrating the whole route. He has a complete plan and my part is merely to participate.

I swim for an hour, possibly two and eventually I spy a dot in the distance. God I hope that is land. This vision inspires me to swim faster. Do you know Bump is right, I don't seem to tire, never in my life have I been able to swim this long without taking a rest. Head down I cut through the sea like an Olympian, only lifting it to make sure I'm still on course to my goal.

The closer I get I can see that the dot is an island. I can also distinguish that the shoreline of the island is a graduated beach, so it will not matter where I land. On my final approach the sea is high and the surf is pounding down onto the shore. The beach appears sandy and quite steep, so having been surfing many times in my life, I know that I will need to leave the water quickly or run the risk that the swell will drag me back into the sea. A minor worry, I will just be pleased to get out of this bloody ocean.

I use the surf to propel me towards the shore; I must admit I'm having fun doing this and if anyone was watching, they would be able to see the glee in my face as I body surf in on a massive wave. As soon as I feel the momentum of the wave has expired, I put my feet down and low and behold, I feel the bottom. With the knowledge that the swell may still cause me a problem, I immediately start wading towards the beach. I am up to my waist in water so finding the initial impetus is difficult, but as I begin to move so the easier my progress becomes.

Finally I trudge out of the sea, stagger up the beach until I am completely clear of the water and then drop to my knees. I feel exhausted for the first time since I have been in this world, I actually do feel tired. I slump down into a sitting position and recline back untill I am lying flat out staring at the sky. Gazing up at the beauty of the light blue sky, it becomes evident to me that I can't see the sun. I sit back up again and take a thorough scan of the complete sky; there is no sun. As I concentrate on the heavens, the blueness flickers slightly changing the shades of this canopy. Very odd, but then again it appears to be par for the course around here; so instead of trying to analyse the idiosyncrasies of this 'domain' as the Optic puts it, my efforts would probably be better utilised exploring my new location.

I head further up the beach until I reach the tree line. These trees are palms; at least they are typical to their setting this time, unlike the oasis. I can see beyond the trees. The centre of the island is a mountain, by its shape possibly a volcano. I assume heading for this will give me the advantage of a totally panoramic view, which would be useful in helping me decide what to do next.

I also need to find Bump. What the hell has happened to her? One minute she was with me; we were clutching at each other. How he managed to remove her and take her place, God only knows. I can only hope she is safe; it's funny, but deep down inside me, I get the feeling she is in no danger at present. I don't know why I have this sentiment but it kind of reassures me for the moment and that's good, because I need to concentrate on what to do next.

I begin pushing my way through the undergrowth which forms a green, waist high carpet between the palm trees. The trees themselves vary in size, some are adult, grading down to saplings, but they are spaced making my passage through them a simple task. Even the undergrowth moves away with comparative ease, so I stride ahead making excellent progress.

Eventually the palms cease and I enter a rocky terrain, once more the larger rocks are evenly spaced so traversing them and heading for the foot of the peak is a straightforward undertaking. This all makes such a refreshing change; so far this part of my nightmare journey has been reasonably pleasant, too easy or have I spoken too soon?

I reach the foot of the high rocky formation. This is indeed a volcano and the way up looks to be far from easy, it's almost a sheer climb. My mountaineering skills were always questionable, limited at best even with all the proper equipment. I'm not sure I have the ability to scale this monster. I decide to try circling the base in an attempt to discover an easier way up, after all surely the whole volcano can't have almost perpendicular sides......can it?

After an hour or so of searching for a less demanding route in which to scale this mountain, I stumble upon a huge opening, about ten feet tall and a good twenty five feet wide. Immediately I spot this cavern, I crouch and take cover. Even as I am doing this, I can't help wondering what the hell am I doing? I've just sauntered around the volcano as though I'm taking a stroll in the woods and anyone or anything could have seen me and now, because the norm has changed, I'm acting like a covert spy. I sometimes really question some of the things my instincts tell me to do. I move from rock to rock maintaining as much cover as possible until I am able to find a position where I can see right inside the large opening.

At first appearance the area inside looks to be incredibly dark, but as my eyes adjust to the light inside, I see a definite worn pathway heading further on into it. Perhaps this is a way up? I warily make my way to the left hand side of the cavity entrance, never leaving my cover until inevitably I have to make a mad dash for the opening. Once there, I wait for my eyes to fully adjust to their new environment and slowly and methodically I survey the whole area.

There is a path of sorts, but it doesn't look like it has been used in a long time. The main cavern is dome shaped with stalactites hanging in picturesque disorder all over the roof. The sides are covered with moisture with various types of moss growing in this damp environment. The ground either side of the path is extremely uneven with stalagmites pushing up and vegetation growing everywhere. The plant life becomes more sparse the further into the cave it goes. The path itself winds through the cavern, inclining and disappearing into the darkness at the rear.

I take to the path deciding to follow its course. The further I advance along the path and into the cave, so the darker and narrower it gets. It's

104

changing now from a cave into a tunnel. I have to use the walls to help guide me along because after a while I am surrounded by total darkness. I can still feel the path is continuing to go upwards and the tunnel itself doesn't seem to have become any smaller. It's amazing what you can tell by touch, which at this moment in time is all I seem to have. The tunnel winds on and up until at last I can see some light. I head straight for it. As I approach the exit, again I wait a few moments for my sight to readjust to this new found brightness and then carefully I ease my way out of the mine shaft and into the open.

The tunnel leads out onto a small ledge. This tiny rocky projection continues rising up the side of the volcano. Without delay I continue on up this precarious trail, keeping as close as I can to the mountainside for safety reasons as there is a sheer drop on the other. At one point I stop and look out over the island. God it's quite beautiful. The side that I am able to see is covered with forest which continues right down to the beach and the sea, but there appears to be no sign of life in any way. I continue.

Eventually the trail expands making my progress a lot easier, until finally it opens up into a clearing. This area predominantly consists of grass and rocks, with the odd tree scattered here and there. I start to walk across it when I realise that this isn't a clearing at all, I'm in the crater and I'm at the top.

I spin round and round, enabling me to take in the whole area. Somehow I made it to the top! I walk from one side to the other, followed by the entire circumference of the crater, gazing out over the land mass. All I can see is the island itself, its features and as you would expect; sea all around it. I check my immediate surrounding area and the crater itself several times, moving back and forth, hoping that I will spot something unusual, something I should investigate. But nothing changes. I have to question why I am here. I can't see what to do next. I amble to the centre of the crater, find a comfortable looking place to sit and slump myself down. I need to think this out.

The Optics both implied that this place is all in my mind; a corner of my brain I think were the exact words and also that the first Optic is in charge of this place and knows of me. Apparently I should and would have had no awareness of him until he was brought into this domain?

Domain meaning my brain, I suppose.

Optic two said that bringing me here was wrong; I should have never met an Optic. Why? He also said that they can only leave when the host, me in this case, dies or if I command it. Command it, what the hell does that mean? Dead I can understand.

Bump it seems, is my twin sister who died at birth but somehow passes her essence; is that the right word, soul, spirit, life force, whatever, into me, along with another Optic. Her Optic? It appears there are quite a few people or things running around inside me really! I can't help thinking that is quite worrying.

The Optics didn't seem to know each other but are here to do the same thing. One's here to control me and the other one is here for Bump. Mine though, seems to want to kill both of us, but the other one appears to be trying to protect her. If that is the case, then she should be okay. Optic one would have to fight Optic two in order to destroy her.

I was also told that, I have to take this journey. The Optic was most emphatic about that, so what is the point of this journey? So far it has been a long haul trek with the odd visit by the grotesque eyeball, who takes pleasure in terrifying the shit out of me, and Bump for that matter.

My main worry, my main question is that if I'm in my own brain taking an active part in this weird game the Optic has designed for me, where the hell am I in reality. I can't be dead or the Optic would be gone. He said that himself, so what is the real me, the flesh and blood me, actually doing?

As I sit puzzling over these thoughts, it also springs to my mind that how with all of these different so called rooms we have travelled through, neither of us has been physically hurt. In reality we would have been hospitalised at least three times and visited an out-patients department several times more but no, we just seem to bounce right back after every incident.

My thoughts are interrupted by a crescendo of thunder and as I gaze upwards, a bolt of lightning rips through the atmosphere and strikes at the ocean. I run to the side of the crater closest to where I saw the bolt strike the water. As I reach the spot the sky darkens over with electrical currents dancing about in the heavens looking poised to burst into action. As the approaching storm gathers momentum the bolts of lightning begin ripping though the air in all directions, manically lashing at the surface of the ocean. This display is quite unbelievable. I have never witnessed anything like this before, but then again I can't ever remember being stuck on an island in the middle of nowhere before either, especially watching a thunder and lightning show to this intensity. A valid point I think, but I'm not going to dwell on it right now. The thunder crashes so loudly that it actually causes me to wince. The bolts of lightning walloping their current into the sea, appear to be coming closer to where I am. It occurs to me that my present location is probably far from the safest if this storm is heading this way. With this thought flickering through my head the rain starts to come down. Initially quite lightly, a few drops here and there, but as the wind increases so the droplets swell in size, the quantity triples and it starts to pour. I need to find cover and up here there isn't any. I head for the path that led me up here. I am becoming acutely aware that I have to get back to that tunnel. It should afford me adequate protection in theory.

With the downpour hampering not only my view but also my footing as the rocky ground has now become quite slippery, I very slowly and deliberately descend the volcano, keeping both my hands on the rock face and my feet as close into it as I can possibly get. Unexpectedly, although I don't know why, I hear a massive clap of thunder and out of the corner of my eye I see a bolt of lightning hit somewhere above me. Its point of impact shakes the entire mountain. I freeze for an instant, awaiting any repercussion of this collision and then low and behold, down comes the debris produced by the lightning's stab at the volcano.

First a huge boulder comes tumbling down, missing me by only a few feet, bouncing off a higher protrusion and falling wide but this is closely pursued by smaller rubble, some of which does connect but causes me no real harm. Immediately the cascade ceases I brush myself off and continue on down, but now with a little more urgency.

The lightening continues with strike after strike, bits of rock, shrub and dirt come flying over the edge, gushing downward to the abyss below.

As I reach the access to the tunnel, another bolt shoots from the sky, which to my horror changes direction mid air and heads directly for my position. I've certainly never seen or heard of anything like this before. Throwing caution to the wind I launch myself into the aperture of the tunnel, just as it hits the mountainside causing everything around me to judder. At the same time I hear crackling noises and glancing quickly back I see minute strands of lightening appearing to search for their prey, like hundreds of tiny electrical tentacles moving along the walls of the tunnel towards me, sparking as they contact with various things along the way. I hurriedly move back away from the advancing electrodes but within a few feet the electric army seems to run out of power and it begins to recede. I watch the glimmering arms withdraw becoming duller as they go. I can't help thinking that they were coming for me, they made a conscious effort to reach me, which could only mean the Optics games are being played yet again.
"OPTIC! Where the fuck are you, you one eyed freak?" I yell out.

No retort comes back, however the lightning bolts pepper the outside walls of the tunnel. One after another they rip and gouge at the caves opening with sparks and blinding arcs of white light, ripping pieces off as the onslaught continues. The smaller lightening stems reach into the cavern but don't seem to have the prolonged energy to reach me.

It doesn't look like the Optic is going to put in a personal appearance this time, but the message he's sending is pretty emphatic. I decide to take no chances and skulk further back into the passageway only in reverse, on my bum, facing the direction of the weathers rampage enabling me to see its advancement if any. Mind you if it keeps this up, it's going to eventually bring down this warren that I'm hiding in. The construction of it isn't exactly engineered to modern day specifications; it looks like it was dug out without any type of support in place.

Having studied the tunnels make up, I think it may be prudent to return all the way back to the main cave as soon as possible. I travel back down the way I came, back into the darkness and all the way I am able to hear and feel the lightning strikes assaulting and rocking the volcano.

Leaving the tunnel and entering the main cave again, it now seems to be much bigger and brighter than I remember it to be. I can see the walls more clearly now. When I first came in here I believed it to be water trickling down the walls but it's not water at all, but lava; or if it was water, it isn't now. The moss isn't apparent any more either. The heat in here is intolerable and the whole area is trembling. I run down the path to the main entrance not looking back for anything. I've got to get out of here because if this thing is going to erupt I really don't want to be in it, or anywhere near it for that matter.

I clear the entrance and presently I am back out in the open. I distance myself from the volcano, stop and look back. The first totally bizarre thing is the black clouds, heavy rain and lightening are still around the volcano's apex, but only there? They seem to be circling it, as if it believes I'm still in there and therefore it has to continue its barrage. Where I am now standing the weather is great, blue sky as before; still no sun though. The volcano itself is shaking and rumbling as though about to erupt. That's problematic because I am almost back on the beach and I don't think I'm far enough away to be safe.

I turn and keep running towards the sandy area. Upon reaching it I bound into the water and dive through the surf. Initially my progress is good, but every now and again I judge my timing wrong and get knocked back a few feet by the waves. As I clear the breakers and swim clear of the swell I turn onto my back and gently paddle myself away from the island.

I watch as the whole volcano becomes a fiery red and white obelisk, spitting out lava, the storm continuing to rage around its peak. I see various types of vegetation spontaneously combust as the intense heat closes in and steam rising as the rains evaporate on contact with the hot stone. Quite a sight. I'm having a day of real firsts today; apart from being in this bloody water yet again.

CHAPTER NINE
THE POWER OF THOUGHT

I sedately swim out to sea on my back, secure in the knowledge that I'm well out of harm's way right out here; or so I believe.

Watching the island almost fade from view, I notice that the storm clouds that were previously surrounding the volcano are now moving away from it en masse. I strain my eyes in disbelief at what I'm seeing, but yes the big black mass of vapours are on the move, and they look like they are heading out to sea. Out to sea in my direction!

I observe the storm for some time moving slowly out to sea, changing direction for a while, then returning on a collision course with me. Are they looking for me? It's as though they are searching the ocean looking for something and I reckon that something has got to be me. As I try to calculate just how far away they are, my calm little swim takes on a slight need to put some distance between me and that storm. I've seen what that thing can do and I don't want to be stuck in this ocean when it gets here, especially if it's going to start firing electric bolts into the water.

I turn onto my front and swim with long hard strokes, ploughing through the water at a great rate of knots. I know I'm making good progress but in this position I can't see where the storm actually is, so I slow down, eventually stop and tread water so that I can ascertain the progress and location of the potential danger. As I turn to discover where it is, I am confronted by a total darkness that was previously a fair distance behind me. Now I'm staring right into it. The storm clouds are directly above me and when I say above me, a little more than twenty feet up. Christ that got here quickly. The clouds are rolling within themselves and I can both see and feel the electric presence forming a ballet inside the darkness of its cover, waiting with unprecedented patience to be unleashed.

I glance ahead of me, the sky is clear and blue but I know deep inside that I'm not going to escape whatever is in store for me here. I take the deepest breath that my lungs will hold, then up end myself and plunge beneath the sea's cover, hoping that this will disconcert the storm and send it searching somewhere else. I agree; a stupid and totally not thought out plan, but the best I could come up with on the spur of the moment.

In the depths I try swimming along under the water, knowing that at some point I'm going to have to surface for air. I try to see through the water to the clouds, feeling a sudden rushing sensation all around me. Firstly I must try to get back to the surface. I need air but the bubbling commotion around me has the ability to hold me down. Now panic sets in as I am caught unable to return to the surface. I am spinning in the water in some kind of liquid eddy. The spinning increases and I realise that I'm being sucked further down towards the sea bed. Trying to fight against this whirlpool is futile, so crazy as it seems, I attempt to relax and let it happen.

I plummet down to the depths of the ocean, as I drift along aimlessly within the vortex. I feel I am pinned against its outer wall. With great effort I force my head and shoulder away from the external side in an effort to get air. Somehow something tells me that whirlpools are almost a clear void in the centre, so therefore it seems reasonable to assume that there may be air in the middle. Great logic don't you think?

My exertion is justly rewarded, as my head clears the water I feel cold fresh air rushing down the twisting eddy towards this seemingly bottomless ocean. I take a deep, deep breath and relax back awaiting the outcome of this journey. I know how to get fresh air now, so trying to do anything else at this moment in time is going to be non-productive. It is apparent to me yet again, that all these diminutive distractions are being put together by the Optic to test me for some reason. Having already discovered this piece of information, as long as the danger is fairly minimal, I might as well just calm myself and enjoy the ride. It is its conclusion that is the worrying part, but trying to anticipate this isn't going to get me anywhere.

For quite some time I fall, spiralling downwards. I have to take air several times more, but even this manoeuvre seems to get easier with practice. The sea bed becomes visible, the sand being violently disturbed by the whirlpools' rotation, the vegetation buffered to and fro, sometimes ripped from the sea bed and hurled around by the eddy.

111

As I near the bottom, I observe a rock formation, also within the boundaries of the vortex, initially clouded from my view by the manic movements of the sand. It is similar to a reef only in the middle is a hole. That looks exactly where I'm headed for. On my final approach, the whirlpool abruptly releases its ardent grip of me. I wasn't expecting that at all and I slump forwards, falling uncontrollably towards the opening in the reef.

The opening is larger than it first appeared and I pass through it without touching the sides, firstly floating and finally falling down. I have entered a chamber that is liquid free and I am now free falling in total darkness. All I can do is to shut my eyes tightly and await the outcome.

Suddenly there is a blast of blinding light and I am sent crashing and cracking through something. Whatever it is, as I pass through or along it, there is definitely more than one of them that I'm hitting and breaking. Finally I land and it is far from soft. I roll until stopped by something solid. I lie very still on my back for a few moments, checking that all parts of my battered body are yet again still functioning, slowly I open my eyes. I'm looking straight up at what broke my fall. I am also able to see the route that I took on my way down.

The tall fir trees must be two hundred feet high with sprawling branches that reach out touching each other. This forest is incredibly densely planted. As I gaze up I can only conclude that I must have hit almost every branch of these trees on the way down, but at least they cushioned my eventual landing. I look all around me. This must be another room; well at least it's not wet. All I can see are these huge firs, great big brown trunks and the pine needle foliage of the branches. I walk over to one of the trees, turn around and sit on its visible root formation. What now? I have managed to arrive in a forest of fir trees immediately after having come from an ocean. Fuck me, the plot thickens, and where's Bump?

I bury my head in my hands and try to concentrate on her. I can see her face, a little blurry but I know it's her. In a flash she becomes crystal clear in my thoughts as she mouths to me. There is no sound, but I think she says, "I am safe".

Quickly I rise to my feet and at the top of my voice yell, "BUMP, BUMP, CAN YOU HEAR ME?" I strain my ears hoping to hear a reply. "BUMP, ARE YOU OUT THERE?"

Suddenly I think I hear something. My head turns towards the direction I perceive the sound to be coming from. I can't hear anything now though, nevertheless I'm pretty sure I heard something so that's the direction in which I will head. At least I haven't got to deliberate over the direction thing.

Off I go with a hastened pace. I begin to travel through the forest, trying as much as possible to head in the same direction as I thought I heard the voice come from. I stop and call out again. Yes I can definitely hear something. Having got my bearing again, I push on. After little more than a mile the forest ends and I am standing in front of a hedge, yes a hedge, a twenty feet high green privet hedge. Forest to hedge, well okay I suppose if I can go from ocean to forest, there is no reason at all why we can't go from forest to hedge. I glance left, right and then up. I can't see any way into it and trying to go over it could be extremely emotional. This is without a doubt the biggest hedge I've ever seen.

"BUMP, CAN YOU HEAR ME NOW?" I bellow.

"Yes she can," comes a reply.

I cautiously turn to see who is talking to me. "Ah, Mr Optic. I might have guessed. So you have Bump. She had better be okay."

The Optic once again is sporting a different disguise. He is now a one eyed caveman with long hair, a full set of unkempt whiskers, crooked teeth and naked. A real picture to behold I can tell you. "Again you assume Being. No I do not have her or she would by now be dead. However I do know where she is."

I study the Optics facial expression. He seems to be annoyed, possibly frustrated or irritated with something.

"So, to what do I owe the pleasure of this latest visit?" I sarcastically question.

"You are here and the female is far over on the other side of this maze. To get to here, all you have to do is fathom out how to cross it."

I turn, look at the huge grass hedge and glance back at him. "A grass maze. How quaint. What else have you got in there to surprise me?"

"Me!" the Optic says most surprised at the accusation, "Nothing. Most of the surprises that you have encountered are the making of your own imagination. All I have been doing is enhancing your experience. I cannot produce anything that you haven't already experienced or imagined. It is your own fears and knowledge that fuel the visions you behold."

"So let me get this straight. I'm in my minds funfair and you are the attendant that makes sure that every ride is to my satisfaction, and that's it. Right?"

The Optic is positively frowning at me, his eye not flickering at all as he glares. "You have no real idea what is going on, have you. Even when you eaves dropped on my conversation with the other Optic, you haven't managed to piece together what's got to happen here and it will indeed happen," he snarls arrogantly.

"You're right. I don't confess to have this all figured out yet but from what you two said, you can't hurt me and the other Optic can't hurt Bump."

"That is unfortunately correct but I can hurt and destroy the female, as her Optic can do the same to you. If we are rid of both of them, then you and I can come to terms."

At this point I become unsure what the Optic is actually getting at. His demeanour is more amicable than on any of our other meetings. It's clear he wants something from me but is hiding it very well at present. I need to be direct and see where it goes. "Look it strikes me that you need my help with something, so what do you want, just say it and then perhaps I can help."

"Help, HAHAHA, from you!" the Optic roars. "No I do not need help from the likes of you Being. Go and find your female, I have told you where," he sneers. With this last command he turns his back on me and slowly saunters off into the forest. Not his normal exit style but dramatic none the less.

I turn back to the hedge, my own personal green wall. Left or right to find the entrance into this maze, that's the choice. It's got to be right because as Bump says, right is correct. The thought makes me smile, I do really miss her. I begin walking around the hedge, pushing it every now and again in case the way in is not visually evident. After an hour or so of simply walking and looking, eventually I find a break in the privet wall. I can't help thinking to myself, why doesn't the Optic just drop me off at the bloody front door, it would be much easier for me to carry out his journey and it would be so much quicker too.

I peer into the entrance and see pretty much what you would expect to see in a privet maze, passages leading both left and right. To the left, not very far along, I can already see another way through into the next corridor, but this being a labyrinth, is it the right way to go?

I enter the maze and stand there contemplating which way to go, it's the old left or right choice again. Do I go with Bumps logic, or do I just go with my instincts. I decide to take the latter option this time. I turn left and walk straight past the first available opening and carry on until I reach the next one. When I arrive at it, with the heel of my foot I gouge out a sizeable indentation in the ground. I then move into the next corridor and keep to the left again. I travel along this passageway for a while. This one has a three way alternative, left, right or straight on into the next corridor along. Straight on seems to be the obvious way to go, because I will be two passages across and therefore nearer the middle.

As I'm contemplating this, so a lightening jolt hits my thoughts, why am I trying to get to the middle? The Optic made it perfectly clear. He said that Bump was on the other side of this maze, not in the middle. I have been systematically trying to work out the way to the centre, probably because that's what you would normally do when you enter into a maze. This time the middle is not the objective; Christ I'm a plonker!

Having sorted out the mistake I've been making, it occurs to me that it doesn't really help me all that much after all. I still have to find my way across this labyrinth to reach the other-side and the chances are that I will pass though the centre of it anyway, at least fairly close to it. I press on marking every doorway between the passages with the same indentation that I made at the beginning. At least if I start going over old ground I should be able to see it.

After a very long while of walking up and down these green corridors that all look exactly the same, I come across an opening that is subtly different from all the rest I have previously passed through. It is a shade lighter than the rest of the foliage. I approach it wishing to examine it more closely, but as I near it, so its colour reverts back to the identical shade as the rest. I stop, peer at it and slowly back track my steps. Within a couple of paces the tint lightens again. Is this some sort of sign, is my first thought, am I getting help here, and if I so, from whom? Or is it merely a trick of my eyes wanting to see something? I allow the situation this brief thought and pass through the opening. After all, if I don't follow the only thing in here that appears to be giving me some direction, I would be a fool. I'll worry about what's up ahead when I get there, or if/when I meet it.

Wandering along the next corridor for a minute or so, passing various openings on both sides until yet again I see another one that is different. As I draw near it again resumes the universal colouring of the rest of the hedges. Again I saunter down the next passageway awaiting my instructions. Sure enough, within a short time there is another distinct opening only this time I don't give it a thought, I just march directly through it and on.

After about half an hour I enter a perfectly cylindrical chamber; this must be the middle I assume. There is only one other door here and that's exactly opposite to where I'm standing. I cross the compartment and resume the search for Bump, happy in the notion that whatever is guiding me, must be on my side; I hope.

I travel along many corridors within this warren but I am directed at every turn by the shades of colour change within the hedge and I make good progress across the maze. Finally I turn a corner with the wall of the hedge behind me, while in front is only what I can call a breaker's yard, a car graveyard, an immense pile of broken and scrapped vehicles, stretching further than I can see, both left, right and beyond.

"BUMP, CAN YOU HERE ME, ARE YOU HERE?" I bawl.

No reply, nothing. The Optic said she would be here, the bastard lied. I feel the anger build in me as I start marching towards the broken vehicles. Where the hell is she? As I reach the pile of cars, I look at them. There are all sorts here and somehow, somewhere I remember this place; I've been here before. It wasn't as big as this, nowhere near as many cars, but this place is very familiar. I just stand there surveying the cars. I have most definitely been here before. I know this place. I have spent many hours here, on and off, searching this place for spare bits for my cars. I can even remember the name of it. It was locally called Berkies Breakers Yard. Everyone I knew came here to glean spares for their cars back in the seventies and eighties, before car manufacturers made it impossible to do anything to a vehicle unless you paid a garage.

I examine the row of vehicles closest to me, and as my eyes pass various makes and models I suddenly notice an old sixties motor with a big chrome front grill, which would normally be shaped to resemble a large shiny mouth, the headlights mimicking eyes, but in this case the shape appears to be all wrong. I slowly stroll over not taking my eyes away from it.

When I'm about ten feet away, I crouch down concentrating on the grill. This grill is elliptical and on this model is should be shaped like a miserable mouth, with the corners turned down, this isn't right at all.

I quickly glance at the cars directly either side of it, they look just as I remember them, so why has this one been changed. It occurs to me that it may be a modification done by the last owner, but I dismiss this as the present grill has disfigured the car, it just doesn't look right at all with this alteration.

What is it about this car? Then it hits me; I stand straight up and place myself directly in front of it, but retaining my ten feet distance. "Well, well, well, don't you just love changing your disguises, you asshole."

There is nothing. No movement, no retort, absolutely nothing at all, the car just sits there. Perhaps I'm wrong, but that grill is shaped like an eye, so I've made the assumption that it is the Optic; call me paranoid if you want.

I watch the vehicle with an unblinking stare for a few minutes then I proceed to approach it with one very slow step at a time. With every pace I can feel my heart beating just a little faster, silly really, but this tension I'm experiencing is self induced, why am I talking to a car? Why do I think it's the Optic? All just a feeling and I'm getting worked up over it. When I'm almost within touching range, I glance left and right to make sure there's nothing around me, but as I bring the grill back into view it happens, there is a very distinct movement, a blink. This startles me and I stumble back, trip over my own retreat and once more fall on to my back side. Next time I will trust my gut feeling. I crawl backwards as I watch the grill gradually draw back its eyelid and fix its glaring stare upon me. I await the dialogue but nothing is said. I continue backing up until I feel that I'm at a safe enough distance away, then stop and compose myself.

The big eye doesn't flicker, it just gawps at me as if it's more afraid of me than I am of it. For a few seconds neither of us move, speak or blink. This situation resembles some sort of stand off, but what I'm having trouble understanding is, why this should be. The OPTIC has always had the upper hand and to date has never had a problem with shoving his opinion right down my throat plus throwing his weight around. So why are we just sitting here? "Where's Bump?" I quietly enquire.

The Optic blinks a couple of times but doesn't answer. I can't help worrying about this situation. What the hell is this megalomaniac up to now. Perhaps he's gone shy? Still no comment, he just keeps on staring at me, with the odd blink thrown in.

I slowly and cautiously get to my feet, place my hands on my hips and yell at him. "Hey dickhead, I'm talking to you. At least have the decency to reply you ignorant bastard."

The pupil moves from left to right and focuses itself upon me again, but still no response. The intensity of his gaze strengthens.

"You said that Bump would be this side of the maze, you lied. Where is she?"

There follows a violent creaking sound as the car shatters, body parts from the vehicles structure fly in all directions. I dive for cover, not that there is much to be found out here between the hedges of the maze and the pile of cars, but the notion seems like a good one at the time. Suddenly the shit hits the fan!

"Lied to you, you insolent Being, lied to you. You are not worthy of talking to, let alone lying to. I ought to just destroy you and then this whole farce would be over."

"No, please, please don't hurt him. He's my brother and my friend. He can't hurt you."

It's Bump, she is here and it's obvious to me that this is her Optic not mine; otherwise she would be dead, or possibly worse and certainly wouldn't be reasoning with him so comfortably. I focus on the area her voice is coming from and I see her in the driving seat of an old Ford. I drag myself to my feet and glance back to the Optic. He has now become an old lady, with long grey hair, dressed in a black robe that covers her from neck to toe; but with still only that one eye. That's always their big give away, the one eye thing. Can't help thinking they could blend in so much better if they did a two eyed version. I walk over to where Bump is sitting in the car; she in turn begins to step down. As I see her I smile. Her face suddenly changes into a pained expression and she is physically forced back into the vehicle.

"No" the Optic says. "If you leave that area you will not be safe. Stay there." His attention then falls to me. "You will not approach her."

The voice doesn't match the appearance. It's that deep gritty commanding do what I say tone, coming out of an old woman's mouth who dresses badly. Again, it just doesn't work. Their briefing was seriously bad, I would say something but I reckon it won't be well accepted.

I turn to the Optic. "Why is she safe just there? And why can't I go over to her?"

119

The Optic places its eye upon me again. "I have shielded her from your Optic, he knows we are around here somewhere and he also knows that you will try to find the female, as you are aware. In essence, you have led him straight to us, but at present, he can only see you, he cannot see us."

I give this some thought. "Okay then, from that statement I really do need to distance myself from you two."

I look back to where Bump is, giving her a big smile. I then return my focus to the Optic. "Keep her safe. Please do that or I will never forgive you."

I observe a mystified expression cross the face of the old woman as she nods twice in acknowledgement, turning away from me and heading to where Bump is. Immediately I begin jogging in the opposite direction.

"YOU BEING!" The Optic calls out.

I stop running and look back. "What's up?" I question.

"The female tells me you are called Andy, is that correct?"

"Yep, that's what my name is,and by the way 'the female' is called Bump. Pretty name isn't it, perhaps you might try using it. Have you got a name Optic?"

The old woman almost, but not quite, smiles, turns away and continues her journey over towards Bump, not answering my question. I turn again and carry on in the direction I was going. I must admit, I haven't got a clue as to where exactly I am going now or indeed what to do next, but from what Bump's Optic said, I need to put some distance between me and them, for safety reasons. Fair enough, this I can do.

CHAPTER TEN
OUTSIDE INPUT

After a couple of miles of continuous jogging, utterly amazed at how fit I feel, I decide that I have put as much distance between Bump and myself that I need to for now, so I slow down and continue walking. She should be safe if my Optic comes for me now.

I have journeyed parallel with the stack of cars to my right the whole way so far, but the hedge of the maze I left behind some time ago. To my left now is a high grass verge that must be some thirty feet high. For the last ten minutes I have been intrigued as to what is over the other side of this hedge, or how far I would be able to see from the top. I gaze up in front of me but my long distance vision is hampered as there is a mist rolling in.

The pile of vehicles have now all become the same make, model and colour. They are all Ford Capri's and they are all white. Just goes to show how many Fords must have been sold at the time. I giggle to myself thinking they must have saved a fortune on the paint jobs, as so many people seemed to have gone for white.

As I continue ambling along I notice the mist is really beginning to close in. A decision needs to be made here. It seems that once more I am being channelled along my route. As long as I continue down the gap between the verge and the cars, I get a strong feeling that my direction co-ordinator is happy. I therefore need to break this continuity and change direction, but which way?

Stopping I survey the pile of broken and discarded auto-mobiles. I then turn my attention to the lush green grass of the verge. The cars would be extremely tricky to climb across and would hamper any real progress, whereas the verge seems a fairly straight forward climb, plus I have been biting at the bit to see what's over the top. The choice seems too simple really, so I'm going to go for the option of clambering over the cars, as that is definitely the most unlikely selection. Besides that I also have that gut feeling that over the high verge is just another problem waiting for yours truly, and we all know what happens when I ignore that gut feeling.

The mist is turning into a thick pea-souper of a fog, gathering momentum rapidly as it rolls in along the road. No time to lose. I head for the cars, pick what looks like the easiest way up onto the pile, and go for it.

Initially the climb is fairly effortless, but on reaching the top I realise that my route forward is over the roofs, bonnets and boots of the many vehicles. This is going to be a little trickier than even I had previously anticipated in the sense of maintaining my footing and balance. I start cautiously making my way over roofs, slide down windscreens and edge along boots and bonnets to the next cars, slowly making my way deeper into the cars graveyard.

After a short time the fog envelops the whole area and I find myself completely enclosed, unable to see a thing and I have to stop. I decide to descend from my position on top of the stack of vehicles and drop down to ground level. At least there I should be able to find a car to get into and take shelter. The fog is incredibly damp, bordering on wet and I find myself drenched in a matter of minutes. My climb down results in a very fast descent as the metal becomes wet and slippery. I lose my grip and footing, tumbling down between the vehicles. Although the drop is no more than about eight feet, I manage to hit or scrape every protrusion available for me to bash into.

Finally I hit the ground in a most ungainly manner, head and shoulders on the ground, one leg resting on a wing mirror and the other through an open car window. Can't help thinking that the drop down to so called safety, could have been a lot better. I pull myself up and out of this awkward position and look around me for a car that I can gain access to. The fog is so thick now that I am struggling to see my hand in front of my face, so I am only able to adopt the touch and feel option. When I find a window that is fully open, I squeeze my way though it and into the car. Once inside, I grab at the window's winding handle, closing it all the way up. Thank God for old mechanical mechanisms, they work without power, and in this case it will shield me from the elements. Thank you old Ford Capri.

Sitting in the front passenger seat, I scan the cars interior. The internal part of this vehicle is still in pretty good condition for its age. Looking at the driving seat and controls I have to smile, the car key is still in it, dangling from the ignition. I scan the back. That's in good nick as well and looks a lot more comfortable than the front. I climb over.

I watch as the murkiness surrounds the car, wafting over everything around me, allowing occasional tiny windows of clear vision, forcing me into trying to ascertain whether I can leave this place or not. There is an eerie quality about the denseness and silence of the fog which causes me some alarm. Can't help feeling that this is just another of the OPTIC's ploys, but to what end I have no idea. I will sit tight and wait for some kind of outcome.

Sitting in the car in complete solitude, I start to ponder on different things. The main issues being; who or what was it that helped me through the labyrinth? Who or what, gave me the signs that led me through its complexity, eventually coming out unscathed? Was it Bump, if so when I saw her, why didn't she say something? Surely she would have, she looked very pleased to see me. Or was it her Optic? I don't think so, he seemed quite indifferent to me until I approached Bump, then he got the right hump. Lastly, was it my Optic? He said he knew where Bump was. It seems to me as though he wants me to find her, almost as if he needs my help to be able to confront her. Perhaps he is hoping that her Optic and I may battle and that the conclusion will be an all win one for him. If Bump's Optic should kill me, I reckon my Optic would be elated, especially as he states that he can't actually harm me himself. He would still have a slight issue with Bump and her Optic both remaining in here, but then again, in theory he could destroy Bump. If I killed her Optic, which is really frigging unlikely, then both Bump and I are at his mercy again and he will be able to play his little games at his leisure. If that should happen, according to what they were chatting about in the clearing, they could both piss off home. Home? Oh what a web we weave, or in this case, what a web I'm being sown into.

Suddenly I feel dizzy. I try to focus on what's outside the car but it's fuzzy and unclear. Initially I put this down to the mist but I soon realise that my blurred vision is completely something else within me. I have a slight ringing in my ears. I shake my head attempting to gain some relief from this feeling but the gentle ringing becomes a faint voice. I put my head in my hands. What the hell is happening to me now? I attempt to hear what is being said but although it seems to be a single voice, it is neither loud or clear enough for me to understand.

Now pain that completely surrounds my head. I can't pinpoint an exact place, it's just everywhere. It thumps in my temples, stabs at the crown of my hair, applies pressure above my nose and forehead, tingles down through the base of my head and into my neck.

The voice has changed tone. The first voice sounded female, this one does as well but I'm sure it's a different person because the tone is completely dissimilar and the speed she is talking at, it's much slower. I am still unable to discern any of the words.

I open my eyes to see if my vision has returned to normal but to my horror all I can see is darkness, all I see is black. I slump sideways across the back seat still holding my head. God I feel dreadful and I really don't understand what is happening to me. I try to relax, slow my breathing down, come on Andy don't let panic take over, stay in control.

The voice changes again, this time it's male. I'm sure it's male, in point of fact, I recognise this voice. It's the accent that I know. "Len!" I call out, "Len is that you?" There is no reply. I feel as if I am calling out really loudly, but I can't hear my own words. Am I in reality actually saying them? "Len, for fucks sake man, answer me, I need your help!" I am convinced inside of me that I yelled that out so thunderously, that everyone, anywhere should have been able to hear me, but again I receive no response.

The pain becomes unbearable, the talking in my head a mass of voices all talking at the same time and completely unexpectedly I hear a voice that I definitely recognise one that I am completely familiar with! It's Barbara, it's my wife, she is here somewhere! I call out to her again and again. I feel the urgent need within me to make her hear and the frustration of hearing no reply. I thrash about in anger. "I can hear you. I can hear lots of people too, but I can hear you. I know it's you, please talk to me, please talk to me, please," I beg. Still no reply and as I lay strewn across the back seat, firstly the voices and then the ringing begin to slowly die away.

I open my eyes again. Now I can see the car I'm in. My vision has completely returned. The pain inside and all around my head is drifting away and I am beginning to feel normal again. Well as normal as I've felt throughout this entire nightmare.

I stare out of the windows that are streaming with condensation. With my arm I rub dry a patch in the interior glass of the rear window to gain a better view outside, only to discover that the outside is also soaked with droplets of water. I clamber over onto the front seats and having wound down the window from which I initially entered, I wriggle my way outside.

The fog has gone; it must have cleared while I was having my funny turn inside the car, but more to the point, all the other cars have disappeared as well. The only car here is the white Ford Capri that I was hiding in a few moments ago.

I now find myself standing right on the edge of marshland. Bloody hell, how do these things happen so fast around here? I do my customary three hundred and sixty degree observation. I can see various pieces of soggy grassland that are just above the water level, the rest of it appears to be either under water or fairly close to becoming submerged.

To the rear of me, not more than ten paces away is that grass verge again with its gradual climb to thirty feet or so. I'm still intrigued to know what's beyond it. This is the first time any part of the terrain has actually remained unchanged for any length of time. Interesting?

To my left and right are the banks of the swamp which continue in an exact straight line as far as the eye can see, keeping perfectly parallel with the base of the verge. This looks to me like a perfect, one or the other, either or either selection. I therefore suppose I am meant to leave this room and have a little wander around a new one.

Yet again, a choice has to be made.

CHAPTER ELEVEN
<u>IT'S ALL IN THE MIND</u>

I begin my steady climb up the grass verge with that niggling feeling of dread inside me. I had a gut feeling it was going to be trouble before, this time the feeling has taken over my entire body, but I'm still going to go through with it. I progress upward, always watching around me, for what, when or even how I don't know, but I definitely feel nervous anticipation that something's about to happen.

On reaching the ridge of the verge, I fall to my stomach, crawling up the last few feet flat on my belly. Finally I can see over the top but I have to admit, I wasn't expecting anything quite like I'm actually witnessing here.

What I behold in front of me is a vast frozen lake, I can only just see the other side. The lake appears to have buildings bordering its icy waters. The edge is no more than a foot away from my nose, so by my understanding, the ridge of this grass verge is more or less a dam holding back the waters and I'm at eye level with it. A scary thought.

To both my left and right runs a narrow path which borders this reservoir, to one side of which is the verge and to the other is the frozen waters. The verge side of the path steepens in both directions, increasing in severity within some ten feet or so. Nevertheless I am going to travel the path in preference to attempting to walk over the icy lake. It might take longer but it looks to be a whole lot safer. I'll take the left path and see what lies ahead.

Carefully I balance my way along the trail as the drop to my left becomes increasingly more sheer. Although I initially only climbed ten feet or so, I now find myself unable to see the bottom. It's turned into an abyss with the path still narrowing further. I test the ice on the lake to see how thick it is, now hoping that it will if needed, enlarge the width of my walking area. On applying my weight to it, I hear a slight crack. I watch the frozen expanse of water closest to me buckle, causing minute fractures within the ice.

Finally I reach the point where I can't go on. Left with no choice, I am going to have to turn back to try the other direction. Perhaps Bump is right, right is correct, so right is the way to go. Turning around on this knife edge is what can only be called an emotional incident, as twice I almost topple onto the ice, but I do eventually manage to turn around and carefully retrace my path back towards my starting point. The trail widens out again the further back I travel, but after some time I realise that I'm not going to completely manage to return to my starting point. I should have appreciated that after what Bump explained to me at the orchard. I obviously closed yet another door behind me and it is now absolutely clear, that I will have to go over the ice to the other side. Hobson's choice, I believe they call it.

All along the route, I test various points for the thickness of the ice and eventually I find one that meets with my approval. No cracking occurs and I hear only a negligible sound of stress as I apply my mass. I remember watching films, fictional and factual about people crossing these sorts of things and they always seem to break somewhere near the middle. With this deliberation in mind, I slide my left foot onto the ice cautiously followed by my right. Maintaining this shuffling motion seems to work ok. I'm making excellent progress, sliding as opposed to stepping, my weight not staying in any one location for more than a second.

The dreaded central point of the lake is almost upon me and again I feel the apprehension begin to build inside of me. I am acutely aware that I am shortly going to reach the thinnest point of ice. Thoughts bound around my head as to what I will do if the ice should break and with these thoughts, I hear the dreaded deep groaning sound of cracking. I speed up my skiing movements to broaden my mass, stretching out my stride to accelerate my pace. As I pass over the ice, I feel the ruptured segments tilt and break off behind me. I dare not glance back, just keep moving and pray to God I make it. I really have no desire to get wet again and certainly not in these frozen waters.

I keep the pace up and after a time, the chase of the breaking ice and the noises it makes, die down and eventually stop. I keep moving, I'm taking no chances here. However I do take the time to quickly glance back and can only conclude that I have been extremely lucky to have outrun the devastation that lies behind me. There are huge lumps of ice now sticking up, with spurts of water shooting up where the breaches have occurred.

Now I must concentrate on what's in front of me. The buildings are more visible and to my slight surprise appear very like those structures in old cowboy town. I really don't think that anything here could be beyond belief now, so the sight before me just seems par for the course. I can't see any sign of people, the place from this distance appears to be deserted. Shame really, it would be nice to see another face, especially a friendly one.

The closer I get so the more I am convinced that this is indeed an old gun slinging cowboy town. I know that in America they maintain some of the old frontier towns so this must be one of them. What the hell am I thinking here, if I am indeed inside my own brain, then this is something that I've either seen or read. This is the first time that I have ever considered this perspective. Still at this moment in time, I really need to get off this lake and onto dry or even firm land, I don't give a shit which.

I press on, finally reaching the jetty which protrudes out into the lake. As I approach it I observe that it sits above the surface of the ice. I can make out a ladder that reaches down, into the frozen water. This I head for. On arrival, I literally launch myself at the rungs. As I grab at them, each one disintegrates in my grasp, collapsing and throwing me back onto the ice. I hit the cold surface flat on my back with an explicit thud and instantly, I hear that inevitable cracking as my impact shatters the ice. I remain very still, listening, only too aware of the condition of the surface immediately surrounding me. After the preliminary creaking sounds, there follows a deadly silence. I remain completely motionless, I truly do not wish to disturb anything, but the slow rasping echo of the ice breaking continues. Caution gone, I jump to my feet and make a mad slippery dash for the shore. The land is about forty feet away and my attempt to run over this distance seems to take an eternity. With every step or slide I take, so I constantly hear the sound of ice breaking. On my final approach, I leap with all my might hoping that I can cover the distance I need to reach safety. As I land, both my head and torso have made it to the shore but my bottom half is still lingering on the disintegrating ice. I can feel the freezing cold water as it soaks my lower half and the numbness begins to set in. I drag myself clear of the water and onto the bank, briskly rubbing my legs to get the circulation going again.

The feeling returns to my feet and legs quicker than I thought it would. I clamber to my feet and start wandering up to the town. There's no greeting party, so I assume the place must be empty, but then again as we all know, assumption is the mother of all cock ups, so I'd best remain wary.

I walk past the jetty, between some houses into what must be the main street. I keep to the middle of the road, looking left and right, unable to see any signs of life. The buildings are all made of wood and as in the films I've watched before of the wild west, there are a variety of stores and businesses including the ever important saloon. I decide that the saloon is where I'll head, if there is anyone here, surely that would be the place to congregate.

While pacing towards the saloon, I note that as one would expect, the street is made solely from dirt. On either side of me there are several buildings within close proximity of their immediate neighbours, forming small blocks. The raised walkways fronting and joining these premises have steps leading down from them into the street, one set allowing access to an alley that runs down the side. On inspection I observe that these steps like the ones at the jetty, are also pretty rickety and in a serious state of disrepair.

On my approach to the saloon, I note three steps up to the staging. On one side there is a hand rail but on the side closest to me, the rail is in four pieces lying on the dusty floor with only the upright struts still in place. On reaching the steps I thoroughly inspect them before I will consider using them; they look in bad shape. I decide to bypass them. I take two steps backward and burst forward, leaping to the top in one go. On landing, I regain my balance by steadying myself on the door frame that surrounds the entrance to the saloon.

In this opening are two swing doors which I peer over to see what's inside. Scanning the saloon, there are tables and chairs, a small stage area with curtains drawn back and secured with sashes, a piano standing in a corner, a sweeping staircase which curves its way down from the first floor and of course, the main bar. The bar is relatively

high and it is obvious to me that customers would only stand while drinking, as there are no sign of any bar stools anywhere. Behind this is a working surface with various bottles placed on it. There is also an enormously long mirror that spans the entire length of the bar. I must have seen this bar in a thousand westerns that I have watched on television over the years
.

I push open one of the swing doors, it makes a horrible creaking sound, promptly coming adrift from its hinges and crashing to the floor. Brilliant, if no one knew I was here, they certainly do now. I couldn't have made much more noise if I had tried. I scan the room, still checking the street outside. If anything or anybody did hear me, they are not making themselves known, that's for sure.

Cautiously I edge around the remaining swing door, ensuring that I don't even breathe on it, and I enter the room. The floor, which is made of spit and sawdust floorboards, creaks under each step I take. I cross the room to the bar. On my approach, I see there is a section of bar which is raised at the far end. I assume this must be the entrance in. I reach the bar without anything else collapsing or falling apart and head for this opening. When I reach it, I go behind, working my way along, looking at the various bottles and pulling at assorted beer pump handles. Every bottle I examine is empty and no beer surges from any of the pumps.

Suddenly my attention is caught by an object partially visible from under the counter at the far end of the bar. It stops me dead. I stand there gazing at the object; I already know what it is. It's the butt of some kind of fire arm. I stride over, pulling it clear of the counter. It's a shotgun. I open it up, checking the barrels. There are no shells in it and it looks as though it hasn't been fired in years, the barrels are filthy and I can actually see cobwebs; no way would I even entertain firing something in this state. I lay it on the counter and leave the bar, walking to the stair case.

As I ascend the steps, so every step and every tread groans with my weight upon it. When I reach the top I survey the saloon area one more time and find to my astonishment that the shotgun has gone, even though I have no doubt exactly where I put it. I check the whole area

130

of the floor below me; it's definitely gone, just disappeared! I feel intense concern start to build inside of me. Is there someone else here? I once again slowly and methodically scrutinise the entire saloon. I cautiously move along the balustrade to gain my widest line of vision. From where I am standing, I am able to see almost the complete saloon; the only tiny part that is not within my sight is the area under the stairs. I cringe taking great pain not to make any noise, I silently move along the landing trying to gain a better view of this hidden spot underneath me. When I reach the vantage point that I am trying to attain, I peer down but I am unable to see anyone or any sign of the gun.

Quickly I evaluate my situation deciding that whoever took the gun has a definite advantage and they must know where I am. I need to change this situation. I move up the hall away from the staircase and try the door handles of every door I come across. The first three are locked, the fourth opens and I enter the room.

A quick look around it reveals nothing unusual, so I cross the room to the window. Looking out I see that I'm located at the front of the building. The window is a sash type. I push up the lower casement and climb out onto the veranda roof. Sliding down, I swing myself back to the ground.

On landing I immediately move to the window closest to me and peer through. I can't see much because the glass is absolutely filthy with dust and grime.

I once more return to the broken swing doors, crash through the remaining door which is still attached and throw myself to the nearest table pulling it over the top of me for protection and cover. The door seems to have survived my entry but the table has ended up as a big flat disc without any legs and I am a crumpled mess at the base of the piano. What a totally crap attempt at a surprise entry, saying it didn't go well is a definite understatement.

Pushing the table top away from me, I pull myself up along the side of the piano and look around the room, half expecting someone to be standing there with a shotgun aimed at me. I can't have got it more

wrong. As I stare at the bar, there is the shotgun, exactly where I put it. Now I feel angry. I stride over to the gun, pick it up and fling it across the room. It hits the opposite wall and clangs as it hits the floor.
At the top of my voice I yell, "WHAT THE FUCK IS GOING ON? WHO'S HERE, SHOW YOURSELF!"

I immediately march out of the saloon, jump down into the middle of the street and spin around, trying to spot any movement, anything I can vent my anger at, but the place is deserted. I stride over to one of the stores, angrily kicking in the door, which just falls to pieces on my impact and I walk in. This is a general store, sacks and jars all over the place. The place is a tip, everything is covered in thick layers of dirt.

I leave the shop, return to the middle of the street and drop to my knees, put my head into my hands and crumple to the sandy, dusty ground. "What is the point of all this?" I ask myself.

"What indeed, a very good question to ask, Being."

I slowly look up to see a young man dressed completely in black. Black cowboy hat, black shirt, black waistcoat, black jeans, black boots, black gun belt and most importantly, he is holding the shot gun.

"Optic?" I enquire.

"Are you pleased to see me Being, you seem to have lost your temper and your will is starting to ebb."

"Now what are you going on about? Why is everything you ever have to say embroiled in a riddle?" I jibe at him, defensively. I rise to my feet and stare directly at the man in front of me. Before he has a chance to answer me, I quickly add, "Two eyes, now that's a definite improvement, you almost look human; it is you isn't it, you are my Optic?"

The young man's face begins to distort, his forehead pulsates, rips open and a single eye bulges through to take the place of the two. "Is that better Being, can you identify me easier like this?"

132

"Well that was pleasant to watch, but I have to say, it's certainly not an enhancement to your boyish looks."

"Why have you lingered here so long, there is nothing here for you, I need you to carry on with the journey; why did you invent this place?" the Optic grunts at me.

Once more his question has me puzzled, why have I invented this place he said, I certainly wasn't aware that I had, but nevertheless it seems he obviously had nothing to do with the instigation of me arriving here. Interesting? "Where would you like me to go next Mr. Optic? Do please feel free to enlighten me because I would hate to invent another scenario that you weren't aware of and waste more of your precious time. Or, then again, perhaps I would."

At this the OPTIC takes an aggressive stride towards me, looking most disgruntled. "Insolence yet again, you seem to have a knack of being able to annoy me. Return to the icy lake. If you look, you should be able to see where you need to go from there."

I turn, looking down the side alley that I originally entered by, to see the jetty and the lake. I turn back to the Optic, but he's gone. Standing still for a moment I evaluate what has just been said. I can't help sensing that something in that conversation put the Optic on his back foot, but I don't seem able to put my finger on exactly what it was.

I head back towards the jetty. Before leaving the alley I see the lake spreading out in front of me, but it appears different this time. I am able to see the other side of it with ease, it appears closer than before. This time the other bank has beautiful green and golden trees adorning it. It all looks incredibly lush and inviting. I know that when I left it earlier it didn't look anything like this. It has so much appeal, that I feel irresistibly drawn towards it. It occurs to me that this is obviously the bait, a lure to ensure that this time I go the correct way. That is what was wrong with the Optic, I have somehow strayed from his path and he needs me to return to it, hence this stunning, idyllic image I am now witnessing on that far bank. Clever!

Now it becomes extremely clear to me. I have to go back into the town and travel in precisely the opposite direction to the lake. It might piss

133

him off, but I have no doubt that if I head in that direction, I will get more accurate answers than doing the Optics bidding.

My initial impulse is to yell out 'fuck you Optic' but if I can achieve some more distance away from his intended route, avoiding a possible confrontation with him, so the better off I'll probably be.

Immediately having made this decision, I turn around, heading back to the town. On reaching it, I cross over the main street and take a side alley opposite to the one I originally entered through. I walk between the buildings, eventually coming out into a vast, open area of sand. Not another frigging desert. It doesn't matter, Bump has taught me that all I need to do is keep going. Here I don't need food, water or rest, just to keep moving. I feel new vigour surge within me, stronger than I have since I've been here. Coupled with this, I am experiencing a real defiance towards the Optic, as if I have discovered some kind of purpose, not that I am sure what it is but even that doesn't seem to worry me.

I stride off into the desert with purpose in every pace. Shortly the sand turns into shrub-land, then marshland and finally to a rocky terrain. It's perfectly flat but it looks and feels exactly like stone. At this point I stop, surveying everything around me. The town has disappeared from view, and along with it, so has the sand. I can just about make out the shrub-land with of course the marshland right behind me. Surveying the rocky area, nothing is evident except the cold grey of the stone. It's perfectly flat and doesn't seem to change in its characteristics in any way as far as I am able to see. Glancing up, the sky is that clear blue with a pleasant warmth, but still with no visible sun. I can't help wondering where the hell I am, but instantly as this thought fleets through my mind, I have to smile to myself as it also occurs that I haven't really known where the hell I am throughout this whole nightmare.

I start to hike over the stone plateau, watching my every step, absorbing the completely unchanging colour and consistency of the mineral make up that I'm walking upon. After quite some time I begin to notice that the evenness of the path seems very slowly to be changing. It's so slight but my balance tells me that I am beginning to walk down hill. I stop and turn, looking back. It's definitely not apparent, I can't see a gradient. I march on and the sensation becomes stronger. Again I stop, turn back, and yes now there is a distinct bow to the landscape. I am walking down hill. The further I go, the more pronounced it becomes, eventually I am consciously taking smaller strides to compensate for the gradient. As I continue slowly and apprehensively, it becomes quite steep. Finally I reach the point where I have no choice but to sit down and shuffle along to make any further progress. The way in front of me is dropping off so sharply now that standing up and walking is not an option anymore. As I peer forward, it becomes apparent that I am no longer going to be able to proceed, as I am slipping with every movement I take. I stop, remaining perfectly still and try to peer over the edge, but I can't. The ground falls away so drastically, making me feel as though I am literally perched with any unnecessary advancement sending me toppling down to where ever this ends.

After sitting motionless for a while, trying to fathom out what my next action should be, I experience a falling sensation. I creep forward a foot or so, digging my heels into the ground in an attempt to stop this forward motion. For a split second I seem to manage this and I smile to myself at this ridiculous achievement. However my glee is short lived, as within only a few seconds my feet start juddering under the pressure I am applying to the surface and inevitably with the severity of the incline, so I again start slithering downwards. I turn my whole body over so that I'm now face down towards the ground and once more I manage to stop my descent. This pause allows me another chance of possibly discovering a method of climbing my way back up. As I lay prone, with both my hands and feet searching for something to gain a grip on, I take a momentary look upwards and it is at this point that I realise I am indeed in deep trouble.

"You do not listen, do you Being, I told you not to come this way." The Optic is standing approximately ten feet above me. Impossibly, he is standing bolt upright away from the stone surface, at right angles with the ground, towering above me with the gradient. He is still dressed as a cowboy, completely in black.

"Do you know Optic, you can be a real frigging idiot at times. SO YOU TOLD ME, SO I DIDN'T WANT TO GO THE WAY YOU SAID. I can go where I fucking please, I'm in my brain aren't I?"

The Optic scowls at my verbal attack. He punches his fisted hands onto his hips, his head peering forward, his eye turning blood shot and his manner extremely aggressive. "Yes, you are in your own brain, but you are in MY DOMAIN, not the part of the brain you have a feeble control over. You have never experienced what is in here or how to cope with its complexities. This part of your brain belongs to me, NOT YOU. You cannot comprehend the scale of intellect or ability this sphere of influence has, and it is controlled by me!"

"So in which case Mr. Optic, why are you so.....FUCKING CONCERNED THAT I CAME THIS WAY, eh?"

The Optic takes a pace towards my position and stops abruptly. He looks back for a second then turns his head towards me, glaring but saying nothing. I feel that he has something to say but he can't manage to get the words out. These actions of his intrigue me, it's as though he doesn't want to approach any nearer to where I am. I witnessed genuine apprehension in his last set of movements. I need to continue my baiting of him but I really do have other pressing needs, the main one being, that I can feel myself slipping again.

"Hey Optic, do you want to give me a hand here? If I fall, I'm going to be even further from where you want me to be." I'm hoping that this taunt will get me some help but he just stands there gawping at me. "I'm slipping asshole, now would be a great time to step in and come to my rescue!"

The Optic starts to back up, then he turns and walks away.

I lose all the limited grip that I had on the smooth stone and I know this time there isn't going to be any reprieve. I'm going to drop like a stone all the way down to who knows where. As the sliding begins, my finger nails scratch frantically at the stone trying to slow my fall. I attempt to dig my feet into the rock. I'm actually kicking at it but to absolutely no avail, my plunge to where ever is now inevitable. As my speed increases I realise that trying to slow my descent is futile so I attempt to turn myself onto my back. Having achieved this manoeuvre, the solid mass that I was pathetically clinging to disappears and I now find myself free falling, and not for the first time I might add.

136

The air rushes past me as I fall. I squint to see if I can ascertain where I am going to land. I can't see anything below, but above me I can see the stone structure that I was clambering about on. It curves outward into a huge bulge and continues to curves back in on itself, resembling the side of an enormous egg.

Trying to obtain a composed position while I free fall is almost impossible. I'm buffered and tossed around with the speed that I am plummeting at. For the first time since I've been here, I see birds. I pass them way to quickly to identify what they are, and to be honest I couldn't really care less at the moment. Nonetheless there are birds! Throughout this entire journey, I have never met any other living thing, unless you include the two Optics, Bump and myself. Where ever I am now, there is other stuff and even as I fall, this has a strange comforting effect on me. The journey down seems to last for an eternity. I realise that I have no control over this whatsoever, so I simply close my eyes and wait for the inevitable outcome. I experience the feeling that I've been here before. In my mind I am awaiting some kind of saving grace; it happened before, why can't it happen a second time.

I hit the ground and nothing saves me. I really got that bit completely wrong. The pain I feel is unprecedented, as though I have been turned inside out, and an army of vindictive bastards have kicked and stamped all over my whole body. I question why I'm feeling this? Shouldn't I be dead? Ah ha, that's it, isn't it! I can't be killed inside my own brain; well not unless I allow it to happen.

CHAPTER TWELVE
<u>MY SIDE OF REASON</u>

Slowly and painfully I sit myself up, gathering my thoughts together.
Well, if I have just passed through one room and into the next one, the
door has definitely slammed shut behind me this time. There is no way
on earth that I'm going to be able to return that way again. The climb
back would be impossible.

I take store of my new surroundings. There is the most definite
indentation of my body shape imprinted in the long grass. If it hadn't
hurt so much and scared me half to death, it would possibly strike me
as funny. The whole scenario could have come straight from a cartoon
strip. My immediate vicinity consists of this long grass. It appears to
be some kind of hay but not being over agriculturally knowledgeable,
I'm not entirely sure. Behind me is the massive egg shaped rock and in
front, beyond the grass is a wall of black. It just looks like an expanse
of darkness curving around towards both sides of me. Again it's once
more obvious that my choices are extremely limited here, so having
given my way forward at minimum a seconds thought, I decide that
the dark wall will be my next adventure.

The tall pasture is easy enough to plough my way through and within a
short while I am very close to the barrier of night. The nearer I get to it
seems to make no difference as to what I can see, either in it or
through it, it remains a dense blackness. No matter how I view it, the
depth of gloom is impenetrable. Arriving at this barrier of darkness, I
stand before it, staring in, trying to see through the black, but there is
nothing, no visibility at all.

I cautiously offer up my left hand to probe the darkness. As my finger
touches the black film, it seems to pass freely into it. My protrusion
feels as though it is being immediately acknowledged, contained and
sealed, but allowed to move freely forward. Pushing my hand further
in, I feel coldness akin to reaching inside a freezer, attempting to get
something from the very bottom of it. The further I extend my hand,
and then my arm into the depth of the lucid obstacle, so the colder it
becomes. I snatch my hand back, clasping it with my other hand and
rubbing to regain the warmth it had prior to my experiment. Within

seconds feeling is restored, with no apparent ill effects from my probing of the wall.

This time I need to push right into this darkness, really wade into it and see what the outcome will be. I take a really deep breath and with some momentum, thrust my hand, my arm and then half my body and head into the blackness. My eyes agape, I am still unable to make anything out. The dark is total, pitch and intense, there is nothing to be seen; this void is nothingness. Sharply pulling myself back, It dawns on me that I must have to pass completely through it, in order to find out exactly what is on the other side.

As I withdraw my entire body from within it, I slump backwards to the ground. Collecting my thoughts I focus my full attention on this divider. I have an extremely strong urge to rush at the black and fight my way through, until I reach whatever is on the other side. Leaping to my feet, this is precisely what I do. Rushing at the black barrier, I hit the wall, close my eyes and feel the coldness engulf me. This time I push forward, step by step, surging forward and on, all the way through, until abruptly I fall painfully to my knees on the other side. I reach out with my hands towards the ground, trying to maintain my balance as I am thrown forwards.

I peer with dazzled eyes into the light to see where I am now. In front of me about ten feet away is a wall, which is no more than three feet high. To my right is a structure that strangely resembles some kind of outside oven, or perhaps even a barbeque. On my left the wall extends a good forty odd feet, with another construction at the far end of it. This looks to me like some kind of terrace. The floor is tiled with a terracotta type surface, smooth and cool to my touch.

I slowly get to my feet. On attaining my full standing height, I am able to see over the wall that surrounds this veranda. The view in front of me is breathtaking. It is night-time and I am incredibly high up, looking down over a ravine completely surrounded by mountains. The moon is still high in the sky but is approaching the edge of the mountain, where the land drops away towards the sea. There is another headland beyond it, gently winding its silhouette downwards to join it.

I slowly walk towards the wall and as I approach, I can see across the entire valley. There are street and house lights illuminating the twilight. To the left a town with a myriad of white light, while in front of me the lights all appear to be yellow. I've been here before, I know this place. I have looked out onto this fabulous scene before, it was stunning then and it feels safe to me now, as it did before when I first set eyes on it. This is Italy, a place called Ravello and its neighbouring town of Scala. I holidayed here once, stayed with friends who own this place. Now why would I be here?

Slowly I walk along the length of the balcony, checking the end structure, and yes it is exactly what I remember it to be; it's a bathroom, the guest bathroom that Barbara and I used when we stayed here. Opposite the bathroom door is the entrance to the bedroom we shared. The outer door is a double louvre, wooden, slatted construction. Inside this are the main glass doors. I walk through both of these and enter the room. It is precisely how I remember it. Opposite me there is a double bed with wooden head and foot-boards. A grand Italian style double matching wardrobe with a mirror in its centre, stands off to the left taking up most of that wall. The ceiling is high, domed and rising from each corner of the room, until forming a smallish square at the top painted a different colour from the rest of the room. I have to smile to myself; I have good memories of being here.

"Where is this place, Andy?"

I spin sharply around with the familiar sound of this voice and its question. "Bump, you scared the crap out of me. Where the hell have you been, are you okay, how the hell did you get here, did you come through the wall of darkness as well?" All the questions come tumbling out at once.

She runs to me and flings her arms around my neck, giving me a huge hug. "I'm so glad I've found you, but I couldn't have done it without the help of my Optic. He brought me here, but said he couldn't stay because of where you are. He seemed nervous about coming with me."

"Where is he then?"

"He's the other side of the wall, the wall that you came through. He wouldn't come any further, that's what I was saying, he seems frightened to come through it."

We walk out of the bedroom and back onto the terrace, over to the wall surrounding the balcony. "You say that you have never been here before Bump?"

She looks out over the ravine and turns surveying the building. "Nope, I have never been here before. It's beautiful though." She takes a couple of minutes more to absorb the whole of her surroundings and turns to me with a big smile on her face. "By the way you are looking at this place, I think you know where we are." She gently says.

"Indeed, I've definitely been here. I don't know about you, but it feels safe here, as if this place is not accessible to the Optic and as you say, your Optic didn't want to come here. The question is why?"

"I don't know," she replies.

I walk back to the point where I originally entered from the darkness. The door if I remember correctly, also leads into a kitchen. I walk through this door and indeed there is the kitchen again, exactly as I remembered it, but my way in from the darkness has now gone.

"Where did you come in here from Bump?" I enquire.

I turn to her, her face a picture of perplexity, her eyes dancing from left to right with her eyebrows crinkled. "I don't know Andy. I was with my Optic, by all those cars where I last saw you. I remember saying that I wanted to see you and him telling me that if I did, it wouldn't be long before I didn't exist anymore. I started to argue and then I was here, right behind you in that other room."

"What do you mean, it wouldn't be long before you didn't exist anymore?" I question urgently.

"I don't know but that was what he said."

"Do you feel okay at the moment?" I ask her.

141

"Yes a little fuzzy, but I don't feel there is anything wrong."

I look long and hard at her, she doesn't look any different to me, but I am concerned about what her Optic said. The Optics do seem to know how this world works, so I believe we need to heed their words to a degree. I decide to keep a close eye on her. "If you feel different in any way at all, and I do mean, in any way at all, I want to know immediately. Do you understand?" She nods. "Right, if this place is exactly as I remember it, we need to go through the kitchen to the back door and then climb, God knows how many steps, to be able to go back down to the town. Are you up for it?"

Bump smiles. "Let's rock and roll."

I laugh out loud at her reply, take her by the hand and leave the safety of the building by the back door, heading for the steps. When I was last here, these steps were a nightmare, so steep and so many of them, they seemed to go on forever, to say nothing of how you had to stop at least a couple of times to get your breath back. We reach the foot of the concrete stairway, and I slowly look up to the first little landing. Yep, just as I remember them. If there was any one thing that I would have liked to be different on this visit here, it would have been these frigging steps.

We start the climb and even though it is night, the moon lights the way. Within five minutes we reach the top, neither of us faltered on the whole way up, it was so easily scaled, which on my previous visit had definitely not been the case. I'm not even slightly out of breath, I don't feel phased at all. Very strange.

At the top we turn right and walk down the remaining steps towards the road. At the road we head toward the street lights and the town of Ravello. From memory it should only take us some twenty minutes or so to reach the outskirts. As we approach the town, it is most apparent to me that we haven't encountered a single soul; no people, no cars and absolutely no noise. This place was never quiet. Even at two o'clock in the morning you would hear dogs barking in the distance at the very least.

The moon with its glowing brilliance lights our way and at no point is our path engulfed in shadows. The way into the town is crystal clear, all the way down from the terraced building. There must be three hundred steps down until we finally enter Ravello itself. I recall the way forward, so I take the lead along the now upward road, towards the square in the centre.

Suddenly we grind to a halt with the sound of one of the towns many churches striking its hourly bells. As we glance at each other, she snatches at my hand, gripping it quite firmly and we listen in silence, counting the bell tolls. ONE, TWO, THREE, FOUR, FIVE, SIX...... and in the blink of an eye, the night and the moon disappear and daylight is fully upon us, with the sun high in the sky. There is definitely something different about this place. With the intense heat the sun is emitting, I would guess the time to be noon or there abouts. I have to admit the change from night into day is really bizarre, but it is preferable to what I was half expecting to happen; the bells to chime thirteen. Now that would have really put the willies up me. Bump releases my hand and continues on up the road towards the square as if nothing unusual has happened at all.

"Hey, didn't you think that was a fast change from night to day?" I nonchalantly ask.

She pauses for a moment, doesn't even turn and replies, "I have seen similar before and now we know that day and night just change like that, I think we ought to press on, as it's easier to make progress in daylight and we haven't a clue how long that will last."

Flabbergasted by her reply, doesn't really describe my thoughts, but yet again, her logic is unquestionable. I slowly jog after her, picking up my pace a little to catch her up.

All the way up through the small, overhanging streets to the square, I don't physically see anyone, but I see ghostly fleeting images every now and again that distract me from my course. I try to focus on them but they just glimmer for a fraction of a second, and then they are gone. For some reason I don't have a bad feeling about them. They appear as images from my first visit. I don't know how I know this, but I do and they make me feel safe and secure.

After a while I semi ignore them, until most unexpectedly, one of the images stops momentarily, smiling at me. It's my wife Barbara.

"You okay Andy, you look very happy about something?" Bump breaks my trance saying.

"Yeah I'm fine, but I think I've just realised that where ever we are within my brain and its subconscious at this moment, this place is protected from the Optics. Everything in here will not be able to harm us."

"That's good isn't it?" she replies. As Bumps words are spoken, she stops walking and slowly turns towards me. I can see she is trembling and her eyes are huge.

"What's going on, what's the matter?" I ask with extreme concern
.
She sits apprehensively on a small wall at the edge of the square and hangs her head in her hands. "I don't know. I feel shaky and I can't see properly. I feel kind of strange, weak."

I cross to where she is sitting and gently lift her head. There is perspiration all over her face which has dampened her hair and she looks ghostly pale. Her eyes are wide with the pupils enlarged. "How long have you felt like this?"

"Since shortly after the sudden change of night into day," she replies.

"Okay, can you carry on or do you need to rest?"

She gives a little chuckle. "After all the grief I've given you about taking rests, I'd better not say that I need one now."

A smile crosses my face. She has cracked an intentional joke. Nevertheless I am still especially concerned for her. She rises to her feet and as she does so, I take her arm and we proceed across the square, through a large tunnel leading onto an open area which looks right out and over the sea. The ocean is full of various shades of blues and greens, enhancing its beauty with incredible style, but as usual there is no sign of tangible life. Like before I see very vague images moving. There are speed boats and yachts skimming across the bay, but they move so quickly that my attention upon them is only for an instant before they shoot back once more into the background.

From this view point I can see the mountain that was opposite the balcony. As it rises up to its first peak, so there is a strange looking, pulsating black wall obstructing the way to the second peak. This wasn't apparent from the balcony when I first looked up there, but now not only is it visible, I am actually able to hear it. I turn to Bump, she too is staring at the uncanny barrier on the mountain. "Any ideas as to what that is?" I ask.

"I know exactly what that is, that is where I have to go, before I no longer exist. That is the same wall of darkness, both you and I passed through to get here."

I look back to the mountain, and yes I see that it certainly seems to have a similarity to the previous wall, even from this distance. "So if you are the other side of that wall you are safe, but this side you can't survive, is that it?" I question.

"It seems to be that way, I don't know why. I don't know why this side is dangerous for me, but even my Optic would not venture this side of whatever that wall is." She pauses for a moment, sighs and continues, "Which is strange, because this side, you feel safe, you are different here, more relaxed. So why aren't I, why's it good for you but bad for me? I'm experiencing feelings that I have never had before."

"I'm going to return you to that divide. We need to get you back through to where you can be safe."

"Safe," she falsely laughs, "No I won't be safe, the Optic is on that side, but I will be well." Her facial expression drops and becomes saddened. I can see her point, it's a bit like the devil and the deep blue sea for her; there is no solace at either place.

"Come on, we will both go through, find this fucking Optic that's causing all the issues here and get rid of him. There are three of us now, you, me and your Optic and as soon as you have convinced him that I'm one of the good guys, the sooner we can do battle. Your Optic must know how to get rid of him, what his vulnerable points are. I reckon he is the key that will end this nightmare."

Her face lights up a little on hearing this and she lays her head on my shoulder. "I told you that you knew how to make everything better, didn't I?" she softly says.

"Indeed you did fair maiden. Are you ready to rock and roll up that hill side?"

Pulling away, her face beaming she says, "Yes sir!"

We have to return exactly the same way we came in order to leave Ravello and get to Scala, so we use the same path until we are able to take a left hand fork that will lead us through the town of Scala and up towards the mountain. As before, our initial route and the town are deserted, but still I see glimpses of things and people that I feel sure I've seen before. At the foot of the mountain we both stop and gaze up to the arduous path before us. I can hear her breathing heavily and throughout the last mile or so she has laboured immensely just to be able to keep going. "We are going to take a rest here whether you like it or not," I order.

Bump affords me a small smile and sits down on a tree stump. "I have never felt like this before. I feel as if I'm being drained of everything I am. It's so hard for me to keep going."

I look down at her, seeing how distraught she has become and also at how exhausted she now looks. "We are over half way there. It's just the climb up that is going to cause you a problem but don't worry, we will do that bit by bit until we reach the wall. Okay?"

Nodding, she slowly gets to her feet.

"No sit back down, take a well earned rest. We will set off again in five minutes," I decide.

She slumps back down. I see the relief in her stance, knowing that she hasn't to continue on quite so soon.

Looking up at the mountain now, I can't see the wall of black, but I know it's up there. I glance back at her, trying to work out in my mind why she is so weak this side of the dark divide. Then suddenly it hits me; why should I be so comfortable here and Bump the absolute opposite. Why won't the Optics enter this side? Christ it's obvious. My Optic attempted to turn me back from heading this way after the town. He seemed extremely apprehensive about helping me when I was slipping down the huge rock face, he didn't want to venture any closer to where I was heading. When I went through the black wall, I must have entered my side of the brain, the part the Optic has no jurisdiction over, so he can't survive in here; just like Bump can't, she is part of the Optics world, not mine. It is becoming very clear to me that the Optic has only limited powers and bringing me into my own subconscious, albeit his side of it was a well thought out plan to get me to do something. What that something is I'm still not quite sure, but nevertheless, a connived strategy with purpose. Me coming this side of the mind was not part of his intention; nor was Bump or her Optic. Things are not panning out exactly the way he thought they would. Bump was referred to as an essence, so therefore I can assume she has no substance in reality only in my mind, but not this side of my mind because I never knew of her existence before we met on the other side. Her well-being can only continue if I can get her back to the other side. For me that is dangerous because I will then be in the part of my brain that the Optic can control. However it strikes me, even if he can rule in his domain, he is still in my brain, I must have certain power that side as well, otherwise why didn't he follow me here? Why has he not just destroyed me, after all, according to Bump's Optic, he has already broken most of their golden rules by coming into direct contact with me? It is just a matter of finding out what the Optic actually wants from me, that's all. Huh that's all, I make it sound like a walk in the park. I look back at Bump. "Come on let's get this done, it's time the Optic and I came to blows over this situation and I'm pissed off trying to avoid him, so let's take the battle to his door."

Bump very shakily gets to her feet. "I think I can make it, let's go."

CHAPTER THIRTEEN
THE OTHER SIDE OF THE COIN

We clamber up the hillside, over the first peak and towards the second, where the dark portal glimmers its slightly differing shades of black. It is within full view now, only some six hundred yards away. Glancing back at Bump, I can see she is near exhaustion, faltering with nearly every step she takes. I assist her until we finally reach the wall.

On our final approach, we are halted a second time by a single church bell chiming. We both stop and gaze down on the town of Scala below us, trying to identify exactly which church or chapel the sound originated from. This time the bells toll from one to twelve and on the twelfth strike, as before, day turns to night in an instant; moon high in the sky, full, beaming its twilight over the village below and the hill that we are perched on.

I glance back to where the dark portal was and it has gone. Bump is also staring at where it was, with her face bordering on panic. "Where's it gone, where's the black door gone Andy?" she screams.

"I don't know, it was there before the bells peeled, I saw it, it just vanished in between trying to ascertain which building the bells were coming from and the final chime."

"But where is it, I have to go through it before I die and I am dying, look at me." I spin around to see what she is talking about and to my horror, she is fading in and out of image, like a camera lens focusing in and out at incredible speed.

"Stay still; please don't move or do anything. I'll find the portal, just stay completely still and conserve your energy. Understand?" She nods, gently laying herself down on the rocky surface which is surrounded by trees.

I carry on up the mountainside to where the black wall was and look further beyond, trying to discover where it could have moved to.

In an moment of inspiration, I turn to where the balcony was, right across the other side of the ravine. We are higher now, being this far up the mountainside and I can see right onto it. I can see where I first entered from, the door to the far left of the terrace, and there it is, there is the dark portal, exactly where it was when I originally came through it. It's now painfully clear to me that during the day time, the portal is up on this mountain and during the night, it is down there on that terrace. Although I feel quite proud of myself for having fathomed so quickly the mystery of the disappearing portal, this is swiftly followed by the overwhelming dread inside of me as I realise that we are now so far away from it.

I jog down to where Bump is laying; she is motionless, almost lifeless. "Bump, Bump are you still with me?" There is a slight movement of her head and a hand motion indicating that she is currently still hanging on.

"Listen, the door back to the other side is on the balcony where you first found me. I think that during daylight the door is here and then at night, it goes back over there. It's obvious to me there is no way you have the strength to get back over there, so we must stay put and wait for the night, then we can go through when daylight returns with the portal. What do you think?"

She turns towards me, her face is now dreadfully drawn, her eyes are blood shot and her colour has taken on a deep grey that fluctuates in different shades. Her whole being is still fading in and out and as this occurs, tiny little electrical flashes appear within and all around her. "Andy don't make it too long, I don't think I have too much time. I feel very strange and I can't concentrate."

I kneel beside her attempting to take her hand but as I go to grasp it, there is nothing tangible to grip; her hand passes straight through mine and lies limply on the ground. This makes me fall backwards in bewilderment. I have never seen anything like this before, only in a film, not in real life; not that I'm entirely sure this nightmare can be defined as real life. "Bump you need to remain perfectly still until day returns. I have no idea how long that is going to be but it won't be too long, just save all your energy and when the wall reappears, I'm going to pick you up and take you back through. Do you understand?"

She gives a slight nod of acknowledgement, enough to let me know she understands.

After what seems like an absolute eternity, the bells start to chime. As before they toll from one to twelve and also as before, daylight returns in the blink of an eye. I slowly and apprehensively look up the mountain to see if the portal has returned. As my eyes reach the point where the black wall was previously situated, I feel a small smile flicker across my face; it's back! I turn to Bump. "Come on its back, let's go!"

She makes neither movement or noise, just remains lying perfectly motionless on the rock. I gradually approach her, gently turning her over onto her back. Her eyes are partially closed and she is soaked in perspiration, her body limp with its mass phasing in and out of perspective, incredibly little substance left. I run my hand around her head. This part of her body still seems to have some weight to it. As I try to gather her up, my hands pass through her as if she has turned into jelly. There is very little of her left on which to grip or hold on to, apart from her head. I remove my shirt, placing her head into it and gathering up as much of what remains of her as I can and I run at the wall of black.

I can both feel and hear myself yelling as I hit the wall. On my entry, I push and shove forward with my frantic endeavour to reach the other side, but shortly my momentum ebbs as I become physically aware of being drawn to a halt. The blackness completely engulfs me, I feel the pressure encasing me, forcing the breath out of me. I push my last and final surge forward in an attempt to escape the darkness when suddenly I sense that something has a hold of me around my waist. We are yanked forward with amazing force and thrown clear of the portal. As I hit the ground, Bump is snatched from my grasp and I continue to roll with the momentum of the force in which I was violently extracted from the blackness.

On coming to a halt, I immediately turn to discover who or what had seized Bump from my grasp. To my surprise, I see a woman leaning over her dishevelled body. "Leave her alone," I yell at the woman.

The woman who is caressing Bump, turns very slowly towards me, her one eye glaring at me. "You fool, she is almost dead. If you had kept her that side a moment longer, she would be gone; her essence would be scattered and irretrievable. Why did you let her stay there for so long?" It's her Optic, in the form of a woman in her forties with short black hair and a dumpy body. Her sole eye is full of tears and emotion.

"I didn't keep her there Optic, I was trying to get her back here as soon as I realised the danger that she was in. Do you really think I would intentionally let any harm come to her, she's my fucking sister, for Christ sake."

Her optic turns away from me and gazes down, almost lovingly at Bump. "She will recover from this because she is now back on this side, you returned her just in time, however now that she has been in your side of the mind, with your memories, she will be different when she recovers. She will have gained some of your experiences and will have more knowledge of you." The Optic quietly states, tenderly she picks Bump up, who in turn seems to be regaining some of her substance, and she walks away along the beach.

It is at this point I survey my new surroundings. The black wall is behind me. In front of me is a beautiful beach of golden sands, with high dunes to my left and gently lapping sea to my right. I rise to my feet and follow the Optic. She walks for a good ten minutes and nothing is said, then she abruptly stops and gently lays Bump down at the edge of a sand dune. She arranges her into a position where she is reclining on her back, with her head slightly raised, having scooped up the sand to form a makeshift pillow.

As I approach them both, the Optic turns towards me, just as it did at the car graveyard, almost aggressively, but then relaxes a little in the knowledge that I'm not going to harm her.

"Is she okay now?" I question.

"She will recover now she is here." The Optic replies.

"What now, what do we do now? You are an Optic, do you know why I'm here?"

The Optic lifts her head and stares straight at me. "You should not be here, you and your Optic should never have met, neither for that matter should you and I. For some reason your Optic has chosen to bring you into his domain."

"For some reason, come on, you must know that reason, why won't you tell me what it is?" I interrupt.

The Optic slowly stands, leaving Bump lying comfortably on the sand and focuses her whole attention upon me. "We Optics are from a race of people far from what you can ever imagine. Our species vary in kind, depending on which status we evolve from. We, as in your Optic and I, are part of the basic species that has to develop in order to take our places with more important issues and certain standings in our own world. Do you understand thus far?"

I nod. "I think so, please carry on."

"Your kind as a race have been visited many times in the past, your people have begun to realise this only now, in fact only over the past hundred or so of your years. Before you started to understand what the universe was, Trilopse my ancestors; much more advanced than I, came here while your genus was still in a very early stage of development but beginning to evolve nonetheless, and evolving quite quickly. Their conclusion was that they must visit every hundred of your years, to keep a watchful eye on how your people developed. They had identified that your brain patterns, although at the time limited and basic, that with the drive of the life force within you, they would soon become quite enhanced, allowing your species to become much stronger and far more inquisitive. Indeed within only a short period of time, your species began to leave other kinds behind with their intellect, so the Trilopse decided to leave some of our race here to maintain a vigil over you, ensuring that you didn't advance too far without our knowledge."

"So let me get this right, what you are saying is that you have not only been watching us, but also living with us and that we had no idea?"

"Correct. You must bear in mind that your kind evolved from the oceans, you adapted to land in less than twenty of your years. From that stage you moved from being semi-reptilian to humanoid, walking and moving about on all four feet until you discovered that you could balance and therefore function more effectively on two. These periods in your evolution moved forward with unprecedented speed. The Trilopse were extremely disturbed by your ability to adapt so quickly and effectively. They assessed your developmental pattern and concluded that if you were allowed to continue with your evolution at the speed it was happening, eventually you would destroy everything within your reach. Ultimately that could mean us as well, along with all other living things that you as a race, might come across."

This revelation from the Optic leaves my head spinning. Her/his/its interpretation of our history from the beginning, is disturbing to say the least, but having said this, I can see that from my limited life and knowledge of history, she is probably right. Nevertheless she has still not intimated why I have been brought to this domain and what the other Optic wants from me. "Optic, do you have a name, or are you all known solely as just Optic?"

It makes a snorting noise, which I assume to be their version of laughing. "Yes we have individual titles just like you do, but our language is impossible for you to learn, as your vocal capabilities are incredibly basic. We can speak your language here within your subconscious but you however cannot speak ours. If I were to say my name, you would not even remotely be able to mimic it," she replies.

"Okay then, I'll name you myself, if indeed that's alright with you?"

The Optic's head slightly swings from side to side, looking directly at me. "I will permit it,"she concludes.

"I'm going to call you Quad if that's okay because you have previously said that the more elevated type of your race is called a Trilopse and tri means three, so quad means four, and in my opinion I reckon you have a far greater intellect than the third model."

The Optic lets out a slight snort, erupting into loud grunts, waving her arms about and turning from left to right. I think I may have amused her. Who said we can't communicate with aliens?

Having let Quad laugh for a while, I carry on with my inquisition. "Right Quad, you still haven't explained why my Optic has brought me into his domain, what is his objective?"

Intensely staring at me once more, it begins to calm down. "When your people developed from basic apes into what you called cavemen, throughout your stone age period, the Trilopse returned to our home. Deep deliberation took place as to how we should proceed with your species. All of our most advanced intellectuals gave great consideration as to what should be done. We as a race have never warred like your people have, we have always been able to overcome issues with debate and subject understanding. For the first time in our history, there were some who favoured destroying this planet to ensure the safety of everything else that exists, a concept that had never been suggested before, but the final outcome was completely different and was a procedure that had also never been undertaken before.

It was found that the main problem with the human race was the extremely powerful brain it possessed. It could function thousands of times faster than any other living organism that had so far been seen. The intellects therefore concluded that the humans brain must be suppressed; hence slowing down its ability and limiting its power to out think and envisage future happenings. The intellects utilised us Optics to become an inbred organism that stops two thirds of your human's brain from working in unison with the other third. This action, when we were utilised, did exactly as they said it would. Your evolution immediately slowed down, almost to the point that there was concern that your race would slip into decline and another species, which you call the ant, would advance further and faster than you, allowing it to dominate this planet. You see ants all work together and although they are a great deal smaller than you in their bodily size, they are physically much stronger and work in almost complete unison. Your species as a whole do not; it takes considerable conflict to make you all join together to one end. However the human race prevailed, without the knowledge that we were restricting your abilities. The Optics' criteria was never to be identified by humans or anyone else. We were to live within our host until their demise, only then could we leave and travel back to our home. On our return it would be hailed as a great achievement. The fact that we had helped to keep our worlds safe would ensure that our status in the order of standing would become elevated and celebrated. Although our life span is over a thousand times more than yours, the time that we Optics spend here in our host drags, we live inside the dormant side of your brain and communicate with nobody else throughout all the time we are there."

I saunter over to where Bump is laying and look down on her. She has stopped sweating, her eyes are closed as though contentedly sleeping. Her body has definite form again and the electrical pulses have disappeared. I can see she is visibly regaining her strength.

"Quad from what you are telling me, the Optic needs to kill me so he can swan off back to his own planet. Is that right? If so, what I don't understand is, since I have been here he has had more than enough opportunities to kill me and as yet hasn't done so. Why?"

"He cannot kill you because if he does, he will be trapped inside your brain forever. To destroy you from within your own subconscious would cause a cranial displacement, and as your own personal Optic he is part of your physical anatomy, he has been with you since you took form in your mother's womb. Only an outside influence can kill you in order to allow your Optic to leave. He can't perform the act himself. I could kill you, but he can't."

"So what the hell does he want, I really don't understand?"

"It is quite simple really, he wants you to tell him to go. That is the only other way in which he can leave."

"If it's as uncomplicated as that, why hasn't he just told me? It would give me real pleasure to tell him to piss off."

Quad raises a smile. "He can't just enlighten you as to how he can leave. As I have already told you, you are never supposed to meet your Optic. Since we were initially placed within your species an Optic has never met its host. I am still not even sure how he has managed to bring you into this domain, so in theory, the opportunity of an Optic managing to get his host to tell him to leave, should be impossible."

These words take a few minutes to sink in, but the concept is just, well totally beyond me. "So what would happen if I did tell him that he can go, what would be the consequence of his departure?"

Quad's head drops and her face scrunches up. "You would be the one and only person on this planet to not have his brain suppressed, so therefore you would have the ability to utilise the whole of its capabilities. In essence you would be the most dangerous Being in the universe. You would be able to see into the future, understand how to control everything and everyone, calculate and interpret every form of equation, no matter what its original orientation might be. Your capabilities would be endless, your intelligence boundless."

Now Quad is looking at me with an extremely concerned look across her face. "Is this something you feel that you would like?" She walks over to where the sea is lapping the shore and wades in. As she reaches her waist, she starts to change her form. The little dumpy lady transforms into a hovering oval shape, a large eye ball, just a smaller version of the original Optic that I encountered in the clearing when I first arrived in this place. Although there is no physical mouth I am able to hear it because it is using its mind and thoughts to converse with me now.

"I can imagine what you are thinking Andy, the mere thought of the unprecedented power you could possess, but let me enlighten you, along with all these abilities comes its own problems, the main one being that no human has ever had the capability to exploit the complete brain, therefore I or no one else has any idea what it will do to you. The chances are that you will not be able to control it. Secondly, your own kind will soon perceive you as a threat. They will not embrace you, they will eventually try to destroy you. You will, without any shadow of a doubt, stand alone. You will not be understood, but you will understand everything and would yearn for the time before you didn't."

The words of Quad echo around my head and I know he is right. "Listen Quad, my Optic is driven by the concept that he wants to go home. I don't really think that having a deep and meaningful conversation about him staying on here is going to do the trick. So have you got any constructive ideas as to what you think I should do?"

156

Quad floats above the water, returning to the sand and once more changing its shape back into the body of the little fat woman. She walks over to Bump who is now beginning to stir, holds out a hand to her which she accepts, and helps her to her feet. She then glances back to me. "In case you haven't noticed, at this moment in time you have more than one Optic inside your brain, so if one of us were to leave, there would still be one left to do the job which we were designed to do. You would live a normal life even though you would probably be the only person in the world with the knowledge that there is something called an Optic and what its function is."

"Are you saying that I should just tell him to go and when he's gone, you simply take over where he left off. What about Bump, you are her Optic?" Bump is now looking back and forth, between Quad and I, trying to ascertain what's actually going on.

"She is indeed my host, unfortunately I am only protecting her essence, she has no tangible brain for me to carry out my true function with."

"But what would become of her if you took over the roll as my Optic?" I question.

"I am not entirely sure, but this side of your brain has been her home for a long time now, I can see no reason why that should change," she reasons.

I walk over to Bump giving her a hug. "You okay," I whisper.

She smiles and nods affirming her well being. "What's going on Andy, what are you and my Optic talking about?" she says lowering her head and then adding, "and thank you for saving me, I thought I was finished back there."

I let out a small chuckle that makes her look up. "You're more than welcome, besides which, a brother will always fight for his sister."

With her face full of glee, she flings her arms about my neck giving me a huge hug.

157

"Right, firstly your Optic has a name, it's Quad. Secondly, he has informed me of how this all started and why they are here. That part is extremely complicated and I'm not even going to try explaining it to you. I'm not even sure I've really understood what I've been told. The one thing I do understand though, is that there is a way to get the other Optic to leave and that is exactly what I intend to do."

Bump's persona changes completely, the anxiety shows in her expression as she pulls away and turns her back to me. "Does your plan include me and Quad, or are you going to confront your Optic on your own?" she enquires.

A small smile flickers across my face. "If Quad is right, then this is a meeting I have to do on my own, but don't worry because if I am correct in my thinking, he's really going to want to hear what I have to say and he should like it. Consequently the danger aspect should be minimal."

I turn to Quad who is watching our every movement. "Quad where will I find my Optic, where do you think that bastard is lurking at the moment?"

"You do not find him, he will find you and probably when you least expect it. The one thing you can be sure of is he will not come this close to your side of consciousness. He becomes increasingly more vulnerable the nearer he is to your personal side of the brain. You are safe here, but you need to venture deeper into his side of the domain for him to come to you."

"Understood Quad and thanks." I turn to Bump. "Stay here with Quad, he will watch over you and keep you safe until I get back, okay?"

She nods, hangs her head and I head off along the beach. After taking twenty paces or so, I hear her voice call out. "Make sure you rock and roll back here soon!"

I laugh out loud and wave. "Won't be long fair maiden, won't be long."

CHAPTER FOURTEEN
A FUTILE ATTEMPT

Pretty soon the beach stops as it reaches a rocky headland, not a steep climb but nonetheless a fairly high one. My pace doesn't change in the least, I simply stride up to the base of the rocks and begin my ascent. Within twenty minutes or so I reach the ridge of the headland looking out over to the other side. Bizarre, where I've just come from is a beach, dunes and the sea but this side of the ridge there are none of these things.

In front of me is a concrete jungle, a city stretching out as far ahead as I can see. The buildings are exceptionally tall sky scrapers made of concrete and glass, soaring up into the heavens, so high that I am unable see where they finish. The street directly in front of me runs in a dead straight line away from where I'm standing and again, I can't tell where it ends. There are numerous cars, lorries and vans all parked alongside the pavements on both sides of the road, without any parking spaces between them at all. Looking left and right leaves me with no doubt that my only option is to travel forward along this road, as on each side of it there are a mass of huge buildings forming an impenetrable wall.

I descend the rocky headland, crossing a small area of grass to the tarmac and the walkway between the buildings, continuing on until I reach the road. I gaze up into the sky, it's clear, no clouds and no sun. Yep, I'm definitely back in the Optics domain. It's seems to me as though he has gained access to all the memories and sights that I have seen and acquired over the years, but he omits some of the finer points, or indeed misses them out intentionally. Maybe he is only interested in gleaning certain information from me. He doesn't seem to have the organisational ability to collate all the facts needed in order to complete any one scene that he is attempting to display and consequently, the end product is a mismatch of various different things.

I position myself right in the middle of the road, right on the long white lines that dictate the centre and casually saunter along, glancing at the buildings on either side of me. The ground level frontage of each of these buildings appears to be some type of shop front. I stop, gazing upwards until the top of the building disappears into the sky. Immediately as I pass so the exterior of the building appears to turn to glass, only reflecting the other side of the street. As usual, there is absolutely no sign of any local inhabitant, neither human or animal.

When I have walked for what seems like ten minutes in a directly straight line and crossed at least six intersections, I stop turn around and look back to where I started. The headland has gone and the end of the road now has a building in its place. It looks like a garage, a bus garage to be more precise. Although quite a distance away I am able to see a big green shutter type door in the centre of its frontage. As I strain to distinguish it more clearly, unless my eyes are deceiving me, I think it starts to move. Movement that's novel, something moving in the distance. I keep watching and indeed the shutter is now over halfway up. I start walking back along the street to investigate when I hear a huge engine firing up, letting out a tremendous roar. I stop dead in my tracks, peering at the doors.

Immediately I change my direction, sprinting to the side, thereby hoping that the parked cars will afford me some cover. I crouch down behind some type of four by four, grey in colour, five doors, fairly new. I quickly glance into the vehicle and notice the ignition keys hanging from the steering column. Moving onto the pavement, I go to the side of the car trying all the doors, but to no avail as they are all locked. The question that springs to mind is, what kind of idiot locks his or her keys in the car, but then again I must admit I've done it before.

My thoughts are disturbed by four or five aggressive growls from the big engine which is still inside the garage. It sounds to me like it's impatiently waiting for the shutter to fully open. Can't fucking wait to see what kind of vehicle comes out of those doors!

I decide to put a bit of distance between me and it, whatever it is. I start moving along the line of parked cars in the direction away from the garage. I reach the next junction, turning the first accessible corner. I stop and move back, cautiously peering around to see the state of play.

The engine gives out three move revs, an incredibly deep and hugely menacing sound, but now loud as it is, I seem to have lost my bearings on exactly where the sound is coming from. I position myself more centrally on the street trying to gain a better view of the garage and then suddenly as the revving persists, I realise that the noise is coming from the end of the street that I've just turned into. From my position I can see both ends of the two streets. Both have identical constructions, the shutters of each are almost fully open to exactly the same stage. I glance down the opposite street, shit the same scenario again. The only direction that is not sporting a bloody garage with green shutters on it, is the way I was originally heading. That's obviously the way to go then! Now I'm on the run.

The engines are now fully revved and I hear the wheels spin as the vehicles commence their pursuit and screech into motion.

I pick up the pace, maintaining my proximity to the parked cars, glancing into everyone of them as I pass trying to see if any of them are open with their keys in situ. At one point I manage to glance behind me to see what exactly it is that is chasing me. With this fleeting look I identify that the vehicle is an articulated lorry of sorts, thundering down the road, violently jerking through the gears to gain its speed.

I decide to give up checking the cars and to gain entry into one of the shops. I try a couple of the doors but surprise, surprise, they are locked tight.

The lorries are rapidly gaining ground on me, having congregated on the main drag that incidentally, I am also on. They have formed a perfectly symmetrical line, giving chase and shortening the distance between us with every step that I take.

Realising that my time is definitely limited if I don't manage to get out of the way of these machines pretty quickly, I choose a glass window that I hope will shatter and launch myself at it. On impact the glass splinters and breaks with my body crashing to the floor inside the building.

Scrambling to my feet, I hear a colossal crash causing me to turn and investigate the commotion, and to my horror I watch as one of the articulated lorries slams into the parked cars, shoving them like insignificant particles into the building of which I am now situated. I retreat with amazing acceleration as the debris of a smashed, tangled car weaves its way through the shop front, crashing to a halt, up ended against the far wall. Well if I had any doubt at all about these lorries being the bad guys, I certainly don't have now.

I carry out a quick scan of my immediate situation and surroundings, spotting a staircase at the rear of the shop. I scramble towards this over the smashed remains of various pieces of furniture and masonry, and I climb the steps as fast as my legs will carry me. On reaching the landing, I glance back to see the first artic reverse away from the window, ripping out part of the frontage as it goes and then a second lorry appears circling in the road, gathering speed, apparently waiting to make a second attempt to gain further access into the premises. I'm certainly not going to wait around to see if this lorry is going to be more successful than the first, so I continue on up the flights of stairs.

After tramping up a couple more flights, there follows an almighty crash. I assume the second artic has slammed itself into the building because the entire structure shudders as I hang on to the banister to retain my balance. Huge lumps of debris begin falling from the upper floors. I position myself against the outer wall of the staircase, where I am able to watch for anything big potentially coming in my direction. The lorry below sounds as though it's shunting itself backwards and forwards, I assume trying to move further into the shop. It's then that the horrifying thought flickers through my brain. What if they are taking a crack at undermining the foundations of this place, in order to bring the whole thing crashing down with me in it? As the dust and wreckage from above calms, I grab the central handrail and with elongated strides I rush up the stairs, taking them two at a time, not glancing back for anything. I have got to reach the top of this building and find a way off!

After charging through many levels, I finally broach the last few steps of a narrow hallway leading to a single door, at what I hope is the top of the building. Not slowing my speed in the slightest, I crash through this door, flinging it off its hinges and run out onto the flat roof.

162

Taking just a few paces I stop, taking account of my new surroundings. The door I've just come through is right in the middle of the roof, with an open expanse surrounding it which is covered in gravel. At the outer limits of the building there is a low wall, no more than two feet high which encompasses the entire circumference of the structure. There is nothing else up here at all.

I make for the edge, apprehensively peeking over to see what's out there. Initially I can see the building opposite. It's about fifteen feet away and I estimate that I can jump across to it without too much of a problem. Then my eyes drop down to see what lies below and immediately I feel giddy, stepping back from the edge. I drop down onto my belly, crawling to the base where I slowly scale the wall and look down again.

Below me are clouds, all I can see is clouds and mist. Shit I must be incredibly high up. I know I climbed a lot of stairs but I didn't realise it was as many as that! As I begin inching backwards, so once more the whole structure starts to shake. I hear a horrifying metallic wrenching noise, another gigantic crash accompanied by creaking sounds as the building seems to shift and resettle after its latest assault. Those artics are certainly giving this tower a battering, its entire axis is beginning to slant. They have clearly managed to undermine the frontage. I strongly feel that it won't be long before this place starts to crumble and I do not want to be on it when it does.

Rising to my feet as quickly as possible, I circuit the perimeter of the roof, checking to see if there is another building closer to me. As my tour of the roof ends, I find myself once more standing in exactly the same spot that I started from. I can only conclude that this must be the only place to attempt my leap from. I take five paces back from the edge, tense my muscles and sprint directly at the small wall. On reaching it, I spring to the top, land briefly and launch myself forward into mid air, free-wheeling across the void, with my arms and legs circling frantically hoping that this motion will help propel me though the atmosphere.

Landing on the other side, I throw myself into a forward roll to break my momentum and I skid across the surface for some six or seven feet. Luckily this roof's surface consists of flat asphalt tiles and not gravel,

163

so my ungainly landing doesn't cause me any injury. When I regain my composure, I tentatively return to the edge where I've just completed my landing, trying to see what's happening down at street level.

The same as before, all I can see is clouds and mist. Suddenly, the high rise I was previously on, shudders. From where I am I see lumps of stone and concrete breaking away from the building and steel girders protrude from the sides of the outer walls. The complete construction begins to tilt and starts leaning my way. For fucks sake, why is it falling my way, is everything just geared up to piss me off?

I can still vaguely hear the articulated lorries nose diving at the base of the building, their engines bellowing at the command of their accelerators as they ravage the foundation like hyenas bringing down a prey.

I survey my new roof top. From where I am standing; which incidentally I realise isn't a great place to be if the other building is going to topple this way; there isn't anything, nothing at all, it's just an expanse of roof with no apparent way down, no door that leads to any stairs, no exit at all.

I race across the full length of the roof top to the opposite side. I can see the next building along. Like before, the gap looks as though it can be crossed, I know that I can jump it and make it to the other side. I decide to take the bull by the horns, no hesitation, I need to get well clear of the high rise building which is imminently in the process of being demolished by the artics.

This time there is no low wall surrounding the rooftop, making this jump a straight leap from this building to the next one. I back away from the edge, throw myself forward into a running pace, gathering my maximum speed possible, initiate my take off and decide to worry about my landing when I hopefully arrive at my destination.

I clear the abyss below me and land. I immediately get to my feet, racing across this new rooftop to its far side, in order to estimate my next jump. On arrival my aspirations are dashed because the next building in line is across the other side of the road. There is obviously a junction down there and the gap between the two buildings is way too far to jump. I would at minimum need a jet propelled boost to get me over there!

I turn away taking a closer look around at my latest rooftop. Just like the first one, there is a small construction, almost dead centre of this expanse with a door in it. Again I assume that this must therefore be my way down. I walk straight to the door and try the handle. Great it's locked and the door, by the look of the hinges and the jams, opens outwards. What a surprise! I tug at the handle for a minute or so, soon realising that there is no way that I'm going to get the bloody thing open. I stand back, stop and deliberate on what my next course of action should be. Within only a few seconds I have made my choice and I begin kicking at the door with all the force I can muster. With a few well placed and completely lucky thrusts my left foot goes right through it, causing me to lose my balance. Initially releasing my foot and leg is quite problematic but as I eventually manage to free myself, I note that the hole I've managed to make in the door is indeed a fracture that I can work on enlarging, creating a large enough hole that I will hopefully be able to climb through. I continue lashing out at the opening, breaking pieces away around it until it seems big enough for me to get myself through. Bending to my knees, I try putting my head and shoulder in the hole, because from past experience if they go through, I know the rest of me should. I pass through without any problem and find myself at the top of a staircase.

I look down between the flights to make sure the coast is clear, even holding my breath so as to listen for any unusual noises. All seems good, so I begin my descent.

After climbing down literally hundreds of stairs, I stop again and check what's below. I can see the ground now, so I can't be too far off street level. I am acutely aware that I haven't exactly managed to put much distance between me and the lorries, so I need to be silent, vigilant and cautious. A few steps down I enter a landing. I decide to take this exit to see if I can find somewhere to observe what the mechanical menaces are up to. The door is open and I very quietly go through it into another corridor. Along this hallway are many doors leading off into offices I should think. I pick a number and walk along

165

until I reach the door that corresponds with the number I have chosen. I try the handle, the door is unlocked, so in I go.

The room is indeed an office, with a grand desk by the window and a leather upholstered chair behind it. There is a leather settee and a drinks cabinet shaped like a globe of the world, another couple of chairs and finally, four large potted plants situated strategically about the room. The walls are adorned with various pictures, some painted and some photographs. I quickly scan these but can see no relevance to any of them. I stride over to the window on the far side of the room. It is massive, spanning the entire wall from ceiling to floor. I can see the road outside. I move to one end of the window, attempting to observe the building which the artics were holding under siege. Two of the trucks are stationary in the middle of the main thoroughfare, they appear as if on guard duty? The third one I am unable to see.

I leave the window, exit the office into the hall and return to the stairwell. I quietly proceed down the stairs until I reach the ground floor, opening the door in front of me gently, I peep slowly around it to see what lies ahead of me. All seems still and too quiet, even the truck demolition team seem to have lost all momentum and remain still. I'm not sure whether that's a good or bad thing really. The floor area is similar to any hotel foyer; an open expanse of tables, chairs, pillars, desks and a bar situated on strategic walls. The entire area is carpeted but the thing that catches my attention is that all the pictures adorning the walls are identical to those in the office upstairs, but repeated over and over again. Most odd.

Out of the corner of my eye I catch some movement. I fully focus my attention on an exceptionally large picture with a hideously ostentatious gilt frame. The content of this masterpiece is an eye, one solitary, larger than life, bloodshot, peering eye and if I'm not mistaken, I could swear that it just moved. I cross the room towards it, not removing my gaze from it for a second. When I reach the portrait, I stare as closely as possible at the image, examining the entire canvas. I even tilt the picture forward from the wall and taking a gander behind it, but it all seems pretty ordinary. I back away from it, transfixed by the huge representation of an eyeball, really grotesque. Who would want to paint something like that anyway?

166

My concentration upon it is interrupted by an engine starting up. It's most definitely one of those trucks. I'd recognise that deep thundering noise anywhere. I move to the big swing doors at the front of the foyer; they are open. Stepping partially out onto the pavement I see two of the trucks, the same ones that were previously in the middle of the road. I can still hear the revving of another engine but I don't think it's coming from either of these two here.

I venture a little further out onto the pavement, attempting to obtain a better view of what's going on, when a screech of wheels causes me to spin around in the other direction. There's the revving engine, the third truck, a very battered and dishevelled piece of machinery it looks too. Nevertheless it's obviously still fully functional and at this moment in time, it's gaining speed and heading straight for me.

My choices here are limited to only two. I either make a run for it at street level or go back into this hotel and potentially go through another truck assault as before. As I glance back into the hotel foyer, the portrait of the eye definitely winks at me. That does it for me, choice made!

I make my run directly at the crazy lorry. As I gather momentum, I also hear the other two trucks start their engines. Great all three are back in play now. As the stampeding truck almost collides with me, I feign a couple of side steps, managing to avoid the trucks intention of running me down, and let it pass me by without injury. I have to take this opportunity to make some distance between me and it. It's obvious to me that it's going to take time for a rig that size to do a u-turn, so I need to make every second count to my advantage.

Initially I run directly along the main drag, taking a left at the first available junction. Glancing back I assume the truck must still be making its turn, as it's currently nowhere to be seen.

The side street is long and straight with more shop fronts, a carbon copy of the main street, except it appears to be a scaled down version, as I am able to see the roof tops this time. After running for a couple of minutes more, I reach some crossroads. I intentionally take a left turn, in the hopes that further on, I'll find another left turn, which if my sense of direction is working at all, should place me behind these crazed trucks.

Shortly I slow my pace a little. Above the sound of my panting, I can still hear the roar of the trucks' enormous engines. I reckon by now that truck must have managed to turn himself around, facing in the direction which he last saw me heading away in. I will need to take another left pretty soon, to enable me to get behind them. Losing them completely would be good! I pass the first couple of left turns because I don't want to emerge too close to them. Finally I estimate that I must have travelled more than enough distance to be clear of where the trucks were, so I take the next left.

Slowing to a walk, once again I start studying the road and my immediate surroundings. I can see the main street about three hundred yards away, the buildings appear to get taller the nearer they get to this. There are pavements either side of this road, with street lights situated evenly all the way along. As before, the frontages all look similar to the others. As I walk past one particular building, I immediately recognise it as an hotel, identical to the one on the main street, that I not too long ago made my mad dash from.

As I near the junction, I am stopped in my tracks by the bellowing sound of horns. It's obvious to me that there is definitely more than one vehicle sounding off to make the row that I am hearing. The noise is deafening even though it appears to be originating from quite some distance away. This temporarily eases my mind.

I reach the corner and cautiously poke my head around it. I can see the two trucks that were in the middle of the road and they are sounding their horns. I can't believe that all this noise is being transmitted by just these two vehicles. Peering at the cab of the truck nearest to me, I can't see anyone driving it but then again now I think of it, I don't recall seeing anyone in that one which tried to run me over either.

I find myself in two minds: do I take a right here and make a dash to reach the point where I originally entered this town or do I go back down this road and see if I can get away from this place that way. Then Bump's words echo in my head, you can't go back through rooms, so therefore there is a fair chance that even if I were to make it all the way down that road, the headland I entered by will now no longer be there.

I glance directly across the road. The way ahead is via a much narrower street, completely different from all the other roads that I have encountered so far. This is going to be my selection. I glance back at the stationary trucks on my left, a quick scan right, then I spring into the fastest, yet quietest pace I can and cross the road. When I reach the other side, I take a swift look back at the trucks which still haven't moved, then I jog off in my new direction.

This street has walls each side, no doors, no windows, no pavements or street lights, just two continuous brick walls. I can't estimate the height of the walls as they disappear into the clouds; I can't help chuckling to myself, wondering who the hell the bricklayer was!

After jogging along for some ten minutes or so, it becomes apparent to me that the street is beginning to narrow. I come to a halt and gaze ahead. Up in the far distance there is a shimmering movement on the horizon. Standing there, I get a funny feeling, one of those feelings that churn the bottom of your stomach. I gradually turn around and to my complete and utter horror, about a hundred yards away is that articulated lorry, the one that managed to get itself seriously battered up while trying to knock down the building. Its engine can't be running because I hear no noise, yet it is slowly and silently moving towards me.

I start walking backwards, not wanting to take my eyes off this thing. I attempt to match its speed so that it shouldn't be able to gain any ground on me. I succeed in doing this for several paces. Abruptly the truck starts its engine in motion with that deep gritty roar. I turn, breaking into the fastest sprint I can possibly muster. I heed the sound of the gear box being shifted from first to second, but I don't turn around to see if it's gaining on me. The flickering movement I could previously see at the end of this alley, is very clearly visible now. I put every piece of effort I can assemble into reaching it before the truck reaches me. The truck sounds its horn, one continual blast, informing me of its presence immediately behind me. I sense that the truck is gaining ground but I am now only a few paces away from whatever that light irregularity is.

As I near to within a couple of feet or so away, I leap at it. My hands enter first, passing through into intense heat, burning as though they are on fire. Immediately, the remainder of my body follows with its continued momentum and the sensation intensifies. I feel as though I'm completely on fire. I can hear the horn and the engine of the truck screaming. It is still in pursuit and doesn't sound about to stop.

Within seconds I have cleared this blazing barrier and I'm rolling forwards on something soft and cold. I look back at the light shifting obstacle to establish whether the truck has followed me through. To my total amazement, part of the cab has in fact come through. The remainder must still be on the other side. Its lights are rapidly flickering on and off, accompanied by the roar of its engine intermittently whining. The horn has stopped and the metal that formed this trucks shape, is melting before my eyes.

Immediately this sight causes me to panic. If the barrier has done that to the truck, what the fuck has it done to me. I begin searching my own body for burns or injuries. Nothing, I'm okay, even my clothes aren't singed or damaged. My glance returns to the truck, it is now a miss-shaped mass of molten metal, very little of it remains that looks anything like a truck. I can honestly conclude that the truck is not a well thing, hopefully dead, pretty much no longer existing. A relieved smile flashes across my face. I cautiously walk towards the dissolving machine. "Fuck you, not so noisy now, are you?"

There is no retort.

CHAPTER FIFTEEN
<u>CONSOLATION FACTOR</u>

Turning away from the dissolved wreckage, I breathe a sigh of relief and embrace my new surroundings.

Snow. I landed on something soft and cold, it was snow. Ahead of me are tall pine trees, reaching high into a very dark grey sky. I've seen skies like this before; it normally means a considerable amount of snow is on its way.

Surveying left and right confirms to me that this expanse of trees stretches forever in both directions. I guess that the way forward is through the forest, still it won't be the first time I've strolled through a forest in this strange old world. It's a funny thing though, here I am in a snow clad environment, yet I don't seem to feel the cold. I walk towards the pine trees.

Just before I enter the woodland, I glance back to where the truck lay melted, it's still there, what's left of it, but the portal through which I entered isn't apparent anymore. I can now see well beyond the truck and all there is, is snow and ice. The truck itself looks as if it has been cut off immediately behind the cab and simply left in the snow to rot. Christ knows where the rest of it is. I shrug my shoulders; nothing seems to surprise me much here anymore.

Walking among the trees it's quite restful and when the snow does start, it comes down with a vengeance, hampering both my sight and my progress forward. I press on regardless, moving from tree to tree, creasing my eyes in an effort to see what's ahead. After about an hour of battling against the elements, the blizzard decreases leaving only a few flakes drifting aimlessly around in the breeze. With such a prolific snow fall, the snow is deep and the drifts are enormous as they lean against all the structures that the snow found. My way forward is heavy going as I have to exaggeratedly step high in order to move onwards.

Eventually I come across a clearing. I am at the top of a hill looking down onto two buildings. They both resemble classic Alpine Lodges covered in snow, with glowing lights in the windows and smoke spiralling from their chimneys. The way down is a gentle slope that gradually leads straight to the front doors of both houses. This view could have been taken straight from a Christmas card. It's so perfectly beautiful and serene, which is more than enough to cause me worry.

I move towards one of the tall pines lining the edge of this hilltop and crouch down observing this idyllic outlook; I just want to see and sense what this place is all about. I make myself as comfortable as I can on the cold damp ground and I watch.

After ten minutes or so, the door opens on the Lodge closest to me. A man in his sixties, I would gauge, dressed in a chequered shirt, brown trousers and boots, walks about ten paces out and then looks directly up to where I am crouched. His hair is shoulder length, very unkempt, but most importantly to me, he has two eyes, a nose and a mouth; this calms my apprehension somewhat.

I know that I'm pretty well hidden at the foot of the tree with the undergrowth around me, but I am also aware that his gaze is focused entirely on my position. For a second, I wonder what he's looking at and I even swing round to see if anything or anyone is behind me. Nothing, so therefore he must be looking at me. I stay stock still, even aware that I am holding my breath. The man beckons to me, waving one of his arms back and forth. I remain still. He then turns his back and returns inside the lodge.

I crawl back into the forest and when I am far enough away from the crest of the hill, I walk along a good hundred yards. Having satisfied myself that I am nowhere near my first hiding place, I again drop onto my belly and crawl up to the edge of the tree line again. This time I discover a boulder situated next to a couple of saplings, perfect cover I think. I make my way over to it. Once more I set myself up in what I believe is the perfect spot in order to see the small settlement below and also for me to remain unseen.

Within slightly under a minute, the same man steps out of a door again, but this time, from the other lodge. He strolls over to almost the exact spot where he stood before. He looks down as though searching for the precise place and then extremely slowly, lifts his head and stares directly at where I am now crouched. This time he clasps his hands in front of him, tilting his head to one side. "Andy I know you are up there behind that stone, why don't you come down here and warm yourself in the cabin?" He calls out.

I stay still, shocked, I really don't know what to make of this situation.

"A blizzard will be upon us in less than one of your hours. Your safety is down here."

He said 'in one of your hours', he's an Optic, that's how they talk. The question is which Optic is he, mine or Bump's? The only Optic that has so far attempted to look this normal, is mine. If he's mine, then this could be the time for our confrontation.

I rise to my feet and negotiate my way around the boulder. Then I nonchalantly amble down the gradual slope, towards the old man. As I get closer to him, he turns his back on me and saunters back the way he came, enters the second lodge, leaving the door open. I reach the place where he was stood and look down, inspecting the area. I'm not sure what I am hoping to find, but on investigation, all I see is footprints in the snow, a mishmash of compressed ice. I shake my head and proceed towards the open door. The warm glow from inside the cabin looks incredibly inviting but I know that I really do need to remain frosty and alert, this scenario is way too friendly or am I just becoming paranoid.

At the porch, I step up to the door and peer in to the left and right. To the left there is a room and the door is wide open. Although the light is on, I can see that the fire isn't lit and the room doesn't appear to be occupied, so my attention immediately turns to the room on my right. I step into the hall. In front of me is a staircase which I pass in order to push the door open into the room with the lit fire.

When I have it pushed completely open, I am able to see the old man standing by the fire. There are four high backed, well upholstered chairs in the room, with a large coffee table in the middle. There are two windows; each one situated either side of the room, opposite each other. I enter the room. "Would you like to introduce yourself old man, especially as you seem to know who I am?"

The old man smiles. "You're welcome," he softly says.

"What?" I snap back at him.

"You're welcome for the invitation to come in here, in the warm."

"Oh, okay my profound apologises, thank you for the invitation. Now we have got that bit over would you like to fucking introduce yourself?"

The old man smiles again, walks over to one of the big chairs and sits down. "You know who I am, we have met before and as I do not consider you to be stupid, I assume that you do actually know exactly who I am, you are just not sure which one," he says and then erupts into laughter.

"So Quad, what are you doing here and where's Bump?" I question probingly.

The old man turns and looks at me. "Where do you think she is, where do you think I would leave her? For her to be safe of course."

I can't dismiss the feeling that I'm having a conversation with my Optic. I don't think this is Quad, I reckon the Optic is trying to trick me into seeing if I know where Bump is.

"Well thank god she's safe, that's all that counts really, wouldn't you say?"

"Yes indeed," he replies.

Just as I start making my way to one of the chairs, the old man turns his head to me, his stare quite intent and his forehead is deeply furrowed. "So you have named the other Optic, have you? How quaint," he jibes.

This stops me dead in my tracks. It is my Optic. "So it is you. I know what you want from me, do you want me to say the words that will make you free or shall I carry on playing your game, you fucking asshole?"

"Nice retort Andy but I cannot help thinking that blurting out the question like that will only cause you more problems. You need to be a little more subtle, a little more evasive."

I hear a muffled titter. My stare leaves the old man, moving towards the source of the laughter. This transpires to be one of the chairs with its back towards me. I can see a hand on the arm of the chair followed by a head, Bump's head to be precise, appears around the wings of the high backed seat. "Hi Andy. It's great to see you. Sorry to muck you about but Quad said that we should test you."

I feel annoyance rise up within me. "Did he now? How outstanding."

Quad gets up from his chair and smiles. "I am fully aware of what you intend to do, but please be aware that your Optic is no fool, quite the opposite really and he can read your thoughts in here. You must learn how to guard them, even try to send him signals that are deceptive. If he recognizes your intentions, you will have lost."

"Well at least I was willing to try and have it out with him. Have you any idea how I was feeling as regards to having this battle?"

"Yes I am sure it took great courage but please tell me, why didn't you face up to him when you were in the city? It was him you know."

My thoughts return to the nightmare chase in the city. "I must admit, I didn't actually realise it was him, I purely figured that he was just controlling the trucks. Besides, I had too many other things to contend with, the main one being not getting myself killed by collapsing buildings or run over by rampaging trucks. As I recall, the whole episode was quite emotional."

Quad's smile broadens. "Why were you so concerned? I have already told you, he cannot kill you, not unless he wishes to languish inside this brain for an eternity, and I can assure you, that is not his ultimate aim."

I walk over to the window that faces the way I entered and I gaze out. As Quad had said, the snow is falling heavily and I can hear the wind whipping up, battering itself at every structure that stands against it. The light is also dropping, bringing in night fall, something that I haven't seen since I've been here. It's always either been day or night.

Pondering over the words that Quad has just said, I feel that the final battle with my Optic is going to be messy with an unsatisfactory finish. I don't seem able to totally grasp precisely what this game is, all I know is that something inside is urgently forcing me into getting this thing over and done with. I turn back to Quad. "How would you play it then Quad? How would you play my part with my Optic? Also, how do you see this finishing?"

Quad gets up and walks back to the fire place, the fire is roaring but he doesn't seem to feel the heat. "I will go against my code to fight another Optic, or for that matter even to conspire against one, for on this unusual occasion I believe that he is not doing these things in the best interests of my people or indeed you. He gives the impression that he is acting with a single mindedness that is dangerous for all concerned. I, like you, are not sure what the best way forward would be. I have come to the conclusion that if we all stand alone, he will probably prevail, not obtaining the outcome he hopes for, but nevertheless he will be the last one standing."

"Why, why will he win? You are an Optic as well Quad, surely you have the same powers as him, so why do you think he is more powerful than you are?" I question.

"It is not about our powers, he and I are the same, we both have the same abilities, but he is in his domain, I am not. When an Optic is placed into his own domain, he will synchronise with his host and therefore his influences become more heightened, more finely tuned. I repeat, he is in his domain, I am not, he will definitely have the advantage and he knows it. Why do you think I have tried to remain invisible from him?"

176

This explanation makes things an awful lot clearer to me but still leaves a big question unanswered. "So are you going to help me, or stay impartial?"

"As I have already said something needs to be done and we all need to stand together. It is the only way we can diversify his capabilities and consequently overcome him."

"Overcome him, what's that mean exactly Quad? Are we going to give him a good telling off or are we going to get rid of him? If this comes down to a vote, I'm all for killing the little bastard, I don't know about you?"

Quad slowly turns his head and stares directly at me. "You have more capacity to fight the Optic than anyone in this domain and always will have. I have even heard Bump tell you this, why have you not found this out for yourself yet?"

I recall Bump on more than one occasion, intimating that I had some kind of power to alter proceedings, but I have never felt that I really could. Now Quad is saying it too. "How Quad, how the fuck do I do this, why have I got more supremacy than you two?"

"It is actually quite simple, if you were to stop and really think about it. We are all inside your brain, in your subconscious. This whole domain is ultimately yours and no one else's. The electrical impulses that stimulate your cells are emitted by you, not by the likes of us. We, in essence, are no more than a parasite that lives off and within you."

Christ when he puts it that way, I can't help but think they are just horrible little insects that need eradicating.

Quad continues. "You need to sharpen and define your abilities. The Optic will not expect this."

I amble over to one of the chairs, scoot it forward towards the open fire and slump down into it, my head spinning with everything that has been discussed here. Bump is sitting right opposite me with a concerned look on her face.

"Watch this Andy," Quad says. As I turn my head to observe, Quad slowly and deliberately puts his foot into the fire and simply stands there, with one foot on the floor and the other one firmly embedded in the flames. "Do you see what I mean? You have the power to do this as well, immediately you appreciate that you can control most things. This is your subconscious, so in fact nothing is real, nothing is tangible, and it is all generated from your mind." I keep watching but Quad doesn't move, not even flinch, he just stands there looking at me.

"So what you're saying to me is that you can't feel that, right?"

"Andy there is nothing to feel, it isn't there. Nearly every scenario that you have visited here is from your memories and thoughts. If you put your foot in this fire and feel something, it is because you expect to. There is no other reason. It is not there."

"Okay it's not there, but would you mind awfully taking your foot out of the fire, because it's really making me feel quite peculiar."

Quad smiles as he removes his limb from the flames. When he has completed this action, he takes a pace away from the hearth and looks directly at me. "Off!" he commands, quietly but emphatically. The blaze extinguishes with his command, all that remains apparent in the grate is smouldering embers. I glance back to Quad, he grins and then says, "Ignite!" Immediately the flames erupt into dancing strands, filling the fire place and emitting heat.

"Impressive Quad, very impressive my friend."

Quad looks at me most perplexed and then his head drops.

"What's up mate, the magic you are weaving it's outstanding," I joke.

He moves away from the fire, sits on the arm of the chair that Bump is reclining in. "Nothings wrong Andy, it is just no one has ever referred to me as their friend before. I know what it implies in your language and I feel almost honoured that you regard me as such."

Bump places her hand on Quad's shoulder.

"Then you have two friends Quad, as I do consider you as such and I feel very lucky too. Perhaps someone ought to tell Mr. Optic about the concept of friends; perhaps he might join us."

Quads eyes meet mine and instantaneously we both erupt into uncontrollable laughter. "What do you think, should we talk to your Optic?" Quad giggles.

"Naw, no point, his only friend is his fucking ego, and he struggles with that."

"I consider that you may well have an extremely valid point. It is a shame really, I am sure he did not start out that way, none of my kind would have. It does make me wonder though, if any other Optics out there are experiencing the same indulgence."

Bump and I look at each other, and we both cast our eyes to Quad. "There's a thought mate, there's a very scary thought. Let's hope not, eh?"

Quad nods. "I suggest we stay here during the darkness, it will not last long. Day light is easier for you two to travel in. Tomorrow we make our plans to end this madness."

I nod to Quad, give Bump a smile, take a chair and recline making myself as comfortable as possible. "Till the morning then," I say, "Or whatever you want to call it."

CHAPTER SIXTEEN
SEEING THE POSSIBILITY

Mesmerised I watch the snow hitting the window making no sound whatsoever. I have always found it to be quite beautiful and eerie at the same time. The others are sat gazing out of the other aspect, their eyes never blinking. The fire continues to roar, although no one seems to feed it fuel, regardless of the pile of chopped logs either side of the hearth. It just continuously pushes out heat at will.

The dawn finally arrives a short while later, slowly bringing up the daylight with the sun climbing higher in the sky. I must have fallen asleep because I can't remember seeing the snow stop.

Quad and Bump are standing by the hall door looking at me. They glance at each other and then Quad says, "You slept Andy, for at least two of your hours, this means that your side of the brain is trying to call you back."

I jump to my feet. "What do you mean, calling me back?"

"You think you were here and asleep, while in point of fact I watched you fade away and completely disappear. This means you were using your brain yourself, you were not in this domain. Do you remember anything, a dream or similar?"

"That's really weird, you asking that, because although I have never been able to remember dreams, normally just little snippets, last night I recall voices, my wife's voice." I then place my left hand on my right forearm. "I was also touched here, I don't know by whom, but I definitely know someone or something touched me."

"You probably were touched, but in the real world, not this one, so you have memories of it. Nevertheless you are back now so we have work to do, a plan to make and then to hatch. Are we all ready to go?"

Bump nods and so do I. Quad leads off and we leave the lodge.
We plough our way through the snow, some of it very deep, past the forest, along a frozen river, until we see a glacier ahead in the distance.

Quad stops momentarily as if he's taking a breather, although I know he's not; I get the feeling that something is perturbing him. He carries on, but now his pace is slower and much more deliberate.

"Hey Quad, what's wrong?"

"Wrong, why would you ask that?"

"A question answered with a question, the first and definite sign that all is not right."

Quad stops, so we all stop. He turns looking directly at me. "Can you see the glacier directly in front of us? That is where he will be, that is where your Optic is."

"So why are you worried about this, I was under the impression that the whole point was to actually find him?"

"You are correct, but we need to ensure that this meeting is on our terms and the nearer we get to him, the more likely he is to know that we are here. That will mean he will try to orchestrate the time and place for our gathering; that will not be good."

"I see, so is there any way we can disguise or hide our approach?"

"It is not me he will notice, nor Bump. We have both been in this domain, his domain for all of your natural life and he did not know I was here until I intervened when she was in danger. Bump came across him a couple of times but he disregarded her presence and he has never been able to find her at will. You however, are the main attraction in here, and as he brought you into his domain, he will recognise your signature immediately."

I digest his words, agreeing totally with the facts to hand. "In which case we don't need to go to him, we need him to come to us and I've just thought of the perfect meeting place. Let's turn back, leave this room and find another, but most of all let's reach a room with a portal through to my side of the brain."

Quad's face shows grave concern, his forehead wrinkles and his brow furrows. "I would like to know exactly what you have in mind. It sounds as though it may be extremely devious. I think I am going to like it."

"Why Quad, you have just cracked a joke."

His face changes completely, a smile flickers across it. "Perhaps I have been around you and your flippancy for too long."

I can't help erupting into laughter. Bump is already giggling, obviously finding it hard to contain herself she roars with hilarity.

The sound echoes across the ice plain, bouncing off the huge white glacier. We are all silenced as we hear a distant rumbling and feel a minor tremor in the ground. I look straight at Bump, then across at Quad. "It's him. If we are going to go, now would be a very good time."

We retrace our footsteps as quickly as possible. I don't even glance backwards. The ground tremors increase in their intensity. An ear-splitting, electrical zinging noise becomes increasingly more apparent. "Quad get her out of here and do it now!" I bawl above the row.

In an instant, Quad transforms from the old man into a large wild cat. The glimpse of him as I run, is akin to that of a sabre toothed tiger. He swipes Bump from her feet, speeds off in front of me and within seconds is gone from view. I continue sprinting as fast as I can. A couple of times I slip on the snow but manage to regain my feet and carry on with my ungainly attempt at escape.

Suddenly right in front of me the snow begins to rise into a mound. This stops me dead and I skid onto my backside. I rise and with the aid of back-pedalling type foot work, half turn, back tracking as hastily as I can. In front of my eyes, the heap of snow continues to grow, bursting into a mass of tiny icicles which multiply rapidly as they fill the surrounding area. The icy shards flying my way, lacerate my face and other parts of my body that are uncovered. The initial pain is excruciating but within a fraction of a second this passes. I know I still need to back off further as I recognize there is plenty more still to follow from that upsurge.

God how I hate being right in circumstances like this. From the depths of the ground and up through the snow comes the Optic. This time it has the appearance of a huge yeti, a white hairy, eight foot tall, shaggy snow beast with of course, his trademark one eye. Just what I really need to see. How I wish I hadn't laughed now.

"ABOUT TIME BEING. I HAD DECIDED IT WAS TIME I CAME TO FIND YOU, BUT YOU DECIDED TO COME TO ME. THAT'S VERY CONVENIENT!" The optic yells.

I cease back pedalling, endeavouring to gain a little more composure. I can't see the point in trying to muddle through this meeting because I want this situation to reach its conclusion. "I couldn't see the point in waiting for you dickhead. You take too long making decisions. I needed to get you out of my life, so I came to kick your arse."

The Optic leans forward, roaring at me, an incredibly fearful sound but I need him to see that I won't bend to his intimidation. "Great show Optic, lots of noise, lots of showy crap and do you know what, it means jack shit to me. You are just a tiny little puss spot on the asshole in my brain and I'm going to pop you. You hear me. DO YOU HEAR ME?!"

The optic begins pacing, bent forward as though ready to pounce. He circles left and right, stomping his feet with every step that he takes. "Still no respect Being, you still show me no respect. I must teach you this."

"Be my guest sunshine, I only show respect to those who earn it and there's no way on Gods earth you have earned it."

"EARNED IT, WHAT DO YOU KNOW ABOUT EARNING THINGS?!" The Optic stops pacing, stands tall and proud, his eye piercing me, his entire body language one of total aggression. He rapidly takes a couple of paces towards me. My first feeling is to run, and I'm pretty sure I start the motion to do exactly that. Then on very quick reflection I decide to stand firm. This might not be the ideal place to have things out with him but the scene seems to be set, so I'm going to do battle.

"What! You want a piece of me, then come and get it. What are you going to do, kill me? I don't think so, not unless you want to stay here, locked in my brain forever."

The Optics eye squints and he stops dead in his tracks. "Oh so you have been talking with the female's Optic and feel you have all the answers. I hate to disappoint you Being, but you know very little. I could destroy you and yes, I would have trouble leaving your essence and returning home. What you have not been told, is that your demise would just prolong my departure. In reality you are almost dead anyway. Besides all of that, I can make this time within my domain, a misery, a painful sadistic wretchedness that will accelerate the termination of your body, leaving me to depart without prejudice."

I can't help feeling that I am really out of my depth now with regards to the intricacies of how the Optics travel plans are interpreted, so therefore I think the better judgement is to keep my mouth shut.

"So therefore Being, it is about time I taught you some manners and respect. Thus far I feel I have been patient with you. Now I am going to show you a small sample of my real power."

I begin experiencing that droning dread deep in the bowels of my stomach. I can't help thinking I would give real money if he would just shut up and get on with it. With this thought, the Optic throws out his left hand to its full extent and as it reaches shoulder height, within the blink of an eye, he has extended it straight into me, piercing straight through my abdomen and exiting from the other side. The pain is excruciating, I drop to my knees. Lifting my head I look into his hairy face which is complete with a sadistic smile. "Is that it, is that all you've got you piece of shit?" I stammer.

With this jibe, he lifts his arm, which in turn lifts me to my feet, but he doesn't stop there, he elevates me at least four feet from the ground. As he lifts, I feel the wrenching and pressure this applies to the entry and exit wounds as well as the turmoil I feel in my guts. The pain is so intense that I am struggling to stay conscious. My ears are ringing and I feel nauseous. He then nonchalantly swings his arm, causing me to slide off his limb and crash to the snow laden ground. I look down at my stomach to see blood issuing all over the place. I clasp my hand over the wound but it is way too big to cover. The blood seeps out regardless of my efforts.

The horror of what I'm seeing numbs my thoughts. Suddenly, for some bizarre reason, I feel a renewed vigour. I glance up to see the Optic thrust sideways with great force, not landing within my sight. I immediately zoom in to the area where the blow to him must have originated from, but there is nothing there, I can see for miles over the snowy plain. My attention is caught by an irregularity within the immediate environment of where the Optic was. An extremely slight mismatch of the light as if something is hiding there within the anomaly. I dare not take my eyes from it in case I am unable to see it again, it's such an insignificant deviation, but it's definitely there.

I look down at my stomach again and find there is no sign of blood. I gradually remove my hands from the injury; there is nothing there, no visual sign of anything at all. How can this be? I delicately pull myself to my feet, half expecting pain with every movement, but as I stand fully erect, it becomes obvious to me that I'm actually not hurt at all. No injuries whatsoever?

My concentration returns to the anomaly but I can't see it now, it must have moved.

Abruptly the ground at my feet splits open throwing me backwards and out of the ground the Optic rises again. As his feet hit the floor the earth trembles with the power. He instantly sees me, ignoring me in favour of searching the surrounding area, evidently trying to locate whatever threw him across the snow plain. As his head spins from left to right, he grunts, I can see he is really pissed off.

After only a few seconds of his scanning the vicinity, the Optics attention returns to me. "So you have friends here, do you Being?" He growls.

"Fuck you, I don't need help with you." This is the best response I can think of due to the fact that I now don't have a clue what to do. It's very evident to me that I'm totally out matched here and I really have no idea how to get away from the Optic, so pure bravado is all that seems to remain.

The optic stomps across, proceeding to grab and shake me like a rag doll. I kick and punch at him, but none of my efforts seem to faze him whatsoever. Then he grabs me by the head, the whole of my head fits into one of his hands, and he tightens his grip. It feels like my head is being crushed in a vice. As I cry out from the pain so the Optic drops me. I'm at his feet so I kick fast and viciously at his shins. This time I get a reaction for my violent exertion because he yelps and moves away. Thinking that I have actually managed to find some form of Achilles heel on this brute, I regain my feet, making ready to attack.

To my astonishment I can see the reason that I'm not being smashed to bits by him; between us is the anomaly. Being this close to it I can perceive it much clearer. I can see the Optic right through it. There is a humanoid shaped outline shimmering and changing within the light, within a fraction of a second. The thought occurs that I was thrashing out at this thing and not actually at the Optic, and it also appears to me that whatever it is, it is on my side. I shuffle myself away from both the thing and the Optic.

The Optic is lashing out in all directions, his paws now adorned with razor sharp claws and it's obvious he doesn't know where his adversary is. His bulbous eye is bloodshot with rage and his roar deafening as he slashes, kicks and head buts at thin air. After a couple of minutes of the Optic fighting with the shadows, with no outcome, a lance of intense luminosity strikes from nowhere hitting him, crashing into his back and knocking him to the ground. I can hear the breath leave his body with the clout of the blow as he emits a grinding groan. In an instant his head swings around and I witness that he has identified the source of his enemy. He leaps to his feet and charges. I can once more see the shimmering. The Optic is almost upon it. As the clash is inevitable, the anomaly flickers and disappears. The Optic clutches at thin air and then turns to me. He holds his paws out in front of him, like a flick knife the talons flip up, one by one. I'm pretty sure that this gesture is meant to intimidate me, implying he's going to do me some real harm as soon as he gets a chance.

I hear a voice whispering. "Andy get out of here now, I do not know how long I can keep his attention." I recognise this voice, it's Quad.

The Optic marches towards me, his arms hanging down at his sides with the claws fully extended. I rapidly commence my retreat, breaking into a run. The Optic pursues.

In front of me is the glacier; great I'm going the wrong bloody way. I start to circle, the Optic is almost on my back when suddenly he is jolted backwards, crashes to the ground, again with a breathless moan but he recovers quickly and is instantly back on the rampage. A second ripple of energy is emitted, this time the lightening bolt blasts him straight in the face. The immense power of this assault lifts him so far from the ground that his feet are higher than his head. I can see he is visibly stunned as he crashes to the ground. I continue with my exit.

After sprinting through the snow for five minutes or so, I find that I am unable to maintain the pace, so I stop. I immediately look back to where the fight is taking place. I can see the Optic still swinging his claws, lashing out and intermittently that flash of light sending him tumbling. I know without any doubt that I must keep going to the tree line in the distance. I have to reach there, putting as much distance as possible between the Optic and myself as I am physically capable of.

CHAPTER SEVENTEEN
THE REALITY

I reach my goal without any further incident and as I approach, I spot Bump just inside the canopy. She sees me and comes leaping through the snow, launching herself towards me. Having given me a huge hug, she pulls away holding my shoulders and starts looking me up and down. "Are you okay, are you hurt at all?"

I remove her hands and hold them in mine. "I'm fine thanks to Quad. He saved my bacon."

She looks at me sideways. "Saved your bacon, what bacon?"

Here we go again, one of those conversations that can never arrive anywhere. "It's a turn of phrase; it means that I would have been a goner without Quad's input."

She stares at me momentarily and bemusedly shakes her head. "Anyway you are okay, what about Quad, where is he?"

"Last time I saw him he was in disguise as the invisible man shoving bolts of lightning up the Optics arse."

Again she looks sideways at me. "Do you know, sometimes you talk in absolute riddles. I can hear the words but they make no sense whatsoever. Is Quad okay and can you answer in English please?"

I burst out laughing. "You are very funny at times. As far as I know Quad is fine. He was still fighting the Optic the last time I saw him but I believe he will come away unscathed."

She nods. "Thank you. I hope he returns soon. Between the pair of you, I spend most of my time worrying."

Smiling I question, "Which way, where do we head for now?"

She turns heading into the forest. I follow.

After an hour or so of walking through the forest without incident, the snow comes to an end, just finishes and before us are open fields. The one directly in front of us is ploughed with reasonably deep furrows, the fields further away seem to vary, some look like they are planted with corn or wheat while others appear to contain potato plants. The first thing that hits me as wrong, is that these two crops should not be at this stage of growth together, they are completely out of sync. As I look out I observe the landscape gently rolling up and down and I recognize the scene before me, not exactly, but I have seen similar many times before at my home in Devon.

We continue on. Trampling across the ploughed field is fairly hard going, but nonetheless a trifle easier than trudging through the deep snow. The sky is clear and blue, again with no sign of the sun though.

Having passed over the first field we approach a gate. The whole area is edged by hedges, Devon hedges where the trees have been cut and laid, allowing them to break down, slowly forming a natural barrier. The gate is chained and padlocked, so we clamber up and over it into the next field; this one is definitely barley. Bump starts to walk straight through it, a direct route across to the next gate. I stop her. "We will walk around the edge of it."

She looks at me. "Why, it will take longer?"

"Yes it will but you don't walk through the middle of a crop, someone planted it, will harvest it and they really don't want people trampling it down. It's rude and not the way of the countryside. We will go around."

Raising her eyes she adheres to my request. As we are circling the barley field, it suddenly dawns on me that this is all happening inside my subconscious, no one is actually going to reap this crop, this scenario is entirely a figment of my imagination. I start to giggle at my stupidity. As we amble along, I pull at a couple of plant tops, rubbing the husks. My God this reminds me of my home.

On reaching the next gate, I stop and survey the way forward. In the distance I can see the top of a church. I point it out to Bump. She gazes at the structure for a few seconds. "It's a church isn't it?" she states.

189

"Yes it is and do you know what that means?"

"Someone built it," comes her reply.

Astounding, you can't argue with that answer. "Well yes, someone built it but it also means there is a village or town over there, a place with dwellings and possibly people."

"Oh okay, shall we go there or should we avoid it? What do you think?"

"I think we ought to head for it, make sure we are not seen, purely to see if anything is happening there."

"Okay, let's rock and roll then." With this she opens the gate, this one's not locked, leaves it wide open and proceeds to walk around the perimeter. I pass through the open gate and out of habit, shut it behind me.

I call out, "We are going straight across this one."

Abruptly she stops, puts her hands on her hips and turns around to face me. "Straight across it, through the crop, what happened to the country way then? You really do have to make up your mind. We've just taken forever to get around that last field because you said it was wrong to walk through it. Now all of a sudden it's okay to go through the fucking crop."

"Calm yourself, don't get a strop on, the country way is the right way but as we are not really in the country, we will go through the middle, okay. And by the way, cut out the language thing, a lady shouldn't swear."

She stomps back to where I am stood, gives me a slight glare and then pushes her way through the golden coloured wheat. I follow heading for the church. Having crossed four more fields full of various crops, we pass through a gate that leads us to a sloping meadow. Beyond this and slightly elevated, is the church with its surrounding village. We will have to drop down through this meadow then up to the village.

We decide to traverse the fields keeping to the hedge rows, this time not to be correct but to partially conceal our presence. Along the hedge rows are sporadic trees, again varying in variety and their stage of growth, some twenty feet tall and others just small saplings still early in their development. The meadow itself is quite marshy and muddy; this would normally imply that the area has seen considerable rainfall recently, but in this world who knows. Perhaps it is all staged like a play, solely for our benefit.

We climb the last remaining field up to the village and to my complete surprise we see a woman leading a horse towards us. My initial reaction is to hide but it occurs to me that we have already been seen and therefore to do this would look a trifle strange. As she draws closer, I raise a smile, nod and say, "Good morning."

She in turns smiles and says, "Good afternoon." She continues walking past us with no further conversation.

We slow our pace to allow the woman and her horse to disappear over the brow. "Do you realise, that is the first other person apart from you that I've seen since I've been here. How about you?"

She stops, turns to where the woman went and then back to me. "Yep, definitely the only other person I have ever seen." Having said this, she matter of factly continues walking towards the village.

"Don't you find that strange, you have been here a lot longer than I have and that's the first person you've seen apart from me?"

She stops again momentarily dropping her head forward. "Not really, perhaps the Optic has decided to populate the place. That would be nice wouldn't it, other people to see and talk to."

This answer is apathetic to say the least, she doesn't seem to notice or care about the goings on, just seems to accept everything as the norm. Even when I point out certain factors to her, she sees no relevance to my concerns. Having pondered this subject matter, I glance up to see that she has reached the gate at the top of the field. I run to catch her up. On drawing closer I observe that she is casually chatting with a man on the other side. I would have said that he is in his sixties,

191

wearing a flat cap, a heavy knitted pullover, cord trousers, Wellington boots and smoking a pipe. I slow my advance, attempting to make my entrance in a relaxed and friendly manner. When he spots me, he lifts a cane he is holding in his right hand and calls out a greeting. "Afternoon young 'un," he says in a real old Devonian accent.

"Good afternoon sir," I reply. "What's the name of this village?"

The old man looks me straight in the eye. "Well, you not be one of them moors walkers then, or you'd know where you be to. This be Witheridge boy."

Witheridge, I know this place too. I lived here, but for some reason I can't recall exactly where or when. "The church sir, is it called Witheridge church?"

The old man chuckles, "It could be I s'pose, but it's not, that be St. Pauls Church."

I start to climb over the gate and as I do, the old man opens it with me still balanced on the top. "Around 'ere, we likes to walk through our gates."

I awkwardly dismount, endeavouring to hide my embarrassment. "Yes of course, it's just that some we've come across have been chained and locked. Sorry about that."

"Looking normally helps young un."

"Yes of course, thank you sir."

"You be welcome." Having closed the gate after us, the old man walks off down the road.

We now find ourselves standing on a pavement, with a road that meanders off to our right away from the village, while to our left the road continues on into the centre. The church of St. Pauls is immediately in front of us, with a padlocked metal gate not ten feet away, which leads into the church's graveyard. We walk towards it, passing its main entrance. I stop and gaze at the incredible structure, admiring the magnificent building with its classic Norman style of architecture. We move on. Immediately past the church, on the right hand side, there is a village square. Again this feels familiar to me.

On the left hand side of the square, built around the entire corner, is a large building that looks quite austere. It was obviously some kind of Inn once in its history, but it is run down now with paint flaking on the windows and discolouration to its painted rendering. Next to that, there is a thatched cottage and finally a Georgian type building on the far corner.

In the middle of the square is a single thatched cottage, standing alone within the fork of the road which encircles it entirely. The opposite side of the square has various thatched and slatted roofed properties that intermingle and somehow find a way to look quite picturesque even though they are a mismatch of different period architecture.

We walk on past the square and within seconds arrive at another large building. This one is made of stone, with tall Georgian widows and a sign hanging over its front door. There is no doubt that this is an Inn. The sign hanging outside its frontage has a picture of a bishop with two other clergymen stating its name to be the Mitre Inn, and the door is open. I look across the road. There are two single storey modern buildings, one of which borders the large building on the corner of the square. The other way, the road continues with a staggered crossroads a little further up.

"No people Bump, there are not any people here."

She surveys the area. "You're right. Is that a problem then?"

"Well I don't know really. We saw the woman with the horse, then the old guy at the gate. Two people in as many minutes and now that we are actually in the middle of the village, it's deserted. I think that something ain't right."

I look back at The Mitre, the door remains open so I walk in. Bump follows.

Just inside the main outer door there is a glass interior one. Trying the handle, it opens. Immediately inside there is an open door to my left and in front of me a stunning period staircase rising three floors with a beautifully ornate ceiling rose at its highest point. I have the feeling I know where I'm going, so I turn into the open door on my left. This brings me into a room with a huge fireplace, five tables and a large wooden canopied bar. It's all too familiar.

Moving towards the bar, I see another entrance behind it, off to the right hand corner. This must lead to another area behind the bar, but additionally and more interestingly I spot a black shimmering darkness, just like the one in Ravello. I back away from it, I don't know why because I already know that signifies the way to my side of the brain. "Can you see it Bump, the black light?"

"I see it but I can't go through it with you or I will die."

"I know sweetheart. We are not going to go through it, but what its appearance does mean is that we are close to my side of this world, so the Optic shouldn't bother us here. At least I think I'm right in this assumption."

She moves to the corner of the bar and sits on a pew, one of two that adjoin the inset of the chimney breast.

"I am exceptionally familiar with this place. I have been here many times, and I mean many times but I can't think why," I say.

Suddenly the glass door in the hall opens and in saunters a well proportioned man, I would have guessed in his fifties. He glances over to Bump and nods, then looks straight at me. "Hi Andy, I'm here to help if I can."

"Quad, is that you mate?" I question.

"Who's Quad? No it's me, Rob."

"Rob, Rob who? I sort of recognise you but I don't know who you are."

The outer door bursts open, abruptly stopping the conversation, and a young man enters. He is dressed in a round necked t-shirt, jeans and trainers and is carrying a black leather jacket.

"Andy this situation is extremely dangerous," he says.

"And who the fuck are you?" I demand.

Looking at his face, both of his eyes appear to melt into one and then return to normal. "Does that give you a clue?"

"Quad is that you?"

"Yes it is and this remains an extremely dangerous situation."

"Why, what's up, where's the danger?" I glance over to the man named Rob. "Is he the danger, is he the Optic?"

Rob moves across to the fireplace looking totally confused and a little scared. "Optic, who's the Optic?"

Quad walks right over to him, peering into his face. Rob backs up until he is actually standing on the hearth stones. "He is not the Optic, he is not real, he comes from the other side." Quad matter of factly informs me.

"Other side, what do you mean, what other side?"

"He is a presence, nothing more, he has generated his attendance here. He is from your real world and is a living being with the ability to enter the worlds of the dead and dying."

I feel anger and fear well up inside me. "Who the fuck is dead or dying then, if I'm dead surely this would all be over?"

Rob navigates his way off the hearth, approaching me. "Andy you know me. We are friends and we want you back. I am here because Barbara sent me in to bring you back."

"Okay Rob, you say we are mates then you tell me, where am I? From your side of this fucking nightmare, what do you see and how do you see me when you are not in here. Please, please just tell me because I have no idea, not a fucking clue."

He turns away from me, moving to the other end of the bar. "You are lying on a bed in a hospital. You were involved in a car accident that left you in a coma, fighting for your life. You have been that way now for six days. A vigil has been kept by Barb and the boys, your mum and some of your closest friends. Barb asked me if I was able to contact you. I didn't know whether I would be able to or not, as you know I only normally deal with the deceased. Somehow, I managed to get in and I found you. I'm not sure if I'll be able to do it twice. To be honest, I'm not completely sure how I got here in the first place."

Quad shakes his head. The words I've just heard are alarming to say the least and Bump is looking at me horrified.

"Rob, I do sort of remember you and I sense you mean me no harm, but I'm not sure how to come back. What you've just told me has really scared the shit out of me. I had no idea. What I do know is that I can't leave until I destroy the Optic."

Quad moves over to where Rob is standing. "You are an outside influence making waves in this domain. You must leave before the Optic discovers you are here. If he grasps your kinetic energies, you will die on your side. Leave now!" Within seconds of hearing Quad's words, Rob starts to become transparent and finally disappears. "His Optic is lacking, he never should have allowed him to have the use of that part of his brain," he tuts.

Quad paces the bar area, goes outside and returns within minutes. "We are very close to your side of the brain again Andy. This would be the ideal place for the final battle with the Optic, if we can snare him into coming here."

CHAPTER EIGHTEEN
THE LURE

For some considerable time we sit in complete silence, Quad's words ringing around my head; how to get the Optic here, what a dilemma.

I look around the bar area with that strong feeling of having been here before. I know the pictures on the walls, the curiosities scattered around the room, the fireplace, even the glasses hanging from the canopy above the bar.

Finally the silence is broken by Bump. "Who exactly was that man Rob?"

I burst into laughter. Quad also manages a smile.

"What's so funny, why are you laughing, I haven't said anything funny have I?" Bump has definitely got the hump so to speak, she is pouting. Jumping up from her seat, she proceeds to stomp out of the room.

"No, no, I'm not laughing at you. I'm laughing at the fact we have all sat here for ages not saying anything because we are trying to think of a way to get the Optic here, and you are still wondering who the hell the other bloke was."

"Well, who was he?"

Quad takes her by the shoulders, sitting her down on a stool. "He was from the real world. He is a friend of Andy's but from the other side, the outside where people live a normal, tangible life. Do you understand?"

She looks vacantly. "No I don't. Is he from Andy's side of the brain, is that what you mean?"

Quad glances over to me and then back to Bump. "Not exactly, no. We are in a world entirely generated by Andy's brain. As a whole, his brain can be broken into thirds. One third of which, Andy has complete control over."

"I wouldn't have said that Quad. That's one hell of a statement!" I interrupt.

He smiles and continues. "The other two thirds, the Optic controls and we are all currently existing within these dimensions. Andy should not be here, he should not be able to survive in here, but the Optic has made this possible. Rob was a projection from the outside world, completely outside the brain. Out there he is real, but he has managed to train his mind to enable him to enter into worlds similar to this one. Do you understand now?"

She looks very thoughtful and then her eyes sparkle as she says. "Well that was a long way of telling me he was only visiting. Huh, I'm not stupid you know."

I look at Quad, whose face can only be described as 'a picture'. He gestures with his arms that he is totally at a loss and who can blame him, I have no idea how she came to that conclusion.

She continues, "The lady with the horse and the old man at the gate, they were just visiting as well, weren't they?"

Quads eyes meet mine and we both stare at each other.

"He is already here." Quad emphatically states, abruptly changing the subject.

"Then why didn't he go for us and why can't he just leave, go on his way without challenging?" I pause for a moment and then add, "And can he split into two entities, to become both a woman and a horse at the same time?"

"He can be anything he wants to be. He could be a herd of stampeding elephants if he wanted to. I imagine he was exerting caution, he will know he is close to your side of the brain, he will not take the chance of being too close to the dark threshold."

I gaze towards the shimmering black portal at the rear of the bar. "How the hell are we going to get him to go through that?"

Quad glances at it, lowering his head. "I do not know but we must find a way."

Once more we all sit around deep in thought, trying to fathom a way in which to entice the Optic into this room and ultimately through the black gateway. Then it occurs to me. "I've got it!" I excitedly shout. They both jump at my emphatic statement. "When Bump and I were in Italy the portal moved its position depending on whether it was night or day, so if that scenario is a constant, then at some stage that there will disappear and reappear somewhere else."

Quad's eyebrows furrow as he frowns. "Are you sure? Obviously as I have not been on that side of the barrier, I have never seen into your side of the brain. You need to be absolutely sure."

"I'm sure. It nearly cost Bump her life because it moved its position just before I could get her through it, and we had to wait until it returned because she was too frail to move."

With this statement she is nodding. "Andy's right, I saw it as well. It does move and it moves a long way."

I experience an intense kind of satisfaction with this realisation until Quad quells it in one foul swoop. "How far away, how far, is far away?"

"In Italy it was at least five or six miles I should think."

"Well that is going to be problematic do you not think?"

"No why? If we can find out where the door will be before the Optic does, we can deceive him into a confrontation in precisely that place before it reappears. That should do the trick. He will be on the threshold of my fucking domain and we can have him." By the time I have finished this oration, I am stood straight up with my chest puffed out full of self satisfaction.

"You okay Andy?" Bump says slowly, with a very disturbed look on her face.

"Yep, I'm good, outstanding really. We now have the basis for a plan, right?"

Quad smiles again, he must be getting used to it. "So all we have to do is to find the portal's other location without the Optic locating it as well? I think it would be better for me to do the searching as I can to a degree, go undetected by him. You two should remain right here next to this portal for your safety."

I glance over to the portal then back to Quad. "I don't want to rain on your parade Quad but if the portal moves, we are not going to be very safe are we?"

He takes a fleeting look at the portal and then levels on us. "Ah yes, a valid point, a very valid point. In which case, may I advise you both to keep yourselves well out of sight. Bump no talking to anyone except Andy. Okay?" Bump nods.

Quad saunters out of the bar and onto the street. Checking both left and right, he crosses the road, walking straight towards the building opposite, his substance fading as he proceeds and consequently disappears through the wall of the house as though it simply doesn't exist.

I turn and grin at Bump. "I wish I could do that."

"You can, you just do not believe it yet."

We remain in the bar, although I do take a quick stroll around the ground floor. It all does seem so familiar to me, everything about it as if I had something to do with the building of the place. Christ, I don't know, it's all dreadfully mixed up and confusing.

Behind the bar is a passage that leads through to the kitchen and beyond this it continues on to a door at the end. I enter this room. It is a long room that appears to extend the entire width of the building. There at the end is a motor bike. This I do know, I feel intense excitement inside me. This is my, MY Honda Gold Wing motorbike. I love this bike, I've travelled for miles on this thing.

I'm about to call out to Bump and beckon her to see my beautiful machine, when she shrieks. "Andy get back in here, the black shiny thing has gone."

I run back to the bar entering behind the counter, passing directly through where the portal would have been. I skid to a halt.

She is stood staring at the place where the dark opening previously was. "It's gone."

As she says this I look to the window. It is pitch black outside, the same as Ravello, the portal moves between day and night. "Okay it's all up to Quad now. He has to find out wherever it reappears and I don't reckon that is going to be a particularly easy job."

"He'll find it, I know he will." As she finishes the sentence there comes a strange creaking sound from outside. I glance towards the window, hop over the bar and head for the front door. I know this was open and I think it's time to get it firmly shut.

As I pass through the door leading from the bar into the hallway, I take a speculative look at both the inner and outer doors. I can't see anything outside from here and I don't feel in the least inclined to go out and have a proper gander. I open the inner door pushing the outer one shut with my foot, ensuring that if I should need to retreat at speed, everything behind me would be clear. With the front door almost shut it jams on something. I give it a couple of hefty kicks but it it's not budging. I move into the lobby between the two doors and apply my weight to the front door, giving it a really hard push. This does the trick and the front door slams shut.

I turn to go back through the inner door, into the main hall. On turning, I find myself at a lower level than the floor of the hall by at least a couple of feet and Bump is standing on the other side. Her face is full of panic, she is hammering at the glass door, shouting to me although I am unable to hear her. I turn to the main door attempting to reopen it. I need to get out of this subsiding lobby but as hard as I tug, it just will not move. At one stage I have my feet placed on the wall either side of the door, heaving at it with all my strength, but it's firmly wedged tight. I turn to see Bump, who has armed herself with an umbrella stand and is smashing it with all her might into the glass door. I am still totally unable to hear any sound even though a couple of cracks are appearing in the glass of the door and I can visibly see the whole door frame shaking. There follows a deep, violent shudder beneath my feet and the ground drops away another foot or so. I am now lower than the hall floor by at least three feet, as though stuck between floors in a lift. I signal to Bump for her to attack the base of the door. She acknowledges this and begins to batter at this bottom section.

After a further two drops of my floor, I find myself now only just tall enough to see Bump's feet. The bottom of the door is almost completely shredded where she has relentlessly been smashing the umbrella stand into it, and as for the stand itself, well it doesn't resemble anything I've ever seen before. As the base of the door disintegrates, sound is slightly restored and I can hear her grunting as she lashes out, the noise of the wood splintering and the glass shattering. Finally the complete bottom section of the door collapses allowing enough room for me to crawl through.

I endeavour to pull myself up and under the broken door but I am too far below it to obtain any substantial purchase to heave myself up. She grabs my wrists in an effort to assist me, but to no avail. I try to walk up the walls with one foot on either side, the same with my hands, shuffling my way up, wedging myself back against the wall.. If I can just gain an extra couple of feet, with her help I should get through. I manage to get further up than I thought I would, get my torso onto the lip and then under the gap of the door. Bump grabs my shoulders and I start to wiggle through.

Before I manage to get my knees onto the ledge, something clasps me around my right ankle. I snatch myself away from whatever it is, but it retains a very firm grasp on me. I can't see what it is because of the position I'm in, halfway through the bottom of a door, bent in an L- shape with my legs dangling, not the greatest observation position in the world. As whatever it is starts to apply downward pressure so I intensify my grip on either side of the door frame. I look at Bump and see a serious look of concern all over her face.

"What is it, what's the matter?" she asks worriedly.

"Something has hold of one of my legs and I can't shake it off."

"What do you mean something, can't you see it?"

"For fucks sake, does it look like I can just take a quick look. In case you hadn't noticed, I'm hanging on here for dear life. If you can, climb over the top of me to see if you can work it out."

She releases her grip almost immediately I've finished the sentence and along with it goes any help that she had afforded me, making it even harder for me to hang on. She inches over me and peers down to see what she is able to make out. In an instant she pulls back, taking hold of me once more, pulling with all her might and a real sense of urgency. This concerns me greatly. "Did you see anything?"

"Oh yes I saw something and I don't think you want to know. Keep climbing."

"Tell me, just tell me!"

She continues tugging at me and I feel as though I'm being torn apart. My grip on the door-frame is decreasing and the power of the clasp on my ankle is agonizing. I start kicking out at the unnamed assailant with my free leg. I feel that I'm making contact and the impact of my thrusts must be hurting but nevertheless the grip remains incredibly strong.

"What the hell is it?" I yell.

She glances at me for a fraction of a second and says, "Let's just say it's only got one eye."

This remarkably brief description tells the complete story and I kick even more ferociously than before. I feel the grip move from my ankle and start its way up my leg. I slow my struggle and allow the climbing Optic to reach my waist and then I begin to knee him with all my might. His grasp of me eases slightly, I kick backwards at him with my heels and I don't stop until I feel him slipping. I then yell to Bump.

"Pull now Bump and whatever you do, don't stop!" She pulls and tugs and I begin to regain some of my lost ground from earlier.

I manage to get myself right underneath the door and as I turn myself into a sitting position, I catch the first sight of the Optics façade. Presently this consists of its hands and forearms which resemble a mass of dried out old twigs, intertwined to make some form of limb. I keep kicking out when the head leaps up at me growling its displeasure before it dips back down again. I feel the weight of the Optic ease. He attempts another leap upwards, I coil back my free leg and wait until he rears his ugly head. Immediately he does, I kick out at it ferociously, connecting perfectly. The Optic lurches backwards, completely releasing his grip. I take the opportunity with both hands and shuffle myself behind what's left of the inner door. Now well clear of the enclosed lobby, I rise to my feet with Bump's help. "Thanks sweetheart," I whisper. She smiles and nods.

From within the lobby and the pit that it has now become, there is an eerie silence and both of us stand still just watching the area. Suddenly there emits an horrendous squeal followed by a manic scraping and scampering. It sounds as though he must be attempting to climb up towards us.

To our left is a large wooden dresser. Moving directly to it, I begin heaving it towards what remains of the inner glass door. Bump realising my intention, is quick to help. We place it completely across the door. When placed sideways as we now have it manoeuvred, it about spans the width of the hall and with a few minor adjustments, we manage to really wedge it in. I then jump up on top of it trying to see where the Optic is. The noises from the hole continue but I can see no sign of anything emerging. Turning to Bump I say, "See if you can find anything we can use as weapons to fight him, the heavier or sharper the better."

She literally shoots off into the bar and I hear various noises of things being moved and tested for their usefulness.

Slowly turning back to the glass door it occurs to me there is currently no commotion at all coming from that direction any more. Suddenly I find myself eyeballs to eyeball with the Optic who has his face firmly pressed against the glass, less than three inches away from me. This shock of this ghastly spectacle so close to my face sends me reeling and I fall backwards off the dresser and onto the floor.

Throughout my fall I don't take my eyes from the Optic, or indeed what I'm assuming is the Optic, because its appearance is completely extreme from all his other disguises. His head consists of pulsating veins, intermingled to form the shape of a head of sorts. Of course there is the inevitable single eye, which is bloodshot within varying colours of the rainbow, a mouth that seems to be constantly dribbling, no nose just an indent and ears that resemble flaps either side of his head. His neck, I liken to many sprigs of thick, wooded ivy, again totally fused together to maintain some form of shape and thus far, that's all I can see of him. His wiry fingertips are probing at the glass, as if searching for a fault with which to break through.

I reverse rapidly up the hall just as Bump returns holding a sickle, an old naval colt and a brass shoe horn. I stumble to my feet and grab the first thing she offers me as a weapon. I raise it above my head and am about to charge forward when I comprehend what I'm holding. I turn to her. "What the fuck am I supposed to do with this thing, help him on with his shoes?"

She looks at me slightly sheepishly and says, "It's heavy, batter him with it."

I hand the shoe horn back and replace it with the sickle. "You batter him with it. I was hoping not to get that close."

I glance back at the door to see that the Optics fingers have somehow managed to penetrate the glass and are sticking through it, wriggling. As he currently has both his hands in the same situation, I let loose a battle cry and run forward swinging the sickle at the protrusions. The blade hits its mark after a couple of swings, ripping and slicing off two or three of his digits, which limply fall to the floor. He generates the most ear piercing scream I have ever heard, so shrill that the mirror adorning the wall behind me is obliterated into a million pieces. The shards fly everywhere and both Bump and I cover our faces to shield ourselves against the debris. When the scream dies down, I look back at the door. Not only did the mirror break under the pressure of the reverberation but the glass in the door also has fractures all over it. The Optic has his back to us but within one swift movement he is facing us poised like a coiled spring, waiting to pounce. He launches himself at the glass door and as he connects with it, there is an almighty thud. Much to my surprise he doesn't come through, although there was a definite grinding noise within the remaining glass that leaves me in doubt that with one more of his assaults, he will most definitely break through.

I advance towards the door again, still wielding the sickle, threatening the Optic with all the menace I can muster. He semi-smiles then frowns, distorting his face into a contorted rage. He draws himself back again and I see him tense his entire body getting ready for his next barrage. Within an instant, he once more throws himself at the glass, this time to my further amazement he still doesn't get through. There follows a violent thud and he drops back with his head down, due to the cost of the impact. His head rises almost immediately again and the hate in his eye is so menacing, that I take a step backwards at the sight.

"Take a mental note Bump, I want the name of the manufacturer of that door, especially the glass. I'm going to have it all over my house when I get out of here in case of nuclear war." I joke.

She looks at me perplexed but true to form, amazes with a positive nod as if she understands what I'm on about.

The Optic lays his hands on the glass very gently, positions them so they are at the top and bottom of the door, glances at me, snarls, lifts up his head and shrieks as he did before. Right in front of my eye the glass finally fractures and starts to shatter. I grab Bump by the hand and fly up the staircase to the first landing. From here we can still see the inner door or would be able to, if the Optic hadn't of just torn it into pieces. He is stood where it once was.

Slowly and menacingly he looks up to where we are standing. "Oh boy, now he really looks pissed." I state the obvious.

Bump turns towards me and says, "Pissed? He looks angry to me." Yet again she has made a joke with no idea at all that she has. Still I haven't really got time to explain.

The Optic begins climbing the stairs, taking every pace slowly and methodically. There appears to be real purpose within his advance. I head back to the top of the stairs in order to greet my pursuer; it's become obvious to me that there has got to be a major confrontation here and now. As he approaches the curve in the stairs, so I am stood waiting with my sickle.

Unexpectedly, I hear a clicking sound from behind me. Turning I see Bump holding the old naval colt, pulling back the hammer and then pulling the trigger over and over again. If this wasn't such a serious and tentative time I would laugh. "It's not loaded. You would achieve more effect if you threw it at him." That is precisely what she continues to do, she flings the gun at the Optic with all her strength, scoring a direct hit. The pistol hits him quite squarely on the chest, halting his progress for a second. He looks down to where the gun impacted, to see that it has lodged itself in his chest, it's wrapped itself up in his wiry make up, with only the barrel still showing. He glares up at Bump and turns his attention to the pistol trying to dislodge it from his body. When he finds that it is too deeply embedded and not going to budge, his focus returns to me. For the first time since this meeting, the Optic speaks. "You will die if you do not release me from my binding." He then glares up at Bump. "You will die anyway and I will enjoy the carnage."

She backs away from the balustrade only to return in a second with various pictures and starts throwing them down the stairwell towards the Optic, connecting with some and getting pretty close with others. After she has exhausted these, she begins another onslaught bombarding him with all the available plant pots and their contents. The Optic thrashes his arms about windmill style in an effort to ward off the attacking missiles.

I move down the stairs towards his position and begin a second assault from the ground as it were, swinging the sickle and lashing out at him as fiercely as I know how to. A couple of times I hit my target but unfortunately not with the blade. The lesser effect of the blow still causes him to back down the stairs.

Bump's final projectile a yucca plant of some considerable size, comes careering down the stairwell with incredible velocity, connecting with the side of his head. This final blow of hers sends him staggering backwards. He passes six steps without touching any of them. The plant pot explodes on its contact with his head and the plant itself tangles with the Optic's current bodily make up.

He hits the floor with a staggering thump, rolling to the foot of the dresser. I follow him down as fast as he falls, with my sickle held high above my head. When I think I'm in range I bring down the weapon as hard as I can at his body. Before my eyes the wiry intermingled structure embarks on yet another change of shape. The strands of whatever he was made up from congeal and solidify into a substantially more solid frame. Nevertheless my thrust is being delivered whatever shape he is and the sickle's blade pierces right into the middle of his back. His entire body tenses, he shudders wrenching backwards, lifting back his head to its furthest extension and he cries out a hideous scream of pain. Turning his face towards me he proceeds to spit yellow fluid at me. His change continues into a metallic robot, an android armoured to the teeth. The blade of my sickle snaps like a twig as he perfects the transformation, but the pointed part of the cutting edge remains embedded in his back.

I don't hang around to see what's going to happen next, I run back up the stairs to the landing, grab Bump by the arm and state the obvious, "Time to go."

She is mesmerised by what the Optic is doing and I glance down to see what is captivating her attention. The Optic is thrashing about, attempting to pull the intrusion from his body but he can't seem to reach it. I managed to hit the central most part of his back and his efforts to reach it are futile. Suddenly he stops, raises his right arm above his head and to my horror, extends and angles this arm therefore gaining the ability to reach the wound.

"Jesus that just isn't right; the blokes a fucking contortionist!"

Bump turns to me, gives me a tiny false smile and says, "Didn't you say something about getting out of here just now?"

I nod. "Too right I did. Let's go up another flight of stairs and see if we can get out up there."

We head further up. At the top I take a quick peep down. The Optic has managed to remove the blade from his back and is now staring upwards at us. He begins to climb the staircase, every step deliberate, menacing and over exaggerated, stamping his feet on every tread.

As we reach the top of this flight of stairs we see a door. It is open so we enter. Inside is a small lobby with doors leading both left and right. I try the door to my left, it doesn't budge so I turn to the right hand one. This one opens and we enter a huge room with low rafters spanning its expanse. To my right, there is another much smaller staircase, to my left a double bed, a television and a bedside cabinet, the usual bedroom furniture, while in front there is a two-seater settee. I turn shutting the door we just entered from, locking it after me. I don't know how much good it's going to do but it's got to help to slow him down for a couple of seconds at least.

I can still hear the thundering footsteps of the Optic drawing closer to where we are. I beckon Bump to follow me. I mount the small staircase and enter a dormer bedroom that is set in the topmost part of this building. There are two single beds, a low dresser and nothing else.

My attention is drawn towards a window in the slanting ceiling. It's a Velux sky light, a window that is constructed into the gradient of the roof. This is definitely our only route of escape now. I inspect the window in an effort to ascertain how it opens. After a couple of tries I fathom that it works on a central swivel, consequently when it's fully open, we will only have half its area in which to climb through.

I send Bump out first being the smallest, and while attempting to manoeuvre my way through the opening, I hear an almighty crash. The Optic has destroyed my locked door, would be my guess, which means he's almost upon us. With a lot more urgency I manage to renegotiate the window, squeezing my way out. Once out, I jump to my feet and realise that I'm standing in a valley between two roofs. Bump is at the far end crouched down. I quickly and quietly shut the window and briskly walk along the lead valley to where she is. "See any way down?"

She shakes her head. "Not from here, it's a sheer drop."

I clamber up the tiled roof to the ridge. Once there I straddle the apex and attempt to peer into the darkness for a way down and subsequently, away from the Optic. I can't see too much, it's pretty black out there, the only light seems to be emanating from the pub itself. I scramble along the ridge to the other end but it's a similar problem, a sheer drop down of at least three floors.

Abruptly, my attention is drawn to the skylight as the glass in it shatters and a protruding metal fist is evidently the culprit. Bump darts towards the metallic arm, manically attacking it with her brass shoe horn. The sound of metal against metal rings through the air, breaking the silence of the night, showing that battle is about to recommence.

Attempting to rush towards them both, my way is barred by something I can't see. I can see Bump thrashing away with her deadly shoe horn not ten feet away but as I try to join forces with her, something is barring my way. I attempt to go around it by climbing up to the ridge, but the invisible wall seems to extend wherever I go. I can see her backing away from the Optic, his complete torso now visible above the tiles and he is preparing to heave himself up, out and onto the valley. I feel panic well up inside me. If I don't get to her, that bastard will kill her and enjoy doing it. What's he done now? How is he stopping me from passing?

He turns his now robotic head towards me and I see the glee in his eye. With one blow he swats Bump out of his way. She is sent halfway along the roof and as she lands she doesn't move. He hauls his entire body from the remains of the window, even the tiled area around the frame is totally smashed and distorted.

I try rushing at the barrier by taking a couple of paces backwards and barging with my shoulder at the obstruction. Every attempt is met with failure as I simply spring back off the invisible wall.

Bumps limp body slides down the tiles and he paces forward to meet it.

Frustration, panic and rage all build up in me at the same time. I emit a deep groan, glaring at the Optic. He stops and turns towards me, his expression a little more concerned now. I clench my fists, hammering at the barrier, my vision tunnels, completely and utterly focusing on him. I feel throbbing through my entire body, my sight is tinged with red and spiralling towards the Optic.

Suddenly he is thrown backwards, lifted off his feet and flung the entire length of the roof. He immediately regains his feet and screams at me, a high pitched screech. I walk in his direction, the barrier now gone. His face is full of apprehension and he glances between Bump and I.

"Don't you touch her you fucking abomination." I turn my attention to Bump and to my astonishment she appears to be almost floating towards me. It's obvious that she is unconscious but she is definitely moving. Am I doing this?

The Optic is looking in every direction as if searching for something and then he turns back to me. "It is not over Being, a little show of unharnessed power luckily applied is not going to help you in the long run. The time is close; you will soon learn and see that I control this domain." With his obvious dubiousness to continue I advance on his position but within the first few paces of my progress, he turns, leaping from the building.

CHAPTER NINETEEN
<u>CONCERNED AREAS</u>

I walk across to Bump who is now struggling to her feet and I help her up. "Are you okay?"

"I think so, just dazed. He really did lash out at me that time." She sits back on the tiled gradient and then with urgency starts to search the surrounding rooftop, obviously trying to ascertain where the Optic is. "Where did he go, how did you fight him off, did Quad return?"

"Hey questions, questions. I'm not sure why he left. He said something about 'unharnessed power' and jumped off the roof. With a bit of luck he fell and broke his neck but I don't think we would be that lucky."

She giggles and shakes her head. "What now, what should we do now?"

"I'm not too sure, but getting off this roof would be an outstanding start. What do you think?"

She giggles again and rises to her feet, wandering over to the skylight window, she crouches down and peers around inside. "There's nothing in here now." Gingerly she climbs in and calls up, "You coming?"

She is quite an amazing girl really, nothing seems to phase her for long. "Running all the way Bump." I can hear her laughing from inside the room. Ambling over to the same opening, I clamber down. It's much easier to get through now the Optic has carried out his alterations. I have to smile to myself, at least one good thing came out of his inopportune visit.

I drop down into the dormer room and take the small staircase down into the larger raftered one below. I stop and gaze around. I just know I've been here before. Approaching the main staircase a weird feeling comes over me. I have to steady myself on the door frame and realise I need to sit down. I can hear voices again. I can hear Barbara and my Mum plus someone else. This last voice I don't recognise. The words they are all saying seem to overlap, I can only distinguish the odd word but no complete sentences. I stagger to the settee and slump into it, holding my head in my hands. "Andy, Andy please stay with us." I can hear those words perfectly. I attempt to look across the room but there is a fuzzy mist swirling around and I am unable to properly focus on anything.

I feel a definite touch on my shoulder and hear, "What's the matter Andy, are you okay?" That's Bump's voice.

"Quiet Bump I need to listen, I need to know what this is. It's happened before, I can hear my wife and others but I can't see them and I don't know why I can hear them now."

Again I hear a statement, this time I'm pretty sure it's my mum talking. "Andy concentrate, we need you to come back, come on son. Please come back."

Then all the voices become muddled once more with no words distinguishable. As fast as the fainting sensation came over me, so it passes and all my senses seem to return to normal. The voices have stopped but I can't help worrying as to what this all means?

Bump is kneeling right in front of me, staring up at me. "What is it, what happened?"

"I don't really know, it's all quite peculiar. I can hear my wife, my mum and others and they are calling me back, but back to where I don't know?"

She looks at me with confusion and concern, takes my hand and says, "It must be the other side talking to you. Don't be afraid, they want you back and the Optic doesn't want you to go. He needs you here for his own ends." I hear her words and understand them but I can't help wondering how she knows this stuff, how she comprehends the intricacies of this side and the other side of both these worlds.

As I'm sitting and pondering her words, my attention is drawn to the window. "Its light, daylight is back. That means the portal should be downstairs. We had best go down there and check."

I stagger to my feet a little unsteadily and we both return downstairs to the bar. As we descend the last flight, I notice the glass door in the hall is back totally intact as if nothing had occurred at all. I pause for a moment, checking out the complete hallway. It's all back to the way it was, even the dresser is in place with all the various bits and pieces on top of it. "There must be one hell of a cleaner and handyman working here." I state tongue in cheek.

Bump looks at me a little oddly and questions, "What do you mean?"

"Well take a look around. We left this place as a disaster area and now everything is back in place as though nothing at all had occurred."

"Oh that. I know that. What's the problem? It happens a lot around here. You should be used to it by now. I'm sure you will get used to it eventually."

As we enter the bar, there it is, shimmering within its deep darkness. Exactly as it was in Italy. It has two ports of call, one by night and the other by day. It's day now so I venture outside, taking a large step over the floor between the glass inner door and the main front door. I'm naturally dubious of this area now.

Outside is a dull day, complete with cloud cover. In point of fact the cloud looks like a sheet of grey, strategically placed, with no substance to it at all, no depth, no deviation in colour and no movement.

I look in the direction of the church and there's no sign of anyone. I peer the other way and it's exactly the same. I call to Bump who joins me outside and we begin wandering towards the main square. We pass the building that spans the corner and I stop. "The Angel, this was called The Angel."

She looks up at the building surveying it, then walks into the square to obtain a better perspective. "Angel as in a winged person, that belongs to and comes from the heavens?"

I look at her in total amazement.

"Why are you looking at me like that, what's the matter?"

"Well in my life I have heard descriptions of many different things, but your depiction of an angel was the most concise one I think I've ever heard."

"Why thank you, it's very nice to receive compliments." With this she strolls off past the Angel, across the road, stopping outside a thatched cottage that stands alone, painted pink and is situated in the middle of the square. "Has this one got a name?"

I amble across the road and join her. "Yes it has but I can't recall it at the moment. I do recognise these buildings and their names, which must confirm that I have been here before. I do know this place."

She smiles at me and says, "It will come back to you."

Suddenly the church bell begins to toll and as I gaze up to the top of the tower, I can see someone up there. "Can you see that Bump?"

She nods. "Who do you think it is, do you know him or do you think it's the Optic?"

"No, I don't think it's the Optic, why would he let us know where he is? No I think that is Quad."

Walking into the middle of the square, I yell up to the top of the church. The person up there climbs on the ramparts, peers down at the drop and then jumps. We both sprint to the church grounds, in through the gate, past the grave stones and towards the church door, coming to an abrupt halt when we see Quad dancing about in the foyer.

"What the hell are you doing, you scared the shit out of us."

Quad stops jigging and quips, "I've always wanted to do something like that, I was flying," and he bursts into rapturous laughter.

Bump and I look at each other. "If I didn't know better, I would say he's on some serious drugs."

"What do you mean, if you didn't know better?"

I turn to her, gazing into her eyes. "We are in my mind, my brain. Where the hell would he get drugs from unless there is a drug dealing Optic in here doing a little moonlighting job. I can't believe I'm having this conversation."

Quad walks out from the foyer and straight up to us. "You ought to try that Andy its good fun. Right, now on a serious note, the other portal appears inside the house which you were just stood outside of. I had to search a wide area. I did not think it would be within such close proximity of its other location. Nevertheless that's where it is at night."

"Okay then Quad, if you think about it, it couldn't be better, there is very little distance involved with tricking the Optic into entering my side of the brain. I take it he doesn't know it appears over there?"

I doubt it, because like me, we can only sense that we are too close to these portals, we can't exactly see where they are."

We stroll out of the church yard and head for the thatched cottage. "The Pound House!" I exclaim.

They both stop and look at me.

"That's the name of that thatched cottage, the one you say the portal appears in, it's called The Pound House. I just remembered."

"Good," says Bump, "Because our recent conversations are beginning to really confuse me."

We reach the front door of the cottage and try the handle. It pushes open, we bow our heads, due to the lack of height of this aperture and we enter. The ceilings are also extremely low, with rafters spanning the width of the rooms.

Quad leads the way turning left into what I believe to be the lounge. He points at the far side of the room where it appears a staircase is situated. "That is where the portal will materialise when night arrives."

I cross to the far side of the room, past various pieces of furniture, to the foot of the stairs and I look up them.

"Not up them, it appears in the wall right there at the base of the stairs." I turn to the wall, pointing to an area of solid stone. Quad nods verifying that I'm in the right place.

I walk back to the middle of the room and sit myself down on a sofa that Bump has already made herself comfortable on. Quad walks to the fireplace and leans on the mantel piece.

"Did you know that the Optic came to get us last night Quad?

His head turns quickly towards me. "No I did not. What happened?"

I relate the story and Bump fills in the odd bit I either, exaggerate or omit, until Quad is fully in command of all the facts. He drops his head to ponder. "So he came within minutes of the night arriving, is that correct?"

We both nod.

"In that case, he either knows the portal emerges there or it is just complete coincidence."

"I don't believe in coincidence Quad and what's more, I really do think coincidence in dire situations should be renamed strategy."

He raises his eyes for a second and then continues in serious mode. "The piece of your story that really does interest me is the part when the Optic left. It appears to me that he was dubious of your rage. He talked of your power, which leads me to think that you successfully manifested your ability to fight him on your own terms, utilising your brain waves to disrupt his will and grip on this domain."

Wow what a statement. I'm not even sure I followed the whole drift.

My thoughts are interrupted by Bump. "Are you saying that Andy has finally found that he is stronger and more powerful than the Optic?"

217

"No not exactly. If that was the complete case the Optic would be controlled by now. What I am saying, even hoping is that he showed the Optic an influence of consciousness that he has never encountered before. Indeed how could he have done, the situation of us all being here together should never have happened, there is no precedent set for Optic and host to meet. He is aware that Andy could produce unlimited abilities and powers because this is his brain, but he also assumes that he will not be able to produce these things because he will not know how to instigate them."

Bump frowns. "I'm lost."

We both laugh.

"So Quad if he knew there was a portal there, in the pub, what makes you think he doesn't know about the one here?"

He moves away from the fireplace and commences pacing to and fro in the middle of the room. "When we were in the bar at The Mitre Inn, we were visited by your friend. This friend would only be able to manifest himself to you, close to a portal. He entered via the portal in the bar and the Optic would have felt the intrusion within the patterns of the brain. He would have known immediately and been alerted to its proximity."

"Are you sure because if he does know, we could have a really big problem?"

"Yes I am sure."

"Will he know we are in this house, will he know we are here?"

"He will know you are here, as for Bump and I, he will not. He may assume but he will not really know."

I rise from the sofa and walk over to one of the windows, looking out. It's still daylight outside but I know it could change to night at any second. "Do you know when night will fall Quad?"

"I am afraid not, that is determined by the Optic and that depends on his agenda."

I sit down once more and we remain in complete silence for several minutes. Then I jump to my feet. "Right! Bump and I need to be over at the Mitre because that's where we must start our battle from and then somehow we have to entice him into following us back here. When he gets here, all you've got to do is push him through the portal. I'll do the rest."

Bump slowly climbs out from her cosy seat on the sofa and says, "Right, I'm ready, let's get back over to the bar and wait for the Optic to arrive."

Quad smiles at me. "Well if that's the plan, as skimpy and sketchy as it is, we'd best get ourselves ready and into position. Good luck you two."

"Likewise Quad," she quips. "Come on Andy, no lagging now, we have a fight to start." She absolutely astounds me at times.

CHAPTER TWENTY
<u>TREPIDATION</u>

As Bump and I walk towards The Mitre, we discuss exactly where we should be when the Optic arrives. We pass a bench which is situated at the entrance to the old vicarage, a short distance away from the front door of the pub. Within the blink of an eye, night falls and the light is gone, we are completely surrounded by darkness. We break into a jog, reaching the front door which provides us with some light from the buildings external down lighters and also the pubs sign lights.

On our arrival Bump turns the handle but the door doesn't open. She tries several more times but fails to open it. I gently move her aside trying to gain entry myself, using good old fashioned brute force and ignorance. It definitely won't open, it seems to be locked. The big question is who locked it?

There erupts a tremendous clap of thunder, so intense that is shakes everything around us. She lets out a scream and I grimace. I look left, right and finally upwards; nothing untoward appears to be visible. It starts to rain, followed by more thunder. Then the lightening begins, with blinding bolts striking at the distant ground. "We've got to get in here and I don't think we are going to do so via this door." She nods

We head towards the car park, situated to the right hand side of the building, sprinting down the short drive to where the tarmac opens out into a compact parking area. There is only one car parked and I recognise it straight away. Through the torrential rain I walk over to the XJs jaguar. "Isn't she beautiful?" I yell.

"It's a car Andy and I think we have more pressing problems than drooling over a machine, don't you?"

I know that she definitely has a more than valid point but can't help feeling her response was a female, unemotional response for something that is an unprecedented piece of perfect mechanical art. "Right fine let's press on then."

Running past the houses which border the parking area, we head into the massive back garden of the furthest house. Yet again this feels completely familiar to me and I am left with no doubt as to which way we should go. We traverse the back of the building until we reach a fence. I climb up, dragging Bump up and over it with me.

We now find ourselves in the back garden of the pub. Its tall structure consists of three floors, all made of stone, looking rather dominating as we stare up at it. Crossing the garden, we reach the back door. Again we attempt to gain entry but like the front, it's locked and bolted shut. I scan all the windows at ground level, the one to the extreme right shows the most potential as to possibly allowing us much needed access into the building.

A lightening shaft illuminates the sky, transmitting its bolt, hitting the chimney of one of the surrounding houses. The stone built smokestack erupts into pieces that are thrown, along with tiles and other debris all over the place.

"That one was close," stutters Bump.

"Too close for comfort, as if we are being targeted." I reply.

I dart to the centre of the garden, where in my haste I had previously half noticed a set of garden furniture. Grabbing hold of one of the tubular framed metal chairs I charge towards my allocated window. Approaching it, I launch the chair directly at the glass. To my astonishment, it simply bounces straight back off without causing the glass to crack in the slightest. The window remains totally unscathed. I return to the garden set, this time grabbing the table, and I rush back to the same window, this time retaining the piece of furniture and smashing directly into it with all my strength.

Another bolt from the skies rips at the side of the building immediately above the window that I'm attempting to cave in. After the electrical spear has subsided, I check to see how I have fared so far and indeed if the lightening has possibly even aided my efforts. To my further amazement, there is still absolutely no sign of damage whatsoever, the window, the glass and the frame are all intact, as though nothing had ever happened to them.

"We are not going to get in, are we? We are not going to be allowed to."

I turn to Bump who is sitting in the doorway looking like a drowned rat. "It looks like that may be the case but it doesn't matter, the Optic knows we are here; the games afoot."

I walk across to her, crouch down and whisper in her ear. "Don't say too much sweetheart, he's here and he's listening." She nods slowly and dejectedly.

"Come on, let's back track and find other shelter." I yell. She gets to her feet and we dash across the garden towards our original entrance. Another bolt issues from the storm, hitting the fence and setting it on fire. We pull back defensively for a second. "Nice hit dickhead, at least we can just walk straight through it this time!" The heavens erupt into a crescendo of thunderous noise. "Temper, temper!" I bawl at the top of my voice and then I laugh to show my utter contempt.

I stamp at the flames which have ignited the wooden fence making a way through and as soon as they have subsided sufficiently, we leave. We race along until we reach the opening leading us back into the car park. We cautiously navigate between the two garages which form this access, peering into the parking area. The jaguar is still there. Everything appears as it was prior to this latest incident.

This time instead of crossing the car park we take the long way around. There's way too much electrical interference for my liking. Skirting the edge of the car park we reach the jag. Crouching down behind it, we watch as two more bolts rip their voltage into the tarmac, gauging great lumps out of it. As I observe the electrical projectiles, it appears to me that either we are not their intended target or that they are grossly misplaced, as they are not striking very close to us. We have been here now for a good couple of minutes, plenty of time for them to have worked out our current location. I place my hands on the bonnet of the car raising my head above it, almost daring a reaction from the elements.

"What are you doing, get down!" Bump implores.

"Why are the lightning bolts, which were obviously trying to hit us, striking so far away? Why aren't they getting closer than they are. Why?"

I move slightly away from the car and the cover it has been affording me, watching the skies for some sort of reaction. I can see from the corner of my eye that Bump isn't happy with my cavalier antics. She has her hand outstretched, gesturing to me to return. Again a shaft of raw light rips at the ground across from me, this time holding its form and travelling inch by inch towards me. Emanating from the main shaft there are many smaller, dancing tentacles of electrical current feeling at the ground, as though they are acting as stabilisers holding the main current steady.

I return to the cover of the car. "Did you see that? It wants to come to us but it won't come in the direction of this Jaguar." Then the whole thing hits me like a hammer. "Oh shit!" I gasp. "I can't believe it took me so long to see it."

I grab hold of Bump's arm pulling her away from the car. The lightning bolt is subsiding with its intensity fading away. I lead her from the car and back out to the road. As I glance back the Jaguar reverses, wheels spinning and tyres burning, from its location facing the stone wall. It is manoeuvring itself, allowing it to make its pursuit. I hear the engine roar, as if the driver is charging through his gear changes, but as I now know the car is the Optics latest disguise, I can only assume he is over eager to reach a position in which to chase after us.

We make the main road and Bump heads for the front door of the Mitre. I chase after her, grab hold of her arm and sprint towards the Pound House. "We'll skip the plan of being in the Mitre!" I yell. "We'll go straight into plan whatever. Let's just get to Quad." She acknowledges my wishes and together we charge off towards the square.

The Jaguar comes screaming out of the car park, swinging itself around, heading in our direction. I glance back at it, the grill of the vehicle is steaming as if the engine is overheating, while within the car itself, I can see a huge eyeball totally focused on me.

We turn the corner, past the Angel and begin crossing the road, just as the Jaguar comes skidding around the same corner. I lurch back to the pavement but Bump carries on across and is hit by the car. She slides awkwardly over its offside front wing and is sent tumbling into the road. The car continues to the end of the square, performing a three point turn in order to face us again.

Immediately I try to help Bump who is hauling herself to her feet. Her hands are cut and she is bleeding from a head wound. Once she's up on her feet, we slowly head for the front door of the Pound House. She is limping, and although we are only a few paces from our destination, our lack of speed has enabled the jag to complete its turn and it is once more aiming directly at us. As we approach the door, it swings open. I know we haven't enough time to enable us both to get through this small entrance, so I throw Bump at the opening and turn away just as the car reaches us. She falls through the door with the momentum of my push, as the jag grazes itself along the side of the building attempting to hit her again.

Meanwhile, I have managed to reach the other side of the road, where I quickly turn to see the jag veering away from the building, having ripped out part of the door frame, and I watch it drive itself straight into a tree stump at the end of the house. The car half mounts the stump and comes to a grinding halt. The engine stalls and for a moment there is complete silence and no movement from anywhere.

I glance towards the doorway of the Pound House and see Quad peering out from inside. "You okay Bump?" I call out. Quad nods his head but doesn't speak.

The Jaguar attempts to restart its engine. I stand, listening to its first attempt and then realise that maybe I should be getting myself into the house too. On the second attempt, the v-six motor bursts into action, pistons thumping back into life. I must admit the sound of a jaguar's engine is second to none and the lines of these vehicles are outstanding, but after this ordeal I'll never look at one in the same way again. Shame really, why couldn't it have been a three-wheeled Reliant Robin or something? Never did like them.

Having now got the thing started, the vehicle lurches back and forth, trying to release itself from its grounded position on top of the tree stump. There emits an ear cringing, metallic grinding as the jaguar finally pulls itself clear of its captivator. Oil or petrol, some kind of liquid is discharging profusely from underneath the car.

By now I have only managed to achieve one pace into the road opposite the house, and I don't think I am going to have enough time to make it over there. Checking in both directions I spot a road that runs alongside the Pound House to my left. I make straight for this. The car has already completed its u-turn and is now in hot pursuit. I clear the corner, darting down this small street, around the next corner still bordering the building and back up to the main square again. I can hear the jag squealing around the corners, bashing into obstacles as it negotiates the narrow roads, obviously very badly. By the time it arrives at the main square again, I'm standing in the fractured front door of the Pound House.

The huge eye in the cockpit of the car is staring daggers at me. The car is motionless but the engine remains angrily revving its heart out. I compose myself with a nonchalant stance, raise my left hand forming a fist and give him the second digit raised insult. The v-six lump goes berserk, revving its insides through the roof, the whole vehicle is shaking with its engine producing horrific grating noises. The hand brake is popped and the car shrieks forward as it thunders towards me.

I dart to my right as the car connects with the building. The entire door and its frame, part of the exterior old stone wall and the cob interior wall come crashing inwards. There is dust and debris everywhere.

Standing in the middle of the lounge with the car partially in the hall, and crazy as it seems, I attempt to locate the staircase. I can see the headlights and its indicators flashing through the dust and then suddenly they fade away. "Being, I have had enough of you, I have had enough of your pathetic little friends and I have had enough of these pitiful little games."

I pull myself up on the back of one of the sofas. "You only had to knock. We would have opened the door you know." I state sarcastically.

Bump starts to giggle but ceases abruptly when the Optic enters the room. The only way I can describe his appearance this time is akin to the Hulk, minus the green colouring and still with the customary one eye. His stature is enormous, rippling with muscles, sporting only a pair of tattered jeans as clothing. He has long blond hair, swept back over his ears and vastly elongated ear lobes which almost reach his shoulders. The mouth is thick lipped, snarling at us, his teeth are all over the place. Quite obviously he hasn't visited the dentist for a while.

I glance to the far wall of the lounge and can just begin to identify the black portal. Luckily the light in here is very poor, disguising and rendering this doorway as to be hardly distinguishable.

The Optic remains motionless for a moment, surveying the whole room twice, his eye scrutinising everything around him. I sense he knows something is amiss.

"Nice change dickhead, from car to the incredible bulk. And what exactly are you supposed to be for Christ sake, you really don't have any dress sense at all do you?"

His eye turns back towards me, bulging with the pent up rage I strongly sense within him. He affords me a dismissive grunt and continues to scan his surroundings.

I need to break his attention. I need to get him focused on me. "And what's this with the car? A jaguar, Jesus, I would have thought a big old Range Rover would have been more suited to you, over sized, boxy, over elaborate and sluggish. Yeah that would definitely be more like you." I sneer at him.

He wrenches his head around, his mouth is seeping with saliva. Boy he looks angry and who can blame him. I'm doing a great job of pissing him off. I would be angry if someone was giving me that kind of grief. "YOU TAUNT ME, YOU DARE TO TAUNT ME. THIS IS THE END BEING, I WILL BE RID OF YOU ALL!" He bellows with his exceptionally deep voice.

Moving to his right, he stays within the extremities of the room, always searching with his one immense eye. As he approaches the television, he sweeps his huge hand, swatting the electrical device across the room, crashing it into the opposite wall, where it splinters into a thousand pieces.

From the corner of my eye I spot Bump huddled underneath the staircase; the one immediately next to the dark doorway.

The Optic passes the French windows and suddenly stops. His face is one of intuitive knowing. He spins around, thrashing at the Georgian glass window, which in turn shatters and splinters into a mass of decimated wood and glass. He immediately returns his attention to me. "Where is he?" he says menacingly.

"Who?" I reply gingerly.

"Where is that parasite that has soiled my domain?"

I know he's talking about Quad, but for the life of me, I'm not sure where he is now and besides, I'm not going to let the Optic know even if I did. I'll play this cool. "Bump's not here, sorry mate."

"YOU IDIOT, YOU KNOW WHO I MEAN. THE FEMALE IS HERE, OVER THERE TO BE PRECISE. I WILL GET TO HER IN DUE COURSE. I WANT THAT OPTIC THAT THRIVES IN MY DOMAIN WITHOUT ANY PERMISSION!"

He really does have a cob on and this whole scenario is getting dangerous. A move needs to be made. "You call me an idiot. I'm not the one who is breaking all the rules of your poxy job. YOU ARE! So don't you get on your high horse as if your shit doesn't stink?"

The Optic lurches towards me in a split second, grabbing me around the throat. His grip is incredibly tight. I know without trying that I won't be able to speak. He lifts me completely off the ground, peering down deeply into my eyes. "You see, you are easily caught. Playing with you has made you complacent."

Just then a table smashes itself over his back. He staggers forward slightly with the impact and simply smiles at the futile attempt to get him to release me. He nonchalantly tosses me across the room, towards the main door, away from the portal. As I land, I glance back to see what he's redirecting his annoyance at and needless to say, it's Bump, she was the one who apparently attacked him with the coffee table. The Optic swings wildly at her and she retreats, managing to avoid the blows. Finally her attempts to back away are blocked, as she reaches the far wall. The Optic lifts his enormous clenched fist and brings it down to bear on her head. She swiftly side steps, kicks out at his nether region and leaps through the black portal.

"NO BUMP, DON'T DO THAT!" I scream but I know it's too late. A horrible dread fills my heart.

He takes a sideways glance at me and then turns back to the portal. Extending his hand, he offers up a digit to touch it. As his finger nears, he pulls it back as if scolded by red hot embers. Slowly he turns to face the room, his face a picture of realization. "She is finished, she cannot survive that side and she cannot come back without your presence. Now I will deal with you. I will not allow you to help her, your side of the brain will be her demise. Did you think it was that easy to fool me?"

The second he finishes his indulgent threats, I see a burst of light from where the French windows were. The radiance streaks across the room within the blink of an eye, crashing into the Optics chest and throwing him halfway into the portal. The Optic emits a stomach curdling shriek but manages to take hold of each side of the doorway, stopping his passage completely into it.

Quad transforms from his light source into an exact carbon copy of the Optic, where upon he continues to crash, thump, kick, head butt and shove at the Optic in an effort to force him through the portal. The battle that rages between them is awesome, with Quad throwing everything he has, trying to cause the Optic to lose his grip and pass through the gateway, into my side of the brain. This fracas lasts no more than a few seconds but it feels, to me like an eternity. Suddenly the Optic, who has received one hell of a battering, heaves himself forward, releasing one of his hands and lashes out at Quad, who on receiving the blow, spirals away hitting the ceiling, then ricocheting off he lands almost next to me. He wearily looks up, bleeding from the mouth and the wound from the Optics blow which has left damage to his head. "He is too strong for me; I cannot beat him in his own domain. Please forgive me?" His head drops forward. "Bump, look after her, do not let him kill her."

The Optic has now managed to free himself from the portal, but he too looks quite drained. He slowly raises his head, looking in my direction. "To coin a phrase Being, is that the best you can do?" He taunts me.

For the second time since I've been here, I feel a frenzy build up within me. I glare upward at him. "Haha no! I can guarantee you haven't seen what I can do yet."

The Optics face grimaces. "Then show me, Being."

I want to retort but the rage inside me seals my lips, I am completely focusing all my energy on him. The feeling both excites and scares me. I move forward slowly, not really aware of my intention, I just feel I have to get to him. He moves sideways away from the dark doorway, almost crouched, his arms outstretched and snarling at me. His poise is aggressive but he makes no attacking movements. I hear Quad behind me. I hope he is trying to motivate himself into helping me when I eventually attack. I know I have to get him through the doorway and now he knows it's there, my task has become a million times harder.

From behind me Quad launches a second assault, passing me at great speed. Within the blur of him passing me, I observe he has changed form as well and it appears to me that he has opted for the Cyclops façade. The two Optics lock together in close battle punching, kicking, biting and wrestling; smashing everything that gets in their way on the battlefield. Every blow that hits its mark, causes a display of sparking light that fizzles and gyrates, making the fight seem almost magical. In reality though, there is no magic here, just two incredible forces clashing, both with one intention in mind, death to the other.

After a minute or so, Quad is thrown with great venom into the ceiling, causing a huge indentation, scattering debris everywhere. As he falls to the floor, the Optic kicks out, thrusting him through the corner of the stair case onto the wall behind. Quad struggles to his feet but collapses in a heap on the floor. The Optic strides across to the limp body and lifting his left foot high he gets ready to stamp on Quads head.

I reach boiling point and rush at him. He extends his right hand, without even looking and pushes me away. I crash through a table and end up at the foot of a bookcase. Clambering to my feet, I see the Optic systematically stomping his foot down on Quad, who from where I am appears not to be moving at all, except from the impact of the Optics attack.

"That's enough, you cowardly bastard!" I bawl.

He pauses from his onslaught on Quad, his head very slowly turning towards me. "Two down, just you to deal with now and it's going to be all my pleasure."

For the second time since I've been here, I feel real rage and fear like I have never experienced before. I become totally focused on the Optic, my vision spirals with that red mist surrounding it. I beckon with my left hand for him to come to me. This motion causes the Optics entire body to be violently yanked towards me. His face says it all. Again I witness a deep rooted apprehension in his eye as he attempts to slow his involuntary progress towards me. I feel power well up deep inside me. He is having trouble coping with this, as he pulls both one way and then the other, trying to evade my concentration. When he is close enough to me, he swings his enormous fists but as they connect, all power seems to have been removed from them. I throw a punch back. There is a blinding light and I'm thrown backwards to the wall, hitting it with great impetus. I hear myself groan with the impact but I distinctly feel that no damage has been done. It's a totally weird sensation feeling indestructible.

The Optic has landed outside, obviously thrown through what is left of the French windows. They are now completely decimated, all that remains is a hole in the wall. He is on his feet and approaching me again. This time I start moving to my left, towards the portal. Seeing my intention, he stops and wags his finger at me. "I do not wish to join the dying female, so let us finish this outside this structure where we have more room."

I stroll towards the dark doorway, not taking my eyes from him for a second. "If you want this over and done with, we will fight here and now. If I walk through that portal, I will not be coming back and I think you are fully aware of what that would mean."

The Optics head circles, his eye still bulging, his mouth still dribbling with his bodily stance alert, ready for anything. "If you pass through to your side of the brain, you leave your so called friends at my mercy and equally, you know what that means."

"My friends! My friends you asshole. You have already killed Bump by flinging her through the portal and as for Quad, he's an Optic, he's the same as you. He's no friend of mine. I've got no problem leaving him here so you two can carry on your pathetic little squabble for eternity. With me gone, your whole plan is out of the window. You end up with nothing!"

He walks over to the fireplace, venting his anger on the chimney breast. Lumps of stone dislodge, splintering and spitting themselves in various directions. He states decisively, "Then it will be here and now."

In an instant he is on me, grasping my throat, squeezing so tightly that I am unable to breathe. I try pushing him away but my earlier powers, now when I still need them, escape me. Perhaps I have lost my anger. I begin thrashing at him in every way possible but I can't shake him, he has a death grip on me and I have no answer to it. I feel intensely weak and light headed and know I won't be able to last for much longer. Suddenly the Optic is shoved sideways. He retains his grip on me but loses his footing. This interlude allows me just enough scope to manage to put my left hand into the portal. On touching it, I feel the revitalising spirit surge into me. Now I take hold of the hand around my throat and simply peel it away. I then sharply tug him past me and step completely into the black portal.

As I enter, I keep hold of the Optics wrist pulling him in with me. When I'm partially through, my progress is halted. I still have hold of him, so my assumption is that he must be holding onto something at the other end. I continue tugging, feeling my strength increasing but still unable to budge him. Suddenly he releases his hold of whatever it was and the pair of us surge through the remainder of the portal.

Within a second of our landing, Quad piles through as well. The Optic leaps to his feet and running at the portal, tries to re-enter it, but as he is almost there so it de materialises and disappears. He stands bolt upright, emitting a howling, blood curdling scream.

I'm just about to attack him again when I suddenly spot Bump. Her physical matter is fluctuating and her eyes are closed. Before I can make a move towards her, Quad is there. He turns to me,"You have to take her back and you have to do it now." I run over to them, attempt to pick her up but she simply slips through my arms, there is absolutely no substance to her. "How Quad how, and where's the portal now?"

He slumps down on to his bottom, hanging his head low to his chest. "She is almost gone Andy, he has finally killed her essence."

I furiously turn to the Optic."That's it; I've had it with you!"

Turning to me, he looks really scared. He begins to glow, this both fades and brightens in intensity and I can visibly see he is distressed by whatever is happening to him. I walk towards him and he in turn, begins backing away.

"You're on my side now Optic, MY FUCKING DOMAIN!"

He drops to his knees, glaring at me. "I cannot survive this side. You must allow me to return. Think of what it would mean if I do not return to my side," he pleads.

"And what would that be, what exactly do you think would actually make me allow you to return to your side. What?"

He rises to his feet and stands proud. "Every human must have an Optic. If I die then you will be without one, this would never be tolerated."

"Oh yes, a host without an Optic, can't happen can it?"

A smile flickers across his face and he nods.

I continue. "But then again, with you dead I would still have an Optic. Quad would be my Optic and I'm pretty sure he'd make a decidedly better job of it than you have."

His face becomes extremely serious. "He cannot be your Optic, he is the females."

"Not since you killed her. He seems to be at a loose end."

He starts walking towards me.

"Careful sunshine," I threaten. "You're on my side of the brain. I can destroy you at will."

He stops dead in his tracks.

I turn to Quad, who is still kneeling by Bumps fluctuating body. "Could you take his place Quad?"

He looks up at me and I believe that if he was capable of crying, he would be doing just that by now. He states very quietly in a broken voice, "She is almost gone."

I join Quad and wrap my hand around hers as best I can. "Sleep little sister and go where ever you want to go, never let anyone stop you again and always remember your brother loves you...... and so does Quad."

For an instant her eyes open, all I can see in them is want, then they finally shut tightly. Very slowly the glimmers of light within her body diminish and she simply disintegrates, pieces of her falling to the ground like tiny beads set free from a broken necklace.

Quads and my eyes meet, we both rise and look at the Optic. He in turn raises his hands to the heavens, then charges at us. Quad throws himself straight at him, they both tumble to the ground. The Optic seems to get the better of Quad, sitting on his chest, thumping him with all his might. Quads face is punched from left to right by the intensity of the blows.

I take hold of the Optics hair and lift him away. As he relinquishes his attack of Quad, I ram my fist into his chest, ripping it up to his neck; he crumples to the ground. This action instils in me a real feel good factor, elation, it's unbelievable and I sense a throbbing convulsion in my head. I point my open hands at his torso, red and black beams spring from them hitting the Optics body in various places, shrivelling it up. The glee inside me is terrifying; I'm actually enjoying the kill.

Quad gets up, moves behind me and quietly states, "He is done Andy, he is finished, dead, please stop."

I pull my arms back, not really knowing what to do with these new found weapons, I fold my arms. "Is he really gone?" I question meekly.

"Yes he is gone, dead and my people will already know that he has been destroyed."

"I don't care, because if your people were that concerned, they would have sorted him out themselves, but they didn't and that cost Bump her life!"

"Indeed it did and it will cost me mine too unless I return to the other domain."

I look at Quad, realising the implications of what he has just said. "Shit you're right, you can't survive here either. How long have you got, do you know?"

"Do not panic Andy. I have more than enough time to wait for the doorway to reappear, as long as it does so within the same time scale as on the other side," he snorts in amusement.

"You'll be okay then because it will. Somehow I know this, but don't ask me how."

"Well if you say it will return, that is more than good enough for me. Shall we sit and wait?" Quad slumps down, reclining back and I in turn join him. "Why not, it's been a hell of a day don't you think? I could do with a rest too."

CHAPTER TWENTY ONE
__OVERTONES__

Within a couple of hours the dark portal reappears, exactly where it was previously. We both rise to our feet and walk over to greet its return. I step forward, ready to enter the shimmering mass when Quad suddenly takes hold of my arm. "Where are you going?"

"Back through."

"Why, why do you need to go back through? What's back that side for you? You need to stay here and wait to be called back to your true world."

I must admit that whilst I was sitting waiting for the portal to reappear, I was wondering what the next thing would be for me to do, but when the doorway did return, to me it just seemed the natural thing to go through it. "Do you mean I am supposed to simply wait here and hope something or someone comes to get me and take me back to my real life?"

"In a word yes. The other domain, the one that you have now requested to be mine, is not yours. We cannot meet again. I need to carry out my purpose and you need to carry on with your life. Because of the way things have unfolded I am now your Optic and my role is to suppress two thirds of your brain until you die. Then I will return home."

"You really are a cheerful bastard aren't you?"

Quad erupts into laughter. "Sorry my friend, but we need to get things working the way they were meant to work."

"Witheridge!"

Quad stares at me. "What?"

"Witheridge, that's the name of the place on the other side of this portal. I used to live there."

"The places you have visited on the other side are all from your memories. Everything that has happened in there is a reflection of your mind, all an Optic does is to control your thoughts."

Quad releases my arm and walks past me right up to the threshold of the portal. Once there he stops, looking back at me."I watched over Bump endlessly and I will do the same for you. Always be safe Andy, I will never let you down."

Before I am able to reply, he strides into the black doorway and is gone. I slowly approach it, gently touching it with the palm of my hand. It's icy cold.

I turn to scrutinise my new surroundings. Since the final battle and because of everything it's drained out of me, this time I haven't yet absorbed any information as to what's around me. As far as my eye can see is a meadow with odd willow trees growing at various stages of their development. The ground ahead looks soft, resembling a quagmire with course grasses growing intermittently from within it. The sky is grey, the clouds are slowly moving across a sun which is hardly visible, except for a haze that is permitted to glow through the dull nimbus carpet. Funny, I thought that my side of the brain, the bit that I supposedly control, would be sunny, happy, clear skied with gently rolling hills, beautiful green trees and roses growing at every avenue. I start laughing out loud. "Just like real life." I must be lonely; I'm talking to myself now.

I start walking to my chosen point, the biggest tree that I can see and it's not a willow. I trudge on. After a few moments of walking it begins to rain. I feel a pain in the back of my head. It's nothing terrible, a nagging little throb that initially causes me to wince. I continue. As I proceed I see low, rolling hills coming into view. They stretch all the way along to the horizon. More or less in their centre is a slightly raised bump, marginally higher than all the rest, with a tiny structure on the top, possibly a tower, but it's hard to say for certain from this distance. I reach my original target, the big old oak tree and I sit, resting at its base. Huh take a rest, I know what Bump would have said about this, bless her.

The hills are a good deal closer now and to my surprise I am able to identify them. These are the Bredon Hills, near Pershore in Worcestershire. I was brought up in Pershore and these hills were visible from my bedroom window. As a kid I've both looked at them and climbed them many times. Quad said everything here was formed from my memories, this memory is a good one and hopefully there's no one to disappoint me regarding these recollections.

After a few minutes I get to my feet and continue heading for the tower on the hill. The numb pain in my head remains, creating a muzzy feeling but as before, it doesn't seem urgent enough to worry about and besides, who am I going to confide in anyway. Again I titter to myself.

Finally I encounter a road. Climbing over a fence, I find myself standing on a white line in the middle of a road. I survey both directions, eventually deciding to take the route towards what looks like an entrance to a farm. This direction will also take me nearer to my childhood hill with its tower.

At the entrance I stop, rotating I complete a three hundred and sixty degree circle in order to evaluate everything around me. No people, no cars, no animals are visible, only the beauty of the countryside. I continue on to the farm. Passing the farm house and various barns, I maintain my course up the hill. The rain is getting heavier, the wind is beginning to pick up speed, causing a slight problem with the visibility. I trudge to the top of the hill until I'm at the base of the steep mound on which the tower is stood. I remember this well, many a time I've scrambled up this to reach the tower. I begin my ascent. Twice I falter, slipping down a little but with child like determination, I scramble on towards my goal. On reaching the top I feel total exhilaration at having achieved my aim. I'm the King of the Castle! Suddenly I hear those exact words, but not from my own mouth. The voice came from the other side of the tower. I immediately go to investigate.

The tower isn't very big at all, no more than twenty five feet square. Within seconds I have completely circled the whole structure. I can't find anyone but the voices are still there, I can hear them quite clearly.

"I'm king of the castle, I got here first."

"You cheated, you had a head start."

"I'm king of the castle, I'm king of the castle and you're a dirty rascal."

These are children's voices and I recognise them. The king of the castle is my older brother Chris and the other lad is me. They come into my view, very faint and difficult to distinguish, but nonetheless they are there. Looking down from the tower, I can also see my parents and grandparents at the bottom, all looking up. "Careful boys and stop arguing." Ha that's Dad. How many million times did he have to say those lines to us?

Both the voices and images continue for some time. I simply sit, watch and listen. Fantastic, I am actually watching me and my family all those years ago, as though watching a rather dated television programme. When they disappear, a kind of sadness overtakes me and I just sit in the pouring rain hoping they will return. What great, wholesome memories.

Shortly I climb back down the mound on its far side, heading towards Pershore as I remember it. The pain in my head has gone, so with a renewed vigour, I press on.

On my approach to the town, there are thousands of apparitions, old cars from my past, people, voices, things that I know, that I am familiar with but can't seem to identify. I travel right into the centre of the town. Since my childhood it doesn't seem to have changed structurally or cosmetically at all. At first this astounds me but then the penny drops; of course this is a memory, so it will be as I saw it all those years ago. All these images are reflections that I am generating, not as when I first arrived here and the Optic was designing the landscapes.

I am stood on the main road across from the square, that as I recall was called Broad Street, watching as a bus, a midland red, pulls in at the bus stop. The bus churns out loads of school kids, all dressed in their uniforms, some of them with caps on, all wearing blazers, most carrying satchels, when one of them looks straight at me. He slowly walks away from the bus stop, heading my way. His eyes don't deviate at all, they are completely focused on me. I look left and right to make sure it's me he is watching and there is no one else there, but as he draws closer, I am left with no doubt that it's me. Reaching me, he stops. His gaze is daunting and I have to glance away a couple of times. His stare doesn't falter, he doesn't even blink. Nothing is said, he extends his hand, gesturing for me to take hold of it. This I do and he leads me towards the far end of town. We walk along the High Street, turning left at the Abbey Garages into Cherry Orchard Road. Immediately I recognise this road. "I lived here, number twenty four, I know this road well."

The boy looks up at me but doesn't stop walking. His mouth opens but his lips don't move. "Keep following me, please do not stop, time is of real importance. It is time for you to return." He closes his mouth and turns away. It's as though someone was talking through him, a robot but definitely with purpose.

We finally reach the house that as a child I lived in with my brother, sister, mum and dad, when the lad stops. He turns his head looking at the building, releases my hand and points towards the house. He turns his head towards me again, stares right through me and opens his mouth letting out further instructions. "Enter by the back door, walk through the kitchen and into the hall. Go into the lounge, the first door on your left and exit into the back garden by way of the french windows."

As he starts walking away, I grab his shoulder. He abruptly stops. "Who are you young man and who sent you to me?"

He doesn't turn, remaining perfectly still. "Time is the main factor here, you must do as I instructed and you sent for me." With this he strides off. I glance back at the house then back to the lad, but he's disappeared. Gone in two seconds flat, where, who knows?
I amble cautiously over. There is an enclosed alley between the garage and the house with a wooden gate as its entrance. I open this and enter. On my left are three doors, at the end a sliding door and on my right a single glazed door that I know from memory leads into the kitchen. I focus my attention on the sliding doors. I remember these well, they

lead to the garden, opening out onto a terrace with three steps down to the lawn. Why would I have been told to take a route through the house to reach the garden, when just going through those doors would get me there a lot quicker? I walk past the main back door and stop in front of the sliding doors. My hand reaches up to take the handle when a shrill scream halts me, holding me perfectly still, petrified by the sound. I spin around to see the boy standing next to the wooden gate at the far end of the alley. "What the hell's the matter with you? You scared the shit out of me!"

The lad opens his mouth again, letting out the same ear piercing scream. He is standing there bolt upright with his hands at his sides. His eyes staring like black holes directly at me, he continues with the screeching noise while pointing at the back door.

"Okay, okay, your route, through the back door, I'll take your route." I head directly to the back door. Looking down at the handle, I glance back to the boy. Again he's gone. "Jesus, you are a pushy little sod!" I yell.

I open the back door. The kitchen is exactly as I remember it, from the sink in front of the window, to the folded kitchen table. It's all there. I cross the kitchen to the other side where the door is into the hall, open it and enter. As instructed I take the first door on my left into the lounge. This is a reasonably large room with metal framed French windows on the far wall. It's a weird feeling looking at a room with so many memories, that it has the ability to jolt emotions buried deeply within you. The gas fire, the three piece suite, the old black and white television, it's amazing to see all this and to be in front of it once more. Such intense happiness and so real. I slowly and lovingly walk across the lounge and reach the French windows. As I place my hand on the brass handle to open it, it feels cold, very cold. I initially retract my grasp but then I recall the boy's instructions. I take hold of the opener again, wrenching it downwards. The door opens with ease.

I step through onto the terrace, glancing down. I can remember stamping on a million ants just here, every time I killed a load of them, more would always appear. I titter out loud to myself. Taking two paces forward, I look out. It's unbelievable! The entire garden in front of me is an exact replica of my memories. But then again I remind myself, of course it would be, that's what these are, exact memories, my mind conjuring up pictures from my past. It occurs to me that I have followed the boy's instructions to the letter but now that I'm actually standing here, he didn't say what to do or where to go next. I stroll along the terrace to the other end, looking down from this aspect. All looks the same as it did from the other end. Well I must admit that now I'm at a bit of a loss, not sure how to proceed.

I begin hearing extremely faint and distant voices, along with the return of that nagging pain from earlier in the back of my head. This time the pain is returning with a vengeance. Between the gabbling voices and the throbbing pain, the end of the garden starts to distort. Initially I consider this due to the pain in my head but as I watch, so it appears to churn and I realise that it's actually happening, it's not a fault with my vision.

The pain turns to an intense thumping, the voices become increasingly louder, all talking over the top of each other, making it impossible for me to understand any of it. The swirling motion at the end of the garden has increased in size and appears to be moving its way up the garden towards me. Suddenly while watching this kaleidoscope type whirlpool, I catch something at the very end of it. Its not close enough for me to make it out at the moment but I figure that from the speed of this thing, it won't be long before I am able to do so. I am brought to my knees by the totally encompassing pain resounding everywhere within my head. The voices however are beginning to clear, I can pick out odd words now, but still no sentences are legible.

Then I hear my name and I swear it was spoken by Barbara, my wife. This causes me to focus my complete concentration on the voices, trying to block out the pain and shut my eyes to everything else around me. There it was again, my name, plus another voice, a male one.

Suddenly the pain stops, from a terrible throbbing to within an instant, nothing. With this release of pressure, I become intensely aware of some kind of whirlwind engulfing me. I open my eyes to find myself enveloped within a spinning tunnel and I can see quite clearly what's at the other end. There's a face, not a familiar face, I don't recognise it at all and it's staring along the tunnel directly at me. "Andy, come on man fight," he says.

Fight, what's he on about? There's nothing that I can see here to necessitate any need for fighting.

I turn my back on the tunnel to face the house but it's not there, it's purely a sprawling, spiralling load of bricks, tiles, furniture and plants all dancing in perfect formation, round and round.

There is a huge jolt that flings me to the floor.

"Please Andy don't go, you must come back, don't leave me here alone." That's Barbs voice!

I look back down the tunnel to where the unfamiliar mans face was. Now it's Barb and she's crying.

"Get everybody out now." That man's voice again. "Stand clear." Another huge jolt. Once more I feel like a rag doll being tossed about. The pain in my head lurches violently back into action and the tunnel moves towards me again. I again try to turn back to where the house was and it's back. All the smashed debris has once more turned into a building. What the hell is going on?

"Bring back his wife." That man's voice again.

Turning back to look down the tunnel again, I find that I'm almost at their end. I reach out to it. For some reason I now feel that this is where I need to be. My hand seems to slowly immerse into whatever is at the end of this tunnel. It feels warm and safe. These feelings compel me to fight my way towards it. This is what he meant by fight, now I can see it. Sensing that I'm almost through, I glance back once more towards where the house was. I can still see it quite clearly and stood on the terrace is me as I was at about thirteen years old, watching me in the tunnel leaving my memories behind. He has a smile on his face and the last thing I see him do before the whole vision disappears, is nod to me.

I try turning forward to see where I'm going but I can't. I'm in some kind of suspended state which is completely black. The weird thing is, I can see myself but I can't see anything else. I feel a serene calmness overtake me with no importance attached to anything, completely stress free, I don't give a toss attitude and I feel just great.

CHAPTER TWENTY TWO
THE ESSENCE

"Hold him, for Christ sake, hold him."

I am aware that at least two people, four hands, are restraining me for some reason. Inside I panic. I must get free.

"Andy it's all okay, don't fight, you are back, you are safe." It's Barbs voice. I can see her quite clearly now and she has her hand gently placed on the side of my face. I'm back, this is the real world.

I relax back onto the bed and see that the two people who were holding me are a nurse and my brother in law, Len. The doctor is at the head of the bed. It was his face that I could see at the end of the tunnel. "Welcome back Andy. It has been a long battle to get you through this."

"Hi Doc, good to be back, you have no idea what a fight I've had trying to get back here."

He smiles. "Right, I'll leave you with your family for a while. I will look back in on you tomorrow."

Barb walks over to him and shakes his hand. "Thank you."

"You're quite welcome." The doctor turns with a satisfied smile on his face and leaves the room.

It's at this point that I survey my new surroundings. I am in a small ward with an awful lot of machines and monitors around me. There are two windows on the opposite wall. I can see roof tops so I assume that we are on an upper floor. There is only the one door in and out of this ward and in total I count eight beds. Three of these are empty, two have patients in that appear to be unconscious but on some sort of life support. Like my bed they have varying kinds of electronic machines around them doing their thing, while the other two beds are occupied but with white sheets pulled completely over the top of them. I can only gather that these people have died. I've previously seen pictures the same as I'm seeing here and that was the case then. Quite harrowing really to be in a room with these, but I imagine this must be some sort of intensive care room where they put people that might not make it through.

I turn and look at the people surrounding me. There's Barb, Len, Vickie my sister, Chris my brother and my mum.

"How do you feel?" Mum says.

"Groggy, confused but pleased to be back."

"We thought for a while there, that we were going to lose you." She rushes forward, giving me a huge hug. "You scared us half to death."

Barb is sitting on the edge of the bed holding my hand looking at me. "You died for a few seconds, did you know that?" she very quietly and seriously says.

"Where I've been, it's been touch and go whether I ever got back here."

A silence fills the room as if the most profound statement of all time had just been uttered.

"Where you have been, where have you been? You have been in a coma for eight days, where do you think you have been?"

"Believe me Barb, I've been on a trek through my own brain and what I'm going to tell you now, you probably won't believe. Nevertheless it seemed completely real at the time."

There are smiling faces in the room with this statement, then of course a flood of humorous retorts and innuendoes with everyone there having their little joke at my expense.

"Okay, okay," I loudly say. "If you don't want to hear my experience, fair enough."

Everyone calms down and the joviality dies away, then Chris says, "Go on Andy, tell us."

I begin my account of what I can remember, trying not to leave anything out. I see the surprise on my mum's face when Bump comes into the story but everyone listens intently without any interruptions. The only intrusion to my oration is when two porters enter the ward. They walk past us, without any acknowledgement, over to the nearest bed which is covered by a sheet. One of the porters takes the clipboard from the bottom of the bed, reads down it, places it back on top of the bed, nodding to his co-worker, they release the wheel brakes and manoeuvre the bed out of the ward.

Whilst they carry out this task out, there is complete silence in the room, with all of us watching as the deed is done.

"Poor bastard." Len concludes quietly.

There are a few raised eyebrows then Chris breaks the silence. "Carry on Andy, so now there's two of these Optic things/"

Everyone's attention focuses back to me. I continue with the facts.........or are they? When I get to the very end, the bit where I came into this room, I scan their faces to fathom out whether there is any belief at all in what I am saying. What I see is a mixture of reactions, from 'great little story' to 'wow it must have been one hell of a trip, what a dream.'

Mum's face looks particularly confused but as she starts to say something she is beaten to it by Len. "So you're saying that we all have one of these things, these Optics and they control most of our brain?"

I smile. "Yes we all have one and no they don't control most of our brain, they suppress two thirds of it."

"To prevent us from becoming too clever, right?"

"More or less Len, yes. They see the human race with the use of its complete, no holds barred, totally functioning, brain power as a threat to everything else that exists."

"Hmmmm. Interesting concept, even quite plausible. You need to write a book."

Everyone in the room laughs, except mum. She looks around the bed at the others giggling, finally settling her eyes upon me. "Why did you say that you had a sister, son? Why would you say such a thing? You have Vickie but there was never another."

I gaze up at mum, slowly sitting myself up. "Mum, Bump was with me in your womb, she was my twin. She called herself Bump because the only words she heard from inside the womb were you saying, 'look at my bump' when you were pregnant. She was never born, she died in physical body quite early on in your pregnancy but her essence, because she was my twin, entered into my brain. She lived in there all this time, more or less alone until I turned up."

The silence this assertion causes is deafening, you could hear a pin drop.

Mums head drops. "What you have just told everyone, it must all be true because you are quite correct, you did have a twin. I was never told whether it was a boy or a girl. In those days they couldn't really tell. I have never told anyone, even your father didn't know, he would have been devastated if he had known. So I kept it to myself for all these years, believing that when I died, the secret would die with me. This story you have just told is amazing, unbelievable, but there must be some fact in it for you to have known of your twin. There is no other way you could have ever found out."

Everyone in the room is looking extremely perplexed with these revelations. I feel that the whole scenario needs cheering up a little. "At the end of the day mum, it doesn't matter. My time with Bump was great fun, she was an amazing lass, as funny as hell at times. If she had been born, she would have been one hell of a character."

A small, sad smile flickers across mums face. "What did she look like?"

I feel my lips tighten, accompanied by a deep sorrowful tug within my guts. "I'll tell you another day mum, not now because at the end of the day, she is gone. Now she is dead."

As these words fall from my lips, the remaining bed across from us, the other one with the sheet pulled up, starts to move. Everyone turns to watch me as I gasp, gawping at the movement and their eyes follow my gaze. Slowly the top half begins to rise as if something under the sheet is gradually sitting up, the sheet falls away and the head and torso of a female in her forties becomes visible. When she is sat bolt upright, her head slowly, almost mechanically, turns towards us. Once she is fully facing us, her eyes spring open, her gaze solely and directly at me.

"No Andy, she's not dead. Bump isn't dead. She has finally been born."